'Jay Taverner' was born in England in the 1990s, when a long-term lesbian partnership finally merged into a single writing personality. Jacky Bratton and Jane Traies keep bees, grow tomatoes, renovate old houses and work in education. They spend as much time as they can in the Marches, the setting of Jay Taverner's novels.

First published 2001 by Diva Books
an imprint of Millivres Limited
part of the Millivres Prowler Group
116-134 Bayham Street, London NW1 0BA

A catalogue record for this book is available from the British Library

ISBN 1 873741 59 6

Printed and bound in Finland by WS Bookwell

Hearts & Minds

JAY TAVERNER

One
Cheshire, England, August 1734

There was certainly something going on at the barn. From the stile above it, looking down into the road, Lucy could see a bright flag drooping from a pole stuck up over the door, and papers pinned up on the wooden wall. She could hear men's voices talking and laughing inside. Strollers, Mam had said. Pomping folk.

The bag of washing rubbed her neck. It smelt of feet and dried piss. She humped it down, and dropped it beside her leg with a thump. Outside the great door, two women sat back to back on the shafts of a queer boarded-in handcart. One was old, with masses of white hair. She was sewing something large and red, smoothed over her spread knees; it had a dirt-blackened hem all round.

The younger woman was thin and fair. Although it was nearly noon, she sat in her stays and petticoats, with her face raised to the sun and her hands idle. Her eyes seemed shut, but her head turned at the thump of the washing bag, and she saw Lucy immediately.

It was too late to back out; and Lucy was interested. She scrambled over the stile, stopping to shake down her skirts and push uselessly at the escaping tangles of her hair.

The younger woman dug her elbow back into her companion's ribs. They both watched as Lucy walked slowly down the field, facing them out. She was glad she'd left the poxy washing behind.

"Mr. Ashton!" the fair-haired woman called out, without turning her head. Her voice was hard-edged; it carried clearly right up the field. "Come out, sir – we have a visitor."

The white-haired woman laughed. Lucy stopped, twenty yards away, as a gentleman in plush breeches and a red frogged waistcoat came out into the sun.

He squinted up at Lucy.

"Zounds, Mrs. A – what's toward? Are we transported to the Afric shore? Is this rural Cheshire, or the banks of Nile? Such an exotic! Speak to us, my dear – or are you not familiar with our humble tongue?" And he bowed, smirking.

Lucy had almost no idea what his words meant, but she knew what he was talking about. The same as most people, when they first set eyes on her. She curled her lip; but she supposed his nonsense was better than the usual sneers and stones or gobdropped amazement. She stood her ground, staring at him hard; and then she made a curtsy, dropping as low as the village pew-opener after pennies from visiting gentry at church.

"Stap me, Mrs. A! The manners of a duchess! Such deportment! What a spine! O, brave new world, that hath such creatures in it!" He turned back to Lucy. "Gad, we could make something of you on stage, my dear!"

This time, Lucy had no idea at all what he was talking about; so she stared the harder.

From the barn came a deep, booming voice, asking what was afoot. Lucy was quite disappointed when the speaker appeared, wiping his mouth, and was a snuffy little man in his shirtsleeves, quite old. He stopped in his tracks and stared at her, thrusting his hands in his pockets. The women exchanged a glance.

Lucy had had enough. "If you please, did you need any washing done?"

Mr. Ashton threw up his hands. "Alack and well a day! How are the mighty fallen – Cleopatra takes in washing." He brightened. "It would make a Haymarket burlesque."

The older woman put down her sewing. "Leave the girl be, George. No, miss, we have no need of a washerwoman. I see to our family's things, and the stage stuffs need special attention."

If the red thing was one of them, Lucy thought, they could do with some of it now. She shrugged, and began to turn away.

The man called Ashton was obviously not done with her yet. "Wait a moment, my dear," he said to Lucy. "We might use her another way, eh, Stukely?"

"She's certainly a beauty," the old man said, in his booming voice. He turned to Lucy, jingling his money. "Would you like to go on the stage, me dear?"

The white-haired woman broke in. "I think not, sir," she said very firmly. "Be on your way, child, there's nothing for you here."

"But you will come and see our show tonight?" said the man with the deep voice. "Two fine pieces, and singing and dancing, and only a penny to get in." He winked at Lucy.

The younger woman spoke. "We don't need washing ourselves, Mrs. S, but I believe Mr. Brown might. He sees to his own linen, and always keeps himself very spruce."

Lucy was not used to people who talked so much. It was oddly exciting. She wanted them to go on. "Mr. Brown?" she repeated.

"He's gone for a walk by the river – out into the fields," said the scruffy man. "You could meet him on his return – I'm sure he'd be delighted to see a pretty face." He turned and grinned at his wife.

Lucy looked from face to face. They are very busy about each other, she thought. She bobbed again, and turned back to her bundle. If these were players, she could do without their sorts of games. But she could not help wondering about them, as she shouldered her smelly bag and turned for home.

The mud-holes left by stomping cows had hardened to rock,

and she trudged along the riverbank head down, to avoid twisting an ankle. The washing weighed like a boulder on her back. Sweat ran down between her breasts. She was fifteen and, as far as she could see, the rest of her life would be drudgery like this. The thought filled her with restlessness. The sudden coming of the players had startled and excited her. Lazy, laughing, chattering in their fast, high voices and flirting their bright feathers, they alighted for a moment in the flat fields and took her breath away. Tomorrow they would fly off, leaving only their shit behind for the likes of her to see where they had been.

She was half a mile from the cottage, still preoccupied with her angry thoughts, when she was stopped in her tracks by the sound of someone splashing in the shallows ahead, just round the river bend. She pushed back the curtain of hair from her eyes. The bather was only a few feet away. Clearly, he had not heard Lucy approach. A long white face floated, eyes closed, above the deep centre of the river. The glass-green stream rippled the pale body below. Lucy stared. Mr. Brown, they had said, walking by the water. His coat and breeches hung on a hawthorn spike; shirt and drawers were flung on the ground. One of his thin shoes, its big buckle glinting in the sun, was only a step away from her bare and dusty feet.

As she stood, uncertain whether to stay or go, Mr. Brown raised an arm over his head, so that bright drops rained on his wet, close-clinging curls, and kicked himself backwards into the black rim of shadow round the willow tree on the far bank. His legs gleamed white in the dark water as he reached out and held on to the trailing gold curtain of willow leaves, shaking the water out of his eyes and laughing for pleasure. He had a smooth, bony face with a high ridged nose, like a little horse. Then, still smiling, he let go of the golden leaves and dived, flashing across the river towards her in a spurt of spray.

It was too late to move: he would see her at any minute. His head came up scarcely an arm's length away from where Lucy stood; as she stared, he found his feet on the river bed, and slowly stood up in the shallows. From the water emerged sloping shoulders, draped with a bright strand of weed; water dripped from dark nipples, raised by the cold on shallow but quite unmistakable breasts. Lucy's widening eyes fell with the sliding stream to a flat belly, where a line of wet curls led downwards. Mr. Brown was a woman.

At that moment she saw Lucy. The shock – was it fear? – in her face was veiled so quickly that Lucy could not be sure it had been there. The gold-flecked eyes shone with mockery; 'Mr. Brown' threw one hand to her brow in a larger than life gesture of despair.

"Discovered!" she cried, "and by a woman!" She turned to Lucy, appealing. "Must all my fortunes founder thus?" She drooped. Then she threw back her head defiantly. "No, no!" she cried, "I have it!" She pretended to strike herself on the chest. "All may yet be well!" she announced, springing towards the pile of clothes.

Lucy did not know whether to laugh or run. This naked, capering stranger was clearly mad; but also wonderful.

As Lucy watched, she picked up from the heap of tangled small-clothes a long band of linen which she began to bind tightly over her breasts. She worked deftly, with the ease of practice, talking all the time. "Truth, dear nymph, like beauty, is in the eye of the beholder." She pulled on the ruffled shirt and struck another attitude. Then, as if she were telling a secret, she added, "Thou shalt know the man, by the Athenian garments he hath on." She frowned. "Though whether these drawers are of the true Athenian cut, I know not. However, I needs must put them on."

This she proceeded to do, but in such a droll way, tripping and fumbling, that Lucy giggled. She had no idea what half the woman's words meant, but she knew she had been made into an audience, and was being entertained. She sat down on the bundle and watched, spell-bound, as the figure before her turned from a woman into a man.

Mr. Brown buttoned his coat, flicked an imaginary mote of dirt from his sleeve and, hat in hand, bowed deeply to Lucy.

Lucy gazed up at him – her? – dazzled and bemused.

"'Tis the habit, as they say, maketh the man," said Mr. Brown, gently. "And so it was a *gentleman* of the theatre you met in the fields today, was it not, my dear?"

Was there a hint, just the slightest trace, of urgency in the voice? Lucy, still under the spell, got to her feet and dropped a little curtsy. "Yes, sir," she whispered.

Mr. Brown smiled, and Lucy was dazzled again. "Thou art a beagle true-bred. Hold, here's half my having." He dug in his pocket. "A complimentary ticket for the Theatre Royal, Barnyard," he grinned. "Seven o'clock."

Picking up Lucy's hand, he kissed it, then curled her fingers round something small and hard. As Lucy looked down at the metal token, Mr. Brown walked quickly away.

Two

She was late, and she had forgotten all about the eggs.

"Do you never hear what I say?" Her mother looked at her with weary reproach, red hands dripping suds and her pale face dripping sweat into the washing tub. "Be sure to ask old Mr. Bristow if they can spare us any eggs from the outlayers, I said."

"Oh, Mam, I can't. He looks at me."

"That's why he gives you the eggs, you daft lummock. You forgot to see if there were any blackberries, too, I'll warrant."

"I'll go back," Lucy said.

"No, Luce, you can't. Don't go tearing off. It's three miles. And it's the first of the month – I remembered while you were out. You need to get up to the church for the dole."

Looking at her mam, drooping with tiredness over the washing tub, Lucy felt a great surge of love and anger – love for her poor little mother, and anger at the rest of the world. She ran and kissed her. "All right," she said.

"That's a good girl."

"But don't blame me if the poxy overseer comes dangling down here after us again," Lucy said, peering into the bit of mirror to try to tame her hair. "It's you he's set his piggy eyes on. I'm bound to disappoint him."

Her mother almost laughed. "Let him come! Noll Wethered? It takes more than a brass-button coat from the vicar and a pair of greasy palms to get on t'right side of me, as I've often told him to his face. Fetch the loaf, our Luce, and leave me to finish this lot before I drop."

Lucy trudged the dusty mile to the village, her mind still filled with Mr. Brown. She stretched her hand out and looked at the place he had kissed. The golden eyes looking into hers had made her warm inside. She felt it again now, thinking about him. Or her.

For once, Lucy ignored the purse-lipped old dames in the bread queue and the comments of the rowdy oafs in the lane. There was one of the players' papers on a stump by the church gate. She stopped and looked. Not for the first time, she wished she could read. But even without knowing what it said, its bold staring letters filled her with secret expectation.

She smirked boldly at Wethered as he gave her the loaf, despite his angry eyes. Let him hate her. She didn't care. She knew something he didn't. She clutched the token in her pocket.

As the afternoon's thundery heat abated, Lucy sat by the stream, keeping out of her mother's way in case she was given another chore that would stop her going back to the barn. Mam was always on at her, and she was worse when she was tired. "What's wrong with you, girl? Why can't you ever see what needs doing? Mooning and moping – I don't know what I've done to deserve you..." on and on and on.

Lucy squeezed her eyes shut, seeing dancing green splodges. Her mam's voice whined on in her head. "I've slaved for you since the day you was born. Your father would be ashamed of you, he would, if he could see us now..."

Lucy ground her teeth. She hadn't asked to be born. As for her father, she'd never even seen him. The only men she knew were the red-faced bandy-legged ploughboys and their ratty, creeping fathers who came down to visit her mother on hot summer nights. Ever since Bet had come back to the village, turned away from her maid's place because she was carrying Lucy, they had survived alone in the hut by the river. And you couldn't live just on the washing and the parish dole. As soon as she was big enough to notice, Lucy had learned to creep away when a visitor came, to hide by the river or sit shivering in the leaky wash-house stuffing her fingers in her ears. She hated them all, loud-mouthed or sneaking, silly boys or respectable fathers of families. At least none of them was her father.

That was obvious enough.

She began to tease out her hair with a gap-toothed comb, and let her thoughts drift back to the players. There was no clock in the cottage, and the church was hidden by the hill. She couldn't bear it if she missed the show. She would wait until the shadow of the big willow reached the drying-poles, she decided, and then go anyway.

She finished combing her hair, pinned her little plain cap back on and leaned out over the water to judge the effect. Dark eyes stared up at her from a snub-nosed brown face. Her face came from him, from the black man with the silver collar that her stupid mother had adored.

The face her father had given her pulsed and wavered in the deep current. She hated it, because she knew everyone else did. Santa Lucia! she thought scornfully. An ugly mug and a fancy name was all she had from Prince Monatuma. Prince? That was another fine story her mother had swallowed. Sam the coachman was what he was, at the big house far away up north. She splashed the face to pieces with her hand.

It must be near to seven o'clock. She stood up and put the comb away. The token was safe in her pocket.

Her mother was dozing by the door.

"The player people said I could go back for some washing," Lucy said casually.

Her mother grunted, and looked up at her. "Take care then,"

she said. "No doubt they're no better than they should be."

"Oh, Mam!"

"Never you mind 'Oh, Mam.' Look out for them, is all I'm saying. Be back before dark." She settled herself to catch the last warmth of the sun.

Lucy waited till she got to the end of the lane before she started to run.

There were people at the barn already. They stood about chatting or looking at the papers on the walls. Mr. Stukely, the older of the two men she had seen this morning, stood at the door taking money from those who went in. Lucy went up to him, as bold as she could, and offered him the token. He looked surprised, but said nothing, only waved her inside with a large gesture of his arm.

The closed space of the barn throbbed with the day's heat and glimmered with a golden haze of light. There were candles everywhere, more than Lucy had seen in one place before: on the walls, in tall candlesticks perched up on the platform at the far end and, overhead, a great ring of candles stuck in a cartwheel that had been hung from the forward beam of the old roof. The light flickered off buckles and buttons, and gleamed palely on the sweating brows of people wearing their Sunday clothes on a hot summer night. Lucy played nervously with her fresh-combed hair and looked about her. There were a lot of people. The village folk were beginning to file on to benches facing the platform. In front of those were two rows of chairs – for the gentry and the big farmers, some of whom stood about in knots, talking. Lucy was shy of sitting with the villagers; and anyway, how were they going to see what happened, with the gentry in their tall chairs and great hats there in front? Would they take their hats off when it began? Not them, thought Lucy. Where could she go, to see and not be seen?

Behind her, the shadowy end of the barn was crammed with

everything that had been cleared from the floor, thrown up on to half a stack of hay and a great old wagon. Up above that, perched on a cross-beam, was Jemmy Hodson, the carter's boy. He grinned, and winked at her with his good eye. He was all right, Jemmy. And the other children kicked him for his blind eye and misshapen face, even worse than they taunted her for her dark skin. So they had something in common. She ducked round into the dark and scrambled up; he shifted along to make room.

"I seen it yesterday," he hissed. "It was powerful fine!"

Beyond the lights on the stage was a huge red curtain. The two younger actors that Lucy had met that morning, the Ashtons, came and stood in front of it and played fiddle music. When all the gentry had at last sat down, the music stopped, and a few people clapped their hands. The musicians disappeared round the side of the platform and, before the front row of the audience could get their chatter going again, there was a great rumbling bang, like the roof falling in, and the red curtain drew back. Lucy clutched at Jemmy's arm, but he laughed, and pointed at the three figures which had been revealed. Tall, cloaked, wearing black masks like the mummers who came round the villages at Pace-egging time, they were huddled over a cooking pot, rocking and moaning. Then they raised their heads. The blank stares from the deep empty eye-sockets of their masks were terrible. They started to chant in eerie voices.

"When shall we three meet again?"

Lucy's blood froze, but Jem was having a fine time.

"They're witches, see? Can't you see the devil looking over their shoulder?" He shuddered delightedly.

Before she could answer, two men strode out from behind a painting of trees and started to speak. The witches stood still. One began to scratch himself.

After a while, Lucy recognised the man who was doing all the talking as Mr. Stukely. As the play went on, she found that it did not matter that she could not understand most of the words; it was quite clear what was happening. Mrs. Stukely, her hair all piled up and stuck with jewels, wearing a rich red gown (surely not the battered thing she had been mending? It looked far finer in the candlelight) urged her husband to murder the king. In the end she had to help him do it, and came back shuddering and rolling her eyes, with blood dripping off her dagger. After a while Lucy almost forgot to look for Mr. Brown, but she thought she saw the lean face and mocking smile several times as the play went on. She was almost certain that he was the one who fought with Mr. Stukely at the end. There was something about the way he waved his arms that gave her a sudden shocking memory of the woman by the river.

After an hour that seemed like a whole lifetime, the story ended and the gentry, clapping politely, got up and walked about. Lucy came slowly out of the spell the play had cast over her, to find that her feet had gone dead. She wriggled them vigorously, ready to get down. "It's not over," hissed Jemmy. "There's more yet."

So she sat tight, pins and needles notwithstanding, and eventually was rewarded by the sight of Mr. Brown, quite unmistakable this time in his brown coat and breeches of the afternoon. He was very dashing, and when Mrs. Ashton appeared in blue silk and a lace cap, crying, he made the most gallant love to her. Two lads near the back of the barn offered loud and rude suggestions as to how he might proceed, but Mr. Brown gazed into the lady's eyes as if there was no one else in the room. Lucy sat breathless, drinking in every word. In the end the lady in blue overcame the opposition of her horrid old father (Mr. Stukely in a full-bottomed wig) and threw herself into Mr. Brown's arms, crying, "At last! I am yours!" Lucy, who knew without a shadow of doubt that she would have done the same, whistled and hooted with the village boys.

The spell was still on her as she joined the crowd pushing and struggling towards the great door. What would it be like to be the player woman, to be wooed every night by Mr. Brown? She clasped her hands together. "At last! I am yours!" she mouthed silently.

It was only as she came out into the warm darkness and saw the bright sliver of the moon that she panicked. How ever long had she been there? And she had not even got any washing from the players. Urgently, she began to push her way through the press of bodies, towards the road.

A hand caught her shoulder. "As I'm alive! Is it the Nut-Brown Maid?"

The pale face was shadowed by the broad-brimmed hat, but she knew him at once.

"And how did you find the play, my dear?"

"Oh, I – I liked it!" she stammered, and then, before she could stop herself, "You were the best!"

Mr. Brown seemed amused, but pleased. "Your perspicacity is beyond that of the London critics," he said wryly. Then, seeing she did not understand, he added gently, "I thank you, from my heart. You must tell me if I can ever be of service to you." He made the slightest of bows, his eyes still on hers.

"Oh no. My mother –" Desperate to go, longing to stay, Lucy hardly knew what she was saying. "Might you need any laundry doing, sir?" she blurted out.

She was startled by the loudness of his laughter. Then he stopped and, bending towards her, touched her face lightly with the back of his hand. She tried not to gasp.

Mr. Brown smiled. "I am sure I must have. The dust of the road, you know – it cries out to be washed away, whatever the cost. Come with me." He turned and strode off, leaving the circle of light at the barn door. Lucy scuttled after, her heart banging with excitement.

The door he led her to was only at the far end of the barn, behind where they had put up their stage; it led directly to a ladder. The smell of hay seeped down from the darkness above. He turned and, putting his finger to his lips, took her hand. They sprang up the rough steps, Lucy grabbing her skirts with her free hand.

The loft was dark, but hay loomed in heaps all around and was soft underfoot. They stepped out from the top of the stair. Lucy was almost laughing; her blood pounding in her ears. She reached out, and Mr. Brown took both her hands, pulling her into his arms. They were so close Lucy could feel his breath. The words came without thinking. "At last – I am yours!"

This time she felt rather than heard the laughter that shook him. "Not yet, I think, madam. But on my word as a gentleman," and his arm tightened on her waist, "I swear you will be presently." Their mouths came together and they sagged slowly sideways into the hay.

The dry stalks pricked the backs of Lucy's legs. She reached to pull her petticoats down, but Mr. Brown's hand was there first. "Too late for modesty, sweetheart." He kissed her again, harder this time, his tongue urgent on hers, until Lucy was giddy with longing. The hand moved on her thighs and belly. The ache of her need was almost pain. Then his hand moved again, and she shuddered and cried out.

"Do I please you, madam?" murmured Mr. Brown.

"Oh, yes," cried Lucy, " yes, yes!" and the world began to spin.

Next morning she washed and ironed his two shirts. Her mother had snorted with disgust when she came home with so little.

"Out half the night, and two plain shirts to show for it, girl!"

They were not plain; both had big front ruffles, edged with lace. She imagined the actor putting them on. The ruffles were to hide Mr. Brown's breasts, of course. She closed her eyes. The memory of him was enough to make her own breasts tighten and the ache start again between her legs. She shook herself back into the present, and went to put the cooled iron on the fire. Her whole body felt different this morning; she felt she sure it must show. It was a wonder her mother had not noticed the change in her. She picked up the other flat-iron and went back to Mr. Brown's shirts, taking pains to starch and press them as full and frilly as she could.

As she walked to the barn, she thought wildly of insisting that he take her with him, begging to be a stroller and stay with him, look after him, share his secret life. And all the while, she knew she would say nothing. She was plenty old enough to know what happens to girls who ask too much from men who enjoy their company for a night. But Mr. Brown was not a man, she told herself. He was – something far, far better. Lucy smoothed a careful hand over the ruffles of the top shirt. That was something she knew now, too. It would not make any difference; he would go away and leave her; but somehow, Lucy thought, one day, she could make use of what she knew for herself. There was a way out, and she could find it.

As she had expected, he smiled and paid her – no more than she asked – and turned away; the company were packing up, and would be gone by midday. Lucy stood for a moment, quite unable to stir, pierced by such desire as she had never known. But when he looked back, it was distantly, without a smile, and she knew she could not speak. She was sure she would never see him again.

Three

It was a cold autumn and a wet winter. Thatches dripped and rotted; half the village sheep took the cough, and many died. Bet's drying ground was a sheet of ice and the cottage floor three inches of mud.

The first snow came in December and Lucy and her mother were cut off behind drifts up to the eaves. Lucy battered her way out to the church door for bread, and begged for firing, but there was none to spare; they were beaten away even from gleaning sticks in the hedges of the neighbouring farms. Lucy's mother whined and cursed the farmers for tight-arsed swine. "Christians? The poor may starve at their very doors." She coughed and spat in the mud.

The thaw over Christmas brought sickness. When Lucy went for bread on New Year's Day, hardly anyone else had turned out. The few who had were huddled in the patch of chilly sunlight by the porch. As usual they ignored Lucy.

"And Dame Hennessy's took very bad," a woman was saying. "Shivering and sweating at once, she were, when I called by."

Her audience nodded; it was almost as if they enjoyed the bad luck of their neighbours, Lucy thought. She sat down on a flat tomb and wondered what had become of Noll Wethered. He was well past his time; perhaps he had gone to carry food to the sick. They might all be shivering here for hours.

"'Tis not only folks as is struck down." The only man in the group spoke for the first time. "Overseer's cow died two days back. Fell down dead like it was elf-shot, just as Wethered went to feed it."

This time the satisfaction was thick in the air: he lords it over us all, Lucy thought.

She looked up as the gate clicked. The overseer, dark and forbidding as usual, with his black hat rammed down on his grey wig, came up the churchyard path. She stood quickly, not to be seen disrespecting the graves, but he ignored her and all the hungry eyes that followed him. As he put down the basket of bread he carried and drew out the great key, he began to mutter to himself. For several moments he stood, staring at the key in his hand as if he had forgotten what it was for, still mumbling under his breath. Lucy wondered if he was praying. Let us in, you daft old bugger, and say your prayers in church before we all starve here, she thought. She could not make out his words. Suddenly he thrust the key in the lock and opened the grinding door. They all moved to follow, but halted as he turned on the threshold and glared round at them. Face to face, they saw something was wrong. The overseer's usual self-important look of doing them all a favour was gone. He was red-eyed; black and white bristles scraped a greasy neck-cloth as his mouth worked, muttering and snarling. Grabbing up the basket, he disappeared into the dark doorway. The little group exchanged glances – but bread was bread, whatever had happened to the giver; the line formed and followed him in.

Lucy came last. The church was emptying as she faced Wethered. There were four loaves left in the basket. He leant forward, hands on hips.

"Well?"

"Sir?"

"What do you want?"

Lucy forced herself to be calm. "I've come for the bread, if you please, sir."

"Oh yes, no doubt you have. And why should you take honest men's bread, filth?"

He brought his face close to hers and she lowered her eyes to avoid looking at him. Just wait, she told herself, just wait. He will give it to you in the end. She gasped with pain as he gripped her suddenly by the back hair, jerking her towards him. She smelt his sour breath.

"Devil's bastard." Spittle flicked her cheek and she shut her eyes, but she could not shut out the venom in his voice. "Who knows what black demon the filthy slut your mother lay with to get you, devil-brood? And now you are growing fat on parish char-ity – growing fast, ain't you?" His free hand went to her breast. "Growing into a foul whore like your mother, to tempt Christian men from their duty?" Still panting out curses, he started to pull at her dress.

Lucy struggled, but she dared not strike him or even push him away, although he hurt her. As she twisted desperately to break free, the church door grated open and the vicar's voice boomed down the dark aisle, calling for the overseer. Wethered let her go. Lucy seized a loaf and scuttled away. She did not even stop to curt-sy when she passed the vicar, who smiled, benign and unseeing, over her head.

So fetching the poor-loaf became an ordeal for Lucy; but it had to be done if they were to eat at all. There was no washing to be had, and the few pence they had laid up from the summer were gone by January, when the snow came again. It snowed for days; that stopped even the hardiest of Bet's visitors. Maybe they were afraid their wives would trace their footsteps in the snow, Lucy thought bitterly. In any case her mother was ailing and fretful, and had no kind words for her daughter, let alone the men.

It was a surprise then when Noll Wethered appeared, on a day of hard frost, when the snow was crisped like a piece of fried bread and his boots punched black holes in its crust. Lucy hid in the wash-house as soon as she saw who it was, but he had come to see her mother, not her. He had brought them an extra ration of bread and a small hard wedge of cheese; and he made it perfectly clear how he expected to be paid. Bet was not well that day, blue-lipped and coughing, but, thought Lucy, she would still have to give him what he wanted.

Lucy looked desperately for an escape so that she would not be forced to listen while he took his pleasure, but the snow was piled against the door and the only other way was into the house where they were.

She heard the overseer's whining whisper, and then her mother's voice, raised in anger.

"God rot you, Noll, for the two-faced rogue you are!" She drew a ragged breath. "Do you dare come here with your talk of holy charity, and all for one thing? Does your vicar know his parish officer goes with whores?" She gave a snort of laughter. "If not, he soon will, for the whole village knows it, even the children: 'Oliver holy, Oliver meek, saved on Sunday and damned all week'," she chanted, then she wheezed with laughter, and the cough shook her again.

"Have a care, Bet. There are few enough will spare you a crust this hungry season. Or trudge through the snow to keep you company. You can ill afford to lose a friend." He had not expected mockery, Lucy thought: his words were threatening, but his voice had an edge of uncertainty.

Her mother's voice was rich with scorn. "I'd rather have your room than your company, Overseer. And if it's company we're talking, shouldn't you be keeping your poor ailing wife company these dark days? The poor frail thing could die in her bed while you're whoring round the parish like a stinking tom cat, catching the fever and God knows what else from the likes of me. Get out of here, and leave me be!"

She had no strength to do more than rail at him and stare him down, but in the end he did go, growling and cursing her. When Lucy came out of the wash-house her mother grinned weakly at her; the bread and cheese were still on the table. Lucy did not know whether to be glad or sorry. Her mother still had some fight left in her; but it was Lucy who would have to face him in the dole-queue.

Sure enough, when she next went down to the church, he had a new torment ready and waiting for her.

"Now then, girl, how old are you?"

"Fifteen, please sir."

"Too old for a child's dole," he said briskly. "Should be at work. Off with you. Next!"

Lucy stood her ground, shaking. "But please, sir, there is no work."

"No work, no bread," said the overseer. His bloodshot eyes gleamed with pleasure.

She could not give in. "My mother is sick, sir – we work when we can – when there is any honest work to do."

She should not have said that. He twitched; she thought he would strike her, but he said, "There is parish work that you can do, girl. Get down to Shippen's yard, the stone-breaking. You can have a loaf when you have carried a day's load of stone to the highway."

So she carried stones, in a rough shallow basket that bruised her hip. Her fingers were soon split and swollen where the cold rocks slid and trapped them. To and fro they went, Lucy and three other women, to dump their stones in the pot-holes of the road, then back to the yard where the men were breaking more stone for them to carry away. Two of the men were turned-away labourers who could wield the heavy hammers all day; then there was Bert, the village daftie, and an old travelling man with a stiff and swollen leg. The overseer came every morning, as soon as it was fully light. Sometimes he would stand and watch them work; but mostly he only checked the road they were mending. So many strides since his last visit, whatever the weather, and woe betide them all if his shoes showed any mud when he stepped off.

On the Friday week after Lucy started work, a bleak February day after a bitter night, Wethered did not appear. When the church clock struck noon, the men in the yard straightened up and looked at each other; but after a few minutes they went back to work, as much to warm themselves as from fear of the overseer.

The light was already going when Lucy, up on the road, heard a distant shout, and a smear of ragged noise on the wind. She cocked her head. The noise seemed to come from the village; then, a few minutes later, from further off: an ugly, persistent clatter, mixed with voices chanting. Drunks from the ale-house, idle in this weather, bullying some poor fool with a skinful and no sense, she told herself. She was glad she was not there.

She emptied her stones into the mud, and turned to go back. Someone was running up the road from the village.

"Lucy!" It was Jemmy Hodson, staggering and gasping with effort. As he came closer she could see that his face was livid, the ruined eye-socket dribbling crusty tears in the cold wind, red spots of panic on his cheeks. Fear gripped her.

"Lucy! They're after your mam!"

Wordlessly she lunged past him and started to run towards the village. He caught her arm and hung on, dragging her to a halt. "No, don't go. He'll kill you!"

She struggled to shake off his desperate grip. "Where?"

"At t'ale-house. No, stop!"

She was off down the road again, half-dragging him with her.

"Noll Wethered," he gasped out. "It's Noll Wethered. He said she was a witch."

Lucy stopped and faced him. Her heart was banging with fear. "Tell me. Quick."

"He came down to the ale-house, dinner-time. He was like a mad man, raving, saying his wife was dead." Jemmy gasped for breath, and went on, "They gave him gin, and then he wept and howled more. So they give him more gin, and they all had some with him, then he says, it's that foul whore, Bet Weaver – beg pardon, Lucy, that's what he said. He said, she ill-wished my Mary. My Mary were hale and hearty last night, he said –"

"Liar! She's been sick abed these three months, and everybody knows it." Lucy grabbed him by the shoulders. "Then what happened?"

"He said, she ill-wished my Mary and now Mary's dead and cold. He said, she's a witch, Bet Weaver's a witch and she's killed my wife. And then they all got to shouting, and telling about your mam –" He staggered as Lucy let go of him and was off again, running.

As they reached the first houses, the village lay quiet. No noise came from the ale-house. The street was deserted; the cottages seemed shuttered and still. Lucy turned on Jemmy, shaking him by his thin shoulders. "What happened? Where is he?"

"S-stop it, Lucy, you're hurting, I was trying to tell you. It was when Noll says, them Weavers is a nest of Satan and a scandal in the parish, and it's the duty of the parish to root it out. And they all grabs up tankards, and pots and pans, and sticks from the hearth –"

He broke off as they both heard, quite clearly this time, the shouting down by the river.

"How many?" she said.

"All of them. All the men that were there."

With clenched teeth she turned her face from the closed

cottages to the night sky. She would kill him if he hurt her mam. She would kill him anyway and be done with him. She grabbed up her skirts and ran.

As she reached the rising ground in front of the cottage, she could hear their racket and see a wavering yellow light. Her bare feet were numb; each pounding step thudded into the knot of fury at the back of her neck. Cresting the hill, she stopped and threw herself flat.

It was like a vision of hell. The cottage was dark inside, but its torn thatch and crumbling walls flickered in the dirty light of a dozen smoking torches. The men who held them pranced and bellowed between her and her home. None of them had looked round at her approach; they were making enough noise to drown the coming of a troop of dragoons.

She could not see her mother, but Wethered stood on a mound close to the cottage, holding up a torch so that it spilled light down over him; his face was ruddied in the torchlight, his eyes like black holes. His mouth opened and shut on a relentless stream of words; Lucy did not want to hear what he was saying. Mam's inside, she thought. I must go round them to get to her. Slowly she backed down out of sight and, bending as low as she could, made for the riverbank downstream where she would be hidden by the trees.

Outside the light of the torches it was now pitch dark. Scrambling painfully through old brambles under the trees, Lucy began to panic. At last she broke through on to the grass of the riverbank and turned to run towards the cottage. One foot hit mud; she slid, overbalanced and fell into the racing river.

She gasped and choked as her head broke the water. Flinging out a hand, she felt cold, slimy leaves slip through her fingers. She struggled helplessly against the current and suddenly found herself rammed back against the bank. Frantically, she twisted round and grabbed at the tussocky grass, her feet slipping in deep mud.

She raised her eyes. She could see the cottage now, because the thatch had begun to burn. She heaved desperately against the pull of the water and, with her last strength, flung herself bodily up the bank. The world exploded in white light, and then blackness.

When Lucy came to, the only sounds she could hear were in her own head: the thud of blood in her ears and the squealing clamour of her own panic. The noise of shouting, the thud of footsteps, had gone. She opened her eyes, not on flickering torchlight but on a steady red glow. The cottage was burnt – was still burning, the doorway like a raw throat opened in a scream. Only the glowing thatch moved, red straws twisting like fiery worms as it sank into the charred space between the ruined walls.

Lucy struggled to her feet and numbly began to move towards it. The heat hit her like a jeering blow. Her head swam; she thought she could hear Noll Wethered's whispering voice, taunting her.

"Did you think you could escape, devil-spawn? Little black whore? I have you now, slut." His voice was thick, insistent – and it was not in her head. He stepped out of the shadows and moved towards her.

Before she could gather her exhausted body to flee, he was on her.

Four
Shropshire, July 1735

"Will you drive us then, Hope?" William laughed as he always did at his own old joke; he never tired of making vaguely admiring fun of Hope's role as the man of her household. She smiled, and swung herself up into the cart. Leaning down, she helped Bell up beside her. The cart rocked as William heaved his great frame up the other side and settled in his place, taking up the reins.

Mercy had followed them out of the inn door, still talking. "And don't you go forgetting my errands, William, like you done last time, m'dear. All your man-talk, and market-talk, do drive plain things clean from your head. But I must have they linen-stuffs, do ye hear, husband?"

William smiled absently and hitched the reins.

Bell leaned down towards Mercy. "We have cloth to buy ourselves today; we need to think of winter gowns and petticoats. It would be no trouble for us to buy for you, and William need not worry."

"Oh, you'm a good friend!" cried Mercy, her round face folding into a smile. "'Tis shirting I need – if you can get it good cheap, bring the whole piece, if you can carry it – and then a length of linsey-woolsey for little Joey, to make him a pair of breeches. He do grow that fast, he be bursting through his small-clothes!" She threw a proud arm round little Joey, a hulking thirteen-year-old

27

already tall enough to look her in the eye. "Why, customers will think I can't keep my boy decent, and him with his shirt-tail coming through his breeches!" She laughed and hugged him. Joey grinned, embarrassed.

He will be as tall as William, Hope thought. And if his mother goes on spoiling him as she does, he'll be as wide around the waist as she is before that.

"See, William, what good neighbours we have. Now do you take care of our Dame, and of Hope, and bring them safe home here to the Crosses for supper." Mercy reached up and patted Bell's knee. "You will take a bite with us before you go home-along? I've a fine rabbit-pie just out of the oven this very morning that I'll save against your coming. Oh, and William, do you look in the market for some fairing or fal-lal for our Nance. She's a good girl, and do work that willingly, with more than enough to do..."

The innkeeper grinned down at his wife and slapped the reins. The old horse lurched into motion; the cartwheels groaned on the cobbles of the yard. Mercy waved, still calling instructions, and Joey nodded and grinned, until the cart turned creaking into the road.

Hope settled herself more comfortably on the smooth board that served for a seat. Her left leg pressed comfortably against Bell's; a small smile flickered between them. On her other side, William frowned in concentration and whistled tunelessly through his teeth. The sun was already hot; the hedgerows heavy with summer green and crowned with honeysuckle. A sense of well-being flowed through Hope. She would have liked to put an arm round Bell, but contented herself with leaning gently against her as the cart rocked and swayed over the baked wheel-ruts of the Ludlow road.

William spoke suddenly. "I do need your counsel, friends." He stared ruminatively ahead. Hope and Bell exchanged looks.

"It be twenty years, come harvest-home," said William slowly, "since Mercy and I plighted our troth. Aye, a full score of years." He stared thoughtfully at the horse's ears. "She'm a good woman, Mercy. I would fain bring her a gift for they twenty years. A token, like." He turned a perplexed face to the two women. "But I swear I know not what it should be."

Bell smiled with relief. "We shall think of something, have no fear – and keep your secret, too."

William's brow cleared. "I knew you would," he said gratefully, and resumed his silence.

Twenty years? The voice of Grace Marjoram, long dead, echoed in Hope's head as if it were yesterday: "Tell Mercy Lewis she should marry. William Jones-the-Mardu will be a good-enough father for her children." And so he had been, Hope thought, with a rush of affection for the big man sitting beside her. Mercy had made a more than good-enough man of him. As to children, well, that had been a different matter. For all their prayers, and all Bell's skill in medicine, only Joseph of all the five had survived infancy. It was no wonder his mother thought him the nonpareil.

Hope shook her head. Could it truly be twenty years? The year that Mercy and William had married had been the same year that she and Bell had come to the valley, fleeing from the violence of war, and from a world which had no place for them or their love. Their flight had carried them along this very road.

For a moment the early morning sun was darkened by a memory of that winter journey; of pain, hunger and fear. How young we were, Hope thought, and how completely alone. War had robbed Bell of home and family: her father and elder brother dead, her beloved younger brother Alistair fled to France. Hope had given up everything to follow Bell into exile. But they had found a new life here, against all the odds. She shuddered, thinking how differently their journey could have ended.

As if she had followed her thoughts, Bell reached for Hope's hand. "All's well," she said gently. Then more loudly, to William,

"Those years have been good to us all, have they not?"

As Bell gazed out at the passing fields, Hope studied the woman who had shared her life for so long. She found it difficult, nowadays, to remember a time when Bell had not been there, her face and body as familiar as Hope's own. Her eyes dwelt with pleasure on the slight, dark-haired figure. It did not seem to her that Bell had changed visibly from the sixteen-year-old beauty with the serious brown eyes who had captured her heart all those years ago. Just then Bell turned, as if she had felt Hope's gaze, and they smiled into each other's eyes.

Ludlow was full. The stalls and booths crowding the market lapped up to the gates of the castle and spilled along the neighbouring streets. William unhitched Tranter from the cart and stabled the old horse at the Feathers, before he went off to the parlour there with the air of a man ready for a good long morning. He had come to settle even with a series of farmers with whom he exchanged dung for oats and barley. They met on market days, and made a comfortable ceremony of their bits of solemn reckoning over several mugs of ale.

"We'll have to fetch him out later to look for something for Mercy," said Bell, "or he'll not feel he's had his proper say."

Hope swung the heavy poke that contained their day's trading goods on to her shoulder and smiled down at Bell. "Let's be rid of these first, though," she said.

Visits to the market town, perhaps four or five times in the year, were infrequent enough to give them the feeling of a holiday. Their life was in many ways self-sufficient. Hope cut and hauled their fuel from the woods around, and Bell could make them a meal from almost anything Hope brought in from her garden. The goats kept them in milk and cheese; and the steady stream of neighbours who came to the cottage seeking medicine or advice from Bell meant that the two women never lacked company or a helping hand if they needed one. For the one or two things they could not provide for themselves, they came to market: their surplus produce and some of Bell's remedies produced the little income they needed.

They set off now for the bottom of the town by the bridge where Weatherby, the chandler and seed merchant, was waiting for their last precious cakes of beeswax. Hope made a profitable deal with him for her early flower-seeds, too: Ludlow gardeners were eager to come by local and unadulterated stocks. Then they pushed their way back up the hill to the apothecary's shop in Raven Lane, where Bell and old Mr. Hopkins discussed yet again the virtues of remedies for dropsy and apoplexy.

There was a submerged current in this long-running debate, which was really about a blue cordial which Bell made, and which a number of Hopkins' customers insisted was their only relief. The conversation was always polite, but never conclusive, since Bell refused to tell him the recipe. It was a little irksome to have to carry stoppered bottles of the stuff into town but, as Bell said, it encouraged confidence in the apothecary and his patients alike. The medicine was one of the well-tried recipes they had inherited from Grace Marjoram, and they had proved its power on several occasions, but Bell was sure that the mystery of its contents added to its effectiveness. "Tell them it's a decoction of common foxglove, coloured with bramble juice? It will lose half its virtue over night!" she said to Hope.

Raven Lane led straight into the market, and they set off from the apothecary's with a lighter bag to find the best of the cloth-merchants. As Hope remembered it later, they were very happy. All around them, people like themselves with a few country goods to turn into cash had mostly struck their bargains with the townsfolk who needed their eggs or butter, and were looking for ways to lighten the unaccustomed weight in their pockets. The crowd were in holiday mood. Gingerbread and hot cakes were on sale at the corner of Castle Street; pot-boys pushed through the press of people, miraculously balancing full tankards on boards held over their heads. Bell slipped her arm through Hope's.

Then they were brought to a halt by the crush, beside a baker's shop with great raised pies set out on a table. The crowd had thickened to a stop.

"What is it? Can you see?" said Bell.

Hope hopped up on to a mounting block by the wall. "Not clearly. Something on the steps of a house there, I think. Oh look, it's two women." She took Bell's hand to haul her up on to the narrow foothold.

The women were dressed in grey, with deep white bonnets, and held books in their hands. The younger of them, a short, dark-haired girl, was speaking earnestly to the crowd.

"Quakers!" said Hope. "It's Quaker preachers, isn't it? I can't hear what she says."

But they watched for a few moments anyway, intrigued by the sight of women, apparently alone, speaking in public. The Quakers were known for it, but it was still surprising. The two women had a quiet assurance of manner which was compelling, aside from anything they might say. The dense crowd was all attention: the preachers had clearly been at it for some time. As Hope and Bell watched, indeed, the sermon came to its climax, with amens and halleluiahs from some of the crowd; the little Quaker stopped speaking and stood quite still, her head bowed over folded hands.

Hope was already looking for space to jump down from their precarious perch when she felt Bell's grip on her arm tighten painfully. She looked down at her friend's face: Bell was white to the lips, her eyes fixed on the figures on the steps. Following her gaze, Hope saw that a man, dressed in the brown broadcloth coat and wide hat of a Quaker, had come out of the door behind the preacher women and was speaking to them. His hand lay on the arm of the younger one. As he turned to hold the door for them to go in, Hope saw him full-face.

She looked back at Bell and then, quite certain now, she looked again at the man on the steps.

"It's Alistair," she said.

Hope and William left Bell in Ludlow. They rode back with bolts of shirting and woollen cloth, a ribboned cap for Nance and a piece of French lace for Mercy; with a cask of brandy for the inn and great blocks of salt for themselves and various neighbours against the coming autumn; and on William's part at least, with a tale of wonder to tell at home. Hope sat silent beside him in the heavy summer dusk as he rolled his amazement round and round his tongue.

"Bydam, 'tis a rare do," he said for the fifteenth time. "I did never hear the like." He shook his head in disbelief. "I had forgot she ever had a brother, like. But I call it all to mind, now. Mercy will remember him. Years ago – when you first came by here, before you settled up the bank. He were the one with the broken head, weren't he?"

"He was," said Hope.

About half a mile further on, William changed his tack. "Wait on, now. I do remember something. His name was on that list they put on the church door at Castlebridge. List of Jacobites. Condemned men." He turned to face her. "But you said he was safe, because he were off to foreign parts." His face creased with sudden concern. "Is he in any danger from the law, being in England again, think'ee?"

The last thing Hope needed at this moment was William remembering more about Bell's family, her past life. She fought to keep her voice calm. "No, I think we need not fear that. There is not much heard of the Jacobites now, not in these parts. And Alistair has a new life, seemingly, among the Quakers." And his sister has a new life, she thought desperately. With me, here. She swallowed to calm herself.

"I hope he don't go unsettling our Dame," said William, "and calling her away. What should we do without her?"

For a moment Hope's throat closed; the hand that had clutched her heart when she recognised Bell's brother squeezed painfully in her chest. William had voiced her deep and abiding fear since she first knew Bell: a fear which the years between had lulled to sleep but never entirely killed. In those far-off days, Bell had been the squire's daughter, and Hope had been a servant. Alistair would not even remember her now, let alone imagine any claim she might have on his sister. She saw again Bell standing on the steps of the Quaker house, upright and tense; saw the door open and the maid-servant admit her; saw the door closed. She forced herself to speak calmly.

"You heard what she said, William. She spends this night with them and comes home tomorrow, when they go off about their preaching. They go towards Montgomery and west. Alistair is to marry the girl we saw speak. When they return from Wales they may take Bell home with them. But only for a visit. Only to see the wedding."

Only for a visit. Only for the wedding. Alistair and his new wife, settled and setting up house. Plenty of room for his still-pretty, unmarried sister. In Coalbrookdale, forty miles away. The cold hand squeezed and squeezed Hope's heart.

Five
August

"This way, ladies and gentlemen, this way! The world's greatest rope-dancer is about to begin his astounding performance, hard by this very inn! The only time outside London! Step this way, now."

A young woman in low-cut pink brocade, with a small lace handkerchief straining to cover her ample breasts, pulled her man in Lucy's direction. Lucy stretched her face into a smile, bowing them round to the field at the back of the inn. Then she moved on quickly to work the rest of the party, a crowd of locals returning in high good humour from a wedding, most fortunately met with at this wayside halt.

"Witness the most perilous and death-defying feats ever brought before the public! Signor Moretti will walk on his hands the entire length of the rope, backward and forward, balancing his whole family on the soles of his feet! One performance only in this place, beginning in one minute!"

She was tired to death. Short of breath and sweating in the late August heat, she flapped the bedraggled frill on her flimsy red bodice away from her neck and longed for a drink. She was the only draw the show had, and little enough to get their attention. She banged her drum with as much of a flourish as she could muster.

"Follow me, ladies and gents. Just behind the inn here – plenty of shade to protect the ladies' complexions!" That was usually good for a laugh at her expense from one of the crowd who thought himself a wit; but these goggling red-faced idiots did not seem to take the point. They were willing enough, though, in holiday mood and full of drink. She banged a roll on the drum.

"The family Moretti, rope-dancers and prize gymnasts! All the way from the Low Countries, by command of the Highest in the Land! An opportunity not to be missed, and here today for your delight, the dangerous and amazing feats which have captivated the Crowned Heads of Europe!"

Personally she thought this was overdoing it a bit, but it was part of the patter which Henri particularly liked. I hope he's got the rope right this time, she thought grimly, or we'll all be sore by bedtime. Her back ached enough these days without his bad temper taken out on her. She lifted the drum on its shoulder-strap to ease herself upright. However loose she tied her stays, there was no way of being really comfortable, standing up or lying down. At night the lump in her belly pressed on some part of her guts, however she burrowed into the straw.

The crowd were on the move now, following the bold girl in pink and her beau. Striking a marching beat, smiling and beckoning, Lucy ran wide round them to lead the way to the place where the slack rope was slung between two trees.

Henri began his first set as Lucy settled them on the grass round the worn carpet. Simple stuff to grab their attention first, summersets and handsprings; then little Dino tied up into a ball with a broad leather strap, rolled round and round on the soles of his father's feet.

Sinking down in the shade of the hedge, Lucy let herself relax. As if out of spite, the baby promptly kicked her in the side. She sat up, squeezing her eyes shut to keep back the tears. How much longer? Watching Henri booting his younger son up in the air and catching him spinning, she counted the time again.

It had been two months before she had realised the baby was there. She was still quite near to home then – to where her home had been. She had not left the outskirts of Chester until she was quite sure that her mother had died in the fire. Then she had taken to the road, tramping southwards, no idea where she was going, just trying to shake free from the nightmare of the burning cottage and what Noll had done to her. By the time the first warmer days had come, she was in an unknown countryside of huge flat fields and red earth, and she had missed two lots of bleeding. People fed her at cottage doors; some even gave her a day's work washing or cleaning, but no one would let her stop, especially when they saw her puking her heart out in the ditches. It had been a gypsy woman who had told her for sure about the baby. She had given Lucy a herb drink she said would make it go away. Lucy half-hoped it would turn out to be poison, so she could die and not have to go on; but it had only made her sicker, screaming with cramps for a day and a night, and left her weak.

Thinking that the parish officers in a town might be less hot on keeping her from settling, she had ventured into Market Drayton. That had been the first of May, which was why she had found the Morettis there, for the fair. She had asked a broom-seller in the busy market whether the players were in town. Not that she had any real hopes of Mr. Brown, but the festivities reminded her suddenly of the bright and beautiful people in the barn. No, he'd said, no players, but there was a tumbling man pulling a crowd up at the common.

And so she had gone and watched the act. Seeing Denis, the older boy, trying to take the hat round in between his parts in the show, she had ventured to smile at a few people on her side of the crowd, taking up a few pennies and giving them to him at the end. And they had let her stay on, grudgingly enough, and mainly because Henri's woman had left him the week before, gone off home to her mother in Llangollen, so they had no one to wash or

cook. She had come to where the people spoke Welsh in the
streets, he said, and could not bear to be a wanderer any more.
More likely she couldn't stand any more kicks or surliness from
you, Lucy thought now, watching as Henri, veins standing out like
rope, balanced on one hand on an ale-jug.

Over the weeks that she had tramped with Henri and his nasty,
dirty little sons, she had learned quickly how to work well for him.
She could draw a crowd, indoors or out, and keep them cheerful
and expectant for the endless time it took him to set up each of
his tricks. She had got better and better at beating up climaxes and
stretching out suspense. Her bottling was clever: she knew exactly
when to run the hat round, how to cut off escapes, smile away
reluctance and capture the last pennies in any crowd. Drum them
up and milk them down, Henri said; and so far he had been
pleased with her quickness. Not bad in – how long? She counted
again: four months. Four months since she joined up with them.
More than seven months since the night of the fire. So the baby
would come out in a few weeks now. She never let herself think
further ahead than that: soon she would be rid of it, rid of what
Noll Wethered had put inside her, and maybe then she could be
rid of the memory of him, too.

She focussed on Henri again. He had got on to the plate-
spinning, the end of the carpet-work part of the act. After that
came the moment the crowd had been waiting for, the famous
rope-dancing. She sighed and hauled herself to her feet, reaching
for the drum.

The rope was set right today, for a wonder, and the show went
well. The crowd were ready to be pleased, nudging each other and
groaning with appreciation as Henri, biceps bulging, strutted to
and fro over their heads, dangling the boys in wicker baskets. By
the time the people had all gone and Henri had paid the innkeeper
his vail for the use of his grass and trees and his stable loft to sleep
in, he had more than five shillings still jingling in his greasy little

bag. Still in their costumes, they packed up the gear and pulled the hand-cart close to the loft ladder.

These were the dangerous moments with Henri, Lucy had learned; days like this when there was money to drink, and not too many shows to exhaust him first. Scrambling up as well as she could with her bundle and her great belly, she crouched quickly in the corner of the loft and felt for her little knife. The boys tumbled in, ignoring her as usual, and fell together in a heap in the straw to wolf down the crusts the innkeeper had given them and their father had stopped them from eating before they performed. Henri heaved himself through the hatch and spat on the floor. Lucy pulled her feet back as she sat, making a show of cleaning her nails with the knife.

"Don't worry, cock-tease, I see it." He kicked her feet as he passed. "I can do better than you tonight. I don't need other men's leavings." He stripped off his tasselled jerkin and tights, flexing his hairy body at her. "And I don't want your brat playing with the end, I can tell you."

The boys laughed. Their father pulled on the shirt Lucy had washed that morning and climbed into his breeches. Licking his comb, he slicked back his long dark hair and tied it with a thong. Then he pocketed the money from the bag, and disappeared down the ladder.

In a moment he was back again. "You boys – remember what I said." He glared at them, then tipped his head back, twice, before he disappeared.

Lucy was tired, and she had eaten; she fell asleep as soon as she had burrowed a place to support her in the straw. She woke again, of course, in an hour or so. The boys, asleep, wore a look of innocence at odds with their waking selves: she watched them in the gloom until she could get off again herself. The second time she woke she had to make water, over in the far corner of the loft. Henri was still not back; Dino whimpered in a bad dream. The third time she barely surfaced: dragged from her deepest slumber by a pain in her back, she eased herself by turning over and was immediately asleep again.

In the morning, she wondered whether the boys had still been there then. Because they were certainly not there now.

Nor was Henri.

And nor was the cart.

She stood in the empty inn-yard in the dawn and cursed, and then wept. She was alone again.

Six
September

Hope raised her head to listen. Not a bird – but what? Parsley, crouched under the purple velvet folds of the next row of cabbages, was looking away towards the southerly woods, her ears cupped foward. Hope straightened her back, gripping the silky handle of her hoe. The treetops across the valley brushed to and fro in a rustle of wind. Nothing else. The cry was not repeated; the birds were quiet, deep in their midsummer preoccupation. She turned back to the weeds, inches high already from only a few days of warm rain. Good to get outside, though. Trapped in the cottage, she had been unable to shake off the unease. It was hard to sleep these light nights; and of course she was unused to solitude. She had not passed more than a day or two alone these many years; not slept alone, until last night.

She shook her head slightly, to dislodge the memory of her parting from Bell. Nothing in all their long life together had taught them how to say goodbye to each other. Her mind flinched from the picture of Bell, restrained – or was it relieved? – by the presence of her brother, bidding her farewell at the gate. Smiling, speaking brightly but quietly, like a lady. She had squeezed Hope's hands, but she was wearing the riding gloves Alistair had brought for her, so that even her touch was unfamiliar. And then she was gone. Transformed into a lady on horseback, and gone.

The thought provoked a little wave of self-pity that immediately shamed Hope into anger. She will be back by Christmas, she reminded herself sternly. What is the matter with me, to feel so betrayed? Twenty years of trust, of growing side by side from children almost, so shaped and fitted to each other that I can't always tell where I begin and end, or which of us had an idea or a feeling first – surely that should be enough to make me feel safe? If he had come back for her in the first year or two, when the old life was still fresh in her mind, before she found her place here, then maybe there would have been cause for fear.

For there had been a time, so long ago they had almost forgotten it, before Bell had accepted her new way of life here. For nearly a year she had refused to settle, to relinquish the dispossessed Jacobite lady and take on the role of healer and wise woman which the local people had seen in her before she would acknowledge it herself. If Alistair had come back then from his exile in France, while memories of the old life still pricked and pulled at his sister... who could tell how differently all their lives might have been shaped?

Hope shook herself. Foolish. Now is not then. She is mine as surely as I am hers. She bent to the cat, which was watching her intently.

"Tell me I'm a fool, Parsley," she said.

As she crouched, rubbing the cat behind the ears, Hope thought she heard the cry again – a sobbing scream, suddenly cut off. Puzzled, she went back to weeding her rows of small cabbages.

Suddenly Parsley leapt into the air, clapping her paws together and catching a butterfly. Hope laughed. They were all good hunters, the cats of this line, taught by their mothers almost as soon as their eyes opened. The first Parsley, the old Dame's cat, that had come to them with the cottage, had been grandam to this one; marked so like her that they had used the name again.

Why are my thoughts so far backward today? Hope wondered.

She walked out from behind the burdened bean rows to look up at Brynsquilver, sturdy against the late summer green of the hanging wood. You could still see the line of the old cottage, embedded in the new walls she had added herself: the new living space to the right, and the workshop and goat-house to the left, under the already brightening berries of a rowan. Not for the first time the thought came to her that the proud and laborious work of her own hands, building stone by stone their independence of the old life, had in fact built a house very like the gamekeeper's cottage she had grown up in. Hope shook her head, to clear it of the past.

"Hope?"

The cat shot down the garden, tail in air, and was clawing up Bron's skirts and into her arms before she was squarely landed from her one-handed vault over the stile. She stood still, steadying the bundle on her right shoulder, gentling the ecstatic Parsley in her left arm. Hope smiled. She had learned long ago that it was no use to be jealous; be it cat, dog or horse, the most devoted beast preferred Bron to its owner. Bron crossed the garden with the same long, loping stride that had no doubt brought her down from the far hill farm where she lived. Parsley rubbed her head against the weather-beaten face and clung to the bald sheepskin jerkin that Bron wore in all weathers.

"Welcome," Hope called, wiping her hands on her backside. "I was ready for a rest." She tipped her head towards the house. "You've time for a cup of something? Our last year's elderflower is still feeling the spring. It would be a good deed to help me drink it." She led the way up the path.

They settled on the bench by the door, and the cat jumped up between them. Neither spoke as Hope hefted the stone flagon and eased the waxed wadding from its neck with her thumbs. The wine fizzed and sprayed the air as Hope poured it into the beakers, enjoying the sharp, flowery scent. They drank in friendly silence. Bron was always quiet – living alone with the sheep and her two dogs since her father died, she did not use words easily – but today she was entirely silent. Hope took a good look at her as she poured the second draught: her face was drawn and unsmiling, closed in as if on some pain.

"Is aught wrong?" Hope ventured.

Bron shook her head sharply. She rolled the beaker between her palms and blew down her nose.

"It's nothing."

Hope waited for her.

Eventually Bron said, "You mind John Hamer? Took Waldon's sheep-walk after old Shep Powell, when Shep's wife died and left him with no children to help him?"

Hope nodded. "Son of a big cattle man down by Leominster, they say. Nasty piece of work, I think. He terrifies that poor little woman of his."

"So he is, nasty." Bron shrugged her jerkin round her ears and swallowed her wine at a gulp. "I reckon he wants me off my place."

"What?" Hope was outraged. "Never!"

"You may say. But I reckon that's his idea. He says things – says I've no right to what was my father's, him leaving no will, and me being only a woman. And every chance he gets, he makes trouble on the hill."

She stopped, her big thumb stroking the pattern cut into the beaker's rim. "It wasn't much at first. There's boundary stones up on the Cefns, been in place all my life – suddenly they're not quite where they were. And this morning I found a ewe, broke her legs falling down a ditch, off a walkover that was steady as a rock last week. Nothing much. But he keeps it up, day on day, all this summer. I get to dread waking up in the morning, not knowing what I'll find."

"But Bron – why didn't you say? Surely you can get the law on him?"

Bron shook her head, and made a strange, defensive gesture as if warding off a blow. "I don't want no trouble. No one would help me. I fight my own battles."

There was a pause. Hope could think of nothing to say.

After a while Bron wiped her mouth and said, "Where's our Dame?"

She was closing the subject of her own troubles, Hope thought. She set down her beaker. "You did not know? She's gone. Gone to Coalbrookdale." She felt Bron tense beside her, and forced herself to go on. "She went away with her brother, yesterday."

"Brother?" Bron's voice was tight with concern, her eyes worried.

Hope thought, she needs Bell to be here, too. "Aye, she has a brother. He's called Alistair. He –"

"I mind," Bron broke in. "She had a brother went to France, after the – back in the year '16. She has not –?"

"No, no. I tell you, Coalbrookdale. The place is north and east from here – two days' ride, they said. She has gone to see him wedded. No more." Who was she seeking to reassure, Bron or herself? She lifted the flagon. "Another?"

Bron held out her beaker. They looked down the garden. Parsley wriggled on Bron's lap, purring, turning her belly upwards to the gentle hand.

Eventually Bron spoke. "I'm on my way down to the road. To Mercy's. For my salt."

"Yes," said Hope, "William had it good cheap for you at Ludlow market – we bought ours the same day." She reached out for the cat, and saw Bron's hand draw back. She had never seen Bron touch another human being. She went on, "That was where we first saw him – at the market."

Bron looked at her curiously, and went on stroking the cat.

As Hope told her the story, she felt again the shock that had run through her when she saw Alistair, heard Bell's little gasp. "He was come and gone in a minute," she said, "but we both knew him."

"Ah," said Bron.

There was a moment's silence, then Hope took up the flagon again and carefully poured out the rest of the wine, tilting her hand back just before the first of the lees curdled the thin gold stream. She set the flagon down with the same care.

"And so I came back here alone," she said. "And when Bell came home the next day, she was full of the plan to go off and see him wed to the preacher girl." She attempted a smile. "We had much ado to make up the linsey-woolsey we'd bought that day into a gown fit for a Quaker feast – and then she needed a warm jacket and petticoat as a riding habit besides." Hope rubbed the stuff of her old gown ruefully between her fingers. "This will have to do me for another year." She looked out across the valley.

They sat together listening to the trees, that were never quite still up here, even on the calmest day. The cry that Hope had heard earlier did not come again.

Eventually Bron said, "You'll be wanting to get on."

Hope followed her down the garden. At the stile, Bron hesitated and looked back.

On an impulse, Hope said, "Look in on your way back, would you?"

Bron nodded, smiled, then vaulted the stile and was gone.

Seven

By the time Hope reached the end of the last row of cabbages, down by the bottom hedge, Parsley's shadow was longer than the little cat herself, sitting upright on the path with ears cocked. Hope leaned her hoe on the hedge and looked out over the gate. Bron was not coming, then; she had chosen the shorter but steeper road home, round Bryn. Pushing back the rush of loneliness which came with the thought, Hope shook out her skirt and set off down the slope. The goats were loud in protest in the lower field: it was more than time to bring them in for milking.

Crossing the old field, where the grass still needed resting, she heard something that stopped her dead. It was the cry she had heard this morning – but now it was clearly human. It came from the old goat-shed. Hope turned and began to run.

She pulled open the sagging door, then found herself suddenly sprawled on her back in the grass, the wind knocked out of her and her right cheek exploding into pain. She grabbed ineffectually at a bare foot that ran over her chest, but had scarcely heaved herself on to her knees when the fleeing figure collapsed with a howl into the grass. For a moment, Hope knelt there foolishly, shaking her head to clear it, before she stood up and walked cautiously towards the girl who had flung her aside.

The face that turned towards her was filthy and blood-streaked, but the eyes were blazing. The girl struggled to get up but fell back, her face contracted with pain.

"You need not run away," said Hope, "I won't hurt you." She stretched out a hand, but the girl flinched away and flung up an arm to shield her face. Then the narrow, distended body arched in a spasm of pain and she turned her face to bite the grass. Hope could see clearly now why she had not been able to run away: she was in labour – deep in, and a failing labour, if Hope was any judge. She was covered in mud, her skirt bloody and torn as if by desperate hands. The memory of the earlier screams came to Hope with dreadful clarity. She must have been in the shed all day.

Hope bent and took her gently by the shoulders. "Look at me," she said firmly. "You must let me be your friend. I have some skill in this." But not as much as Bell, she thought desperately. Why aren't you here? I knew I would need you...

Four hours later, the girl was weaker, but no nearer to the birth of her baby. She lay before the fire on a straw pallet spread with Hope's old shawl. Between her fierce, futile pains she lay more and more still, far gone in exhaustion. Hope was exhausted herself; her small experience of birthing had been no preparation for this. The old women of these hills kept their power over their daughters by making this their mystery, and even Bell, trusted wise woman for all other ills and ailments, was not their first choice for a childbed. Hope had delivered children, two or three, and had helped Bell with a dozen more; but she had seen nothing like this deathly straining for hour after hour, with nothing coming but blood. She knew much more about goats; she had turned back-facing kids, though nannies were feeble things, and still might die on you. This girl seemed unlikely to do that, after all she had so far endured, but Hope did not know how to help her.

She was standing, irresolute, at the foot of the stair, when the door opened suddenly and a tall, slightly stooped figure was outlined against the red and gold of the sinking sun.

"Bron! Thank God!"

Bron looked startled. "What's the matter?"

Before Hope could answer, the girl screamed. Bron's eyes widened; she stood, frozen, as the girl thrashed on the floor. Hope thought suddenly, she has never seen this. How could she, living all her days on a hill farm so far from other human dwellings, and no mother, no women there, only her father and brother since she was a child? Bron was staring, horrified; for a desperate moment Hope thought she might turn and go. She felt a great need to keep her, to have company, however little help it might be. Words tumbled out of her.

"I think the babe is turned wrong," she said. "It won't come. And I don't know how to help her, I..." She stopped and ran her hand through her hair. "I don't know what to do, Bron."

Bron's eyes had not left the writhing body on the floor. Hope could not tell what she was thinking. Then, still without speaking, Bron crossed to the hearth and knelt down. She took the see-sawing head between her hands; she was making a little crooning noise, between whistling and humming. She was not flung off, or bitten; the flailing body relaxed, and the hands that reached up held on, thin brown fingers gripping into Bron's old jerkin as if it were the last handhold in the world. Bron stroked the matted black hair out of the girl's eyes, then gently, and still making the same reassuring, wordless noise, ran her large red hands over the swollen belly. "Wrong-turned, yes," she said, "and wedged so. I must turn it, or it will kill her. Hold her, if she will let you."

It was over surprisingly quickly. In less than an hour the tiny boy lay whining feebly in a bushel basket, his misshapen head shaking slightly all the time. The girl was asleep. As soon as she was rid of the pain, she had fallen into a sleep so deep they had feared she was dead; but she was breathing steadily.

Bron returned from washing herself clean at the spring, and stood uncertainly about, as if the passing of the crisis had turned her suddenly back to her old awkward self. Although it was past ten o'clock, she refused Hope's offers of food or a bed for the rest of the night, and vanished into the darkness to walk the six hilly miles home.

Hope threw herself into the chair by the last embers of the fire, and fell into a fitful doze, waking every hour or so to look at her two unexpected guests: the tiny, wrinkled baby and the sleeping girl. Hope gazed down at her in the half-light: how old was she? She looked no more than a child, one thin arm clutching the blanket around her, the other pillowing her head. Sixteen? Seventeen at most, Hope thought, and not from these parts, she was sure. She had called herself Lucy. What had driven her from home in this state? Hope had known of parents who turned their erring daughters out of doors for falling with child, but surely no woman, be she mother or stepmother, could see the girl cast out at the very hour of labour? Well, the girl would tell if she wished; and if not, this was not a house which exacted payment for its hospitality in the form of unwilling confession.

Just before dawn, Hope rose again and, as quietly as she could, began to mend the fire. When she came back from the spring with fresh water, she knew that the girl was awake too, though her tightly closed eyes defied Hope to speak to her. There was a strong tea of herbs which Bell always made for women in childbed, and Hope brewed it now. When it was ready she touched the girl lightly on the shoulder.

"Drink this while it is warm. It will make you feel stronger."

Lucy shrugged away, her eyes still closed.

Hope suppressed her rising sense of irritation as uncharitable. "It will make you feel better," she repeated, "and will help your milk to come. You have not given the child suck yet, and you must look to your own well-being if you are to help him."

Lucy opened her eyes. There was no expression in them. "I don't want him," she said. She turned her back on Hope and stared into the fire.

Hope was saved from an immediate reply by the baby's wail.

She crossed to the basket and picked him up, bringing him back to his mother. "He wants you." She spoke as lightly as she could. "Look, he's hungry."

"Then it can starve," said Lucy with passion. "And best if it does. I'll not feed his brat! I've suffered pain and grief enough through him, without this. I'll not touch it, I tell you. Make it be quiet!" She kept her face turned away, but Hope heard the choking tears, and her heart filled with pity for the pain in the girl's voice.

She laid the baby on the blanket beside its mother and tried again. "However bad his father, the babe bears no blame, Lucy. It is an innocent creature, and looks to you for its life. Come now, take pity on him; he is yours now to care for, whatever the past."

As she spoke, the baby's face contorted in what looked like fury, and it began to cry in earnest, that insistent newborn cry that must be answered. In spite of herself Lucy turned towards it. She looked at the wailing baby for some time before she reached out and picked it up.

"Ugly little turd," she said savagely. "Just like its father."

Over the next few days, Lucy's behaviour towards the baby swung violently between love and rejection. She tried, with a dogged determination that wrung Hope's heart, to feed the child, but he was so weak that sometimes the mere effort of sucking seemed too much for his small energy.

"Oh, please, please feed, little baby," Hope heard her begging the child one morning. "Don't you die, too, and leave me all alone again!" But by the afternoon she was out of patience with it again, pulling the fumbling little mouth from her sore nipple and thrusting the child back into its crib, wishing it dead and its father with it.

Hope had made her up a bed in the little lean-to off the kitchen, with the basket crib beside her, and Lucy stayed there, refusing to get up and walk about, or even to wash herself. She lay staring into space, unresponsive to any attempt to draw her in to conversation. She steadfastly refused to give her son a name, referring to him as "the baby" when she was in humour, and "it" the rest of the time.

Just occasionally, a thought would stir her to life and she would attack Hope with questions.

"Where's your man?" she asked suddenly on the second morning.

Hope blinked. It was so long since any had asked her such a question. Everyone for miles knew her and Bell, and was accustomed to them. "There – there is no man lives here," she said.

Lucy's smile transformed her thin face. "Good," she said decisively. "I'm glad." She thought for a moment. "You been a widow long? Do you like it?"

Extraordinary child, thought Hope; it was impossible to be offended by her. "I do not live alone," she corrected gently. "Another woman – my friend – lives here with me."

The big dark eyes regarded her with a frank interest. She struggled. "We have not either of us been married. We – we choose to be so – we keep each other company," she added lamely.

"My mam wasn't married. But she never chose it. She would have married him, if they had let her..." Her voice trailed away and she returned to her brooding silence.

The next afternoon, however, she returned to the attack. "Where is your friend, then, who lives here? Was that her helped me when...?" She gestured at the baby.

"Oh, no," said Hope, startled, "that was Bron."

"Who's she? Is she a wise woman? A witch? She made the baby come, didn't she? How did she know I was here? Where is she now?"

Hope, concentrating on rubbing out seed-pods by the light of the window, took the easy questions first. "Bron is my old friend. She lives a way from here, in the hills – a farm her father left her

– she keeps a few sheep there. She likes animals better than people, I think. She came by on her way from market, to have a drink with me, because she knew I was alone."

Lucy took all this in and considered it. "She didn't know I was here, then?"

Hope smiled, remembering the look of horror on Bron's face when she saw Lucy. "No," she said.

"But she has the Power, anygates," said Lucy firmly.

Hope didn't bother to argue. Bell always said that there were no witches, except in the minds of those who needed to believe in them. Even after all these years, many of their neighbours thought Bell herself to be a witch, though the magic she dispensed in healing them was no more than a well-practised skill in herb-lore, tempered with a large measure of common sense. To her face, they called her Dame, and treated her with the respect due to a cunning woman; what they called her in private she neither knew nor cared. There seemed no point in discussing such things with this strange girl. Hope went on cleaning her marigold seeds to store.

"So where is she, then, your friend who lives here?" Lucy was nothing if not tenacious.

Where, indeed? thought Hope with a sudden twist of loneliness. Coalbrookdale could be at the other end of England, for all she could make a picture of it, or imagine what Bell might be doing there. Is she glad to be there? Does she miss me as much as I miss her? Is she thinking of me now?

"Gone to see her brother wedded. To a Quaker," she said shortly, and went out into the garden.

Eight
Coalbrookdale, October

Bell sighed: the parlour was empty. She had hoped that Susannah would be down by now, but the neat, pale room showed no sign of anyone having been there yet this morning. Bell was still alone with the thoughts of home that had woken her at sunrise.

She looked round the room. This was a strange house, but she would have been hard put to find words for its strangeness. It was neither very large nor very small; comfortably and solidly built, but too plainly furnished to be grand. It was unlike either of the places where she had spent her life so far and, in spite of the kindness of her hosts, in spite of being with Alistair again, she was a stranger here. She had a sharp pang of longing for home: not just for Hope, whose absence she felt all the time like a physical pain, but for her own comfortable cottage, low and dark, nestled like a sleeping cat in the lap of the hills. She crossed to the window and looked out.

At Brynsquilver, if you wanted to watch the weather coming or simply to breathe the air, you stepped out, into the garden, and the whole valley seemed just another part of where you lived. Here, Bell looked out through the thin glass of a fine casement window on the first floor. The house, a square lump of modern brick, stood awkwardly angled on a bald slope, surrounded by slipping shale banks held in place by weedy clumps of coarse yellow ragwort and faded willow-herb. The track that passed the front door was made of cinders: each morning the maids swept black grit out of the door, and the men of the family took off their boots before they were allowed upstairs to join the ladies in the parlour.

The noise of the front door opening made her look down. Alistair stepped out, hat in hand. Unseen, she could watch for a moment this stranger who was her brother. He wore his own hair these days, not the fashionable wig of his youth. From above, she could see that the light curls, restrained by a sober black ribbon at his nape, were already threaded with grey. He had never been tall or heavy, but he had grown more solid with age. His shoulders in the brown coat were broad and a little stooped. He looked what he now was: a serious, respectable Friend, fast approaching middle age.

As Bell watched, trying to call out of the man below her the boy she had known twenty years before, the front door opened again. Alistair turned towards it, his face lighting up in a smile that took her suddenly back to Wiston and their childhood. Impulsively, she put out a hand to open the window, but drew back as Susannah emerged into the sunlight. She had obviously come to see Alistair off to his day's work and Bell did not want to break into their parting.

They did not touch each other, or even stand very close; a passer-by might have taken them for polite strangers, had he not seen their faces, as Bell could. She was glad that, at last, Alistair had found someone who loved him as much as Susannah; whenever he was near, adoration shone out of her like light. Bell hoped that her brother, so much older in years and experience, could understand his young bride's feelings. So much had happened to him in the years since he left England; half a lifetime which neither Susannah nor Bell had shared. Bell turned away from the window, thinking about the things Alistair had told her of his life in France and his new life here.

She looked around the room: she must find something to do. At home she was never idle, and she felt restless and underused. The house was full of reading matter, but she had soon discovered that there was a limit to the number of religious pamphlets she could absorb. On the work-table lay a pile of linen: Susannah's wedding things were not yet complete. Bell carried a great sheet to the window seat and stroked it into folds on her knees. Susannah's orderly stitches showed her where to begin: just a plain hem, nothing fancy, no frills or tucks. Bell smiled. She was still not used to the deep seriousness that governed every least detail of the Friends' lives. In many ways their plainness appealed to her; her own life in recent years had been simple enough in all outward matters, after all. The gown she and Hope had made for her great journey to Coalbrookdale had been plain as any she saw here – though she doubted that Susannah or her mother would have chosen quite such a rich shade of blue.

It was in other matters than dress and decoration that Bell still had reservations. She had taken a genuine liking to the Beestons, but found it hard to accept what sometimes seemed to her their wilfully simple view of a complex world. However, there is nothing wrong with plain linen, she told herself mockingly; Hope would certainly approve of it. She was unprepared for the spasm of loneliness and longing that seized her at the thought of Hope. Shaking her head to stop tears, she turned again to look out at the alien landscape.

The hills here were ugly: barren but busy, spoiled but not empty or deserted. All the dale, right down to the wharves upon the Severn, was dotted with buildings and cut by muddy roads that scrambled along the hill. There were fine houses – Bell had already seen the new mansions of the Darby family, above them at the head of the dale – but everything was heaped together and built in the same haphazard way, just where it pleased the builder or, she supposed, where it suited the works.

The making of iron dominated every action here, of man or beast. Wherever a flat space could be found or hammered out, furnaces, cottages, smithies, stables or grand houses were thrown together upon the dishevelled hillside. They thickened towards the bottom of the slope, like peas sinking in soup, until the dale around the ponds was closely lined, sometimes two or three brickish rows deep. Immediately below her window she could see the chimneys of Samuel Beeston's forge, already smoking, and the head of the great wheel already churning at the building's end. The high black wall that held back the waters of his forge pool cut off further views up the valley, to her right; she could barely glimpse from here the sheet of dark water that shuddered, iridescent with coal-dust, in the slightest wind. At night you could hear the trickle of its outflow as it tumbled gently down to the river, but now already the shouts of the men and the day-long thump of the hammers drowned out peaceful natural sounds.

As Bell watched, a pony train wound by on the cinder track: three animals almost invisible under huge panniers of charcoal. A dirty girl, in short skirts and the sleeveless shirt that Bell had seen on many of the youngsters at the works, laboured behind them. She had a baby on her hip. Bell tried to imagine the cottage life here, crammed into the huddled huts and working at the same task every day, or through the night, to keep up with the demands of the fires. The thudding of the hammers made Bell feel tense and tired, so what must girls like this one feel? As if to mock her concern, the lass suddenly broke into a ribald song. Bell smiled at herself, and went back to her hemming.

It was not long before Susannah came smiling into the room. There was a pleasant glow to her usually pale complexion, and a lightness to her step. "I am sorry to leave thee so long alone," she said earnestly. "Thou has breakfasted, I hope?"

"I have indeed." Bell returned her smile. "Sukey found me sweet rolls and some new milk. You look after your guests most kindly."

Susannah looked pleased, but replied with her usual seriousness, "Our duty teaches us to give hospitality to both friend and stranger. I am glad it pleases thee. What would thou like to do today? Mother says I may be excused helping in the kitchen to keep thee company."

Bell frowned. "I am a trouble to you. If I am to stay here until you and Alistair are married, you must let me help you as I should if we are to be sisters. I like best to be busy. If your mother says we need not cook today, there is your needlework. Look, I have begun already. And we can talk, and get to know each other better."

Susannah beamed. "That is kind of thee, friend Isabel. Thank'ee."

They sat sewing for a while in the companionable silence which Bell had come to associate with Alistair's new family. Unusually, it was Susannah who spoke first.

"We should not waste our breath in idle talk," she said, "but there is so much I would dearly love to ask thee." She stopped, biting her lip.

"About Alistair?"

Susannah nodded, but did not find words for her questions. To help her – and because she wanted to know what the girl felt – Bell said, "You must know more about his recent life than I do – he has been here in Coalbrookdale for more than a year, has he not?"

Susannah answered eagerly. "He came from France with Friend Colston, in first month last year, after Friend Colston had journeyed to see the works in Lorraine. Alistair," she smiled at being able to say the name out, "was seeking a new field for his inventions. His French acquaintance were slow in making use of his ideas, he says, and there were – other troubles for him, too." She looked up from her sewing. "He has told you that he was married before?"

"Yes," said Bell. She looked quickly at Susannah, then added, "and she died soon afterwards."

"In child-bed, yes. She was very young, and Alistair grieved sorely for her." She sighed. "And then her parents sent and took away the little boy, to bring him up a lord in their fine castle; and so Alistair lost them both."

Bell looked up, stunned. She had assumed, and Alistair had not denied, that the child had died with its mother. The pain of the story was sharpened by the sense that it was all part of his life that she had not shared, and could not intrude upon.

Susannah went on, "That was when he began to travel, I think. But he found little happiness along the way. So he was glad to settle here, where so much is stirring, and Father took him into this house and into the works because he has no son to work with him, nor any so likely as Alistair to build new things in the forges and help the business grow." She looked up at Bell, her face glowing with pride. "He quite soon became a convinced Friend. He is a serious, thinking man – you know that, of course – and his acceptance at Meeting came within the year." She paused, and sewed slowly for a several minutes before she said, "Was he always a serious man, Friend Isabella?"

Bell was not sure what she could say. "I recognise him very easily as he has become," she offered. "He was certainly always an inventor, and a great reader and thinker of new ideas. And an enthusiast. That was how he came to be obliged to flee to France."

Susannah dropped her hands, and gazed earnestly in Bell's face.

This is what he has not told her, Bell thought. She wondered how much he would want her to say; but the girl has a right to know him, she thought, and to know that he has not always been 'convinced' of such things as the Quakers so solemnly believe. "You know that all our family were followers of King James, of the banished Stuart house?"

Susannah's attention was intense. She nodded without speaking.

Bell went on, "Both my brothers were active in the cause; James was in the army and Alistair was studying at Oxford when the fighting started. My father was arrested for treason, and died in prison. When the cause was lost, all we had was lost with it – home, lands and living."

She stopped. There was no need to burden the girl with the story of her older half-brother and his ugly death. Bell doubted if Susannah understood even as much as she had said of the politics of twenty years ago. The notion most people had now of the Jacobites was of a sad collection of old men toasting past glories, or worse, of wild Scotsmen plotting against the king from their Highland bogs. It was more important that Susannah should understand how her husband-to-be had come to leave his country so completely, and for so long.

Bell went on carefully. "After the fighting in Scotland, there was no news of Alistair, and I was sure he had been killed or captured, but later I had news that he had escaped to France. That was all I knew. Many gentlemen fled to France in '16, where they could find others loyal to the cause, and support from the French aristocracy and king."

Susannah's dark eyes were thoughtful. "1716 was the year I was born," she said. "I shall be twenty years old next fourth month."

"When Alistair and I last saw each other, I was sixteen, and he was two years older," said Bell. She looked at the young woman opposite her. I might have had a daughter nearly as old as you, she thought. How strange.

Susannah broke in to her thoughts. "And you thought you would never see each other again. How wonderful is divine providence, that has brought you together again! Dost find thy brother much changed?"

Bell smiled. The politics were not what Susannah wanted to know about. "Of course; twenty years is a lifetime, for many, after all. We have both made new lives. And yet, when I saw him in Ludlow market, I knew him at once. And when I heard him speak,

I was quite sure. His voice is the least changed part of him. If I shut my eyes when he is talking, I can see him, just as he was."

"Tell me," said Susannah wistfully.

Bell felt suddenly inadequate. Memories of Wiston, where she had grown up, had been with her all the time since she had been with Alistair again: she woke most mornings from dreams of the great oaken hall with its sprawl of barns and stables, its low, flag-stoned kitchen and dark, winding stairs. Trying to see through the eyes of Susannah's need, she pictured Alistair in the summer before he went away to Oxford, before the events that were to change all their lives. "He was always fair-complexioned, as he is now," she said, "but slender and quick. He loved to be busy. His ideas burst out into actions, making things – contraptions, engines, things that worked. My father thought it a foolish game for a squire's son." She smiled. "We never thought how such things would become his life."

"Blessed are the ways of infinite wisdom!" Susannah said fervently.

Bell was silent. She must not allow herself to be jealous, she thought. They were two women thinking of one man; but he was not really the same. Would she ever know her Alistair again – or he her?

There was a loud crash from the works outside the window; iron bars were being delivered in the yard. The working day was in full, noisy motion. The distant shouts of the bargemen were drowned out spasmodically by the crash of iron, and the singing of the pack-horse drivers had gone on ever since she had looked out. And through it all came the giant purr of the waterwheels, and the insistent, regular thump of the great hammers that they drove. Bell shook her head, as if to empty it of the noise. Susannah looked concerned.

Bell tried to smile. "That dreadful hammer!" she said lightly. "How do you bear it, every day?"

Susannah was quite blank for a moment. "Oh! I think I do not hear it. I suppose we are accustomed to it." She jumped up and looked out. Turning back, she said, "Friend Alistair is proud of the improvements he has made to the hammer engine – perhaps if thou could see it, thou would not think it so dreadful?"

"Yes," said Bell, "I will ask him. He always liked to show me his precious inventions."

Nine

A boy was sweeping the gritty yard outside the forge. He greeted Alistair enthusiastically.

"And good morning to thee, my friend," said Alistair. "This is good work."

The boy nodded and grinned. "When Matt see how good I done it, he says, do it regular. He says, ha'penny a week, if I stick to it."

"I hope thou will, then, for the ha'penny will be welcome at home. How does thy mother now?"

"Better, sir, thank'ee. But not strong yet." He frowned, concentrating. "She says, thank Mrs. Beeston for the things she sent."

"I will give her your message, and do thou give my regards to thy mother. Is Friend Matthew within?"

"Aye, in the finery. They got a good blow on there today."

Alistair turned to Bell. "We should be in time to see the furnace opened. Come."

The boy saluted them and went back to his sweeping as Alistair pushed open the blackened door.

They stood just inside the finery, clear of the men and machines. Four men were crouched, like hunters with weapons in hand, round a little door. The light of the fire within slitted out round the edges, painting their sweating, blackened faces with bars of red.

The heat was stifling, but the men were heavily clad, with smock-frocks over their clothes and leather aprons over all. Broad-brimmed hats protected their faces from the blasting heat.

Suddenly one of the men shouted, and a lad whom Bell had not noticed started to haul down on a chain. The door ground up, opening a white-hot mouth. Heat struck Bell's face like a blow from a fist. The men plunged the long rods they held down the fiery throat. Bell had a sudden vivid memory of hell's mouth, painted on the wall of the old church at Wiston, with the devils, black and red, wielding their pitchforks. She turned to her brother, but before she could speak, the leader shouted again and, grabbing up a huge pair of tongs, plunged them into the mouth, for all the world like the Devil's tooth-drawer. Another man, shambling grotesquely on a short leg, pushed a low cart towards the fire; they heaved and strained, and suddenly a great hot ball, glowing like the sun, fell out into the cart. Bell drew back her skirts as they rushed it across the floor to an anvil, spilling dazzling drops of white-hot metal in its path.

The boy let go his chain with a clatter, darkening the room, and threw his weight on to a wooden bar beside him. With a grinding shriek, a giant head like the cruel beak of a huge bird fell from the roof. Bell gasped and clutched Alistair's arm. The great hammer reared and clanged down again and again on to the molten mass, shaking the teeth in her head. Even through closed eyelids, she could feel the glare of the spurting fires.

The sweating, panting men flipped the great lump over and over with their eight-foot tongs, delivering every side of it to the pitiless blows. Golden gobbets spurted out; there was a general smell of singeing. Suddenly one man leapt aside, batting at the heavy leather gaiters that protected his feet and legs.

Alistair put his arm round Bell. "Would thou like to see how it works?" he shouted – as if, she thought, the work was not being done in here. The black sandy floor was hot through her boots as he led her round behind the boy who worked the chains and levers, to a dark space full of noise and movement. As her eyes adjusted, she recognised the pulsing thud that they heard day in, day out, up at the house. It was not the hammer itself – the cruel beak had struck with a ringing crash, and had already stopped. The regular beat came from the huge contraption in front of her: man-high leather bags under great wooden plates that rose and fell alternately. Bellows, Bell saw, just like the ones that lay in her own hearth, but made for giants.

Alistair touched her arm and pointed upwards. High above she could see pale natural light, and the edge of the great wheel. A sinuous arm of water punched down into one splashing bucket after another, as the wheel creaked round.

Alistair yelled, "Dost see how cunningly the machinery works? This same wheel drives both the trip hammer and the bellows."

Bell smiled and nodded. The heat, noise and stench were making her feel sick.

"There's a system of cams – look, here, behind the bellows."

She could make out little in the gloom, where a huge wooden beam turned over and blunt wooden teeth thudded against each other. Suddenly yet another man appeared, poking at the bellows with a stick. Soon four or five men had joined him to inspect it, talking earnestly in signs and grimaces. Alistair walked over to them. There was more prodding and shouting. He could be there for hours. Bell caught his eye, smiling her apology, and headed for the air.

Outside, the boy was still sweeping, and the sky had clouded over. She breathed in the cool air, pulled her cloak round her. Her brother had changed very little in twenty years, she thought, smiling: he could still lose himself in a project and forget his dinner. She began to climb the bank towards the house.

Images of the foundry stayed with her. As she lay awake that night, she saw again the great white-hot ball of molten iron, the grimy, sweating faces of the men and the fall of the hammerhead, and marvelled for the hundredth time at the foreignness of this place. It had taken only two days to ride here, but distant lands could not have been more full of wonders or more strange. She wondered what Hope would make of it all, and wished again that they could have seen all these sights together, to talk about in the evenings by the fire.

Not tired enough to sleep, unable to lie comfortably in the unfamiliar bed or to shut out the night noises of the Dale, she tossed restlessly, thinking of Hope lying lonely in their bed at home. What had possessed her to leave the cottage in the valley and come here to stay among strangers? For even Alistair was a stranger now, preoccupied and still a little shy. The Beestons were kind in their solemn way, and perhaps it was ungrateful to long so desperately for her visit to end. But they were not easy. For all her sweetness, Susannah was not a companion to whom Bell could feel close. Her mother, Rebecca, a tall, faded woman with a permanent worried frown, had been as welcoming as her nature allowed, but was so very solemn of manner that Bell felt frivolous and self-conscious in her company. Bell had hardly seen Samuel Beeston, Susannah's father, except at meals. Always the dignified iron-founder or the weighty Friend, he seemed full of business, as if he scarcely noticed her over the rim of his good white stock. In the daytime Bell could usually find some small thing to occupy herself or something new to think about. But the nights seemed endless.

She told herself that it was a good lesson for her, to get used to being alone sometime. What would happen, after all, if Hope were to die? Then she was annoyed at herself for having such morbid thoughts. The pious Quakers made one think altogether too much upon one's latter end. Soon Alistair would be wedded to his little bride, they would move into the new house that stood ready for them, its plaster well dried out already, as Susannah had told her, and its furniture selected from the Beeston plenty. Some was even new: twelve fine chairs had arrived only the day before, unloaded from a Bristol barge and carried up from the Severn by an admiring crowd of boys and girls. Most things were done; there was only a little extra sewing for Susannah herself. The wedding would be in early December. Even if Bell had to wait a week for someone with whom she could ride west, she would be home by Christmas. She turned her heavy pillow, and tried to empty her mind of the blazing images of the day.

Before the week was out, she was to learn that the heat and stink of the forge was far from the worst that the Dale had to offer. There were five days of solid rain, and the great wheels which drove the hammers creaked around faster and longer on each successive day. Then on a Saturday (or seventh day, as her hosts called it) she woke to find the world outside the windows lost in a thick fog. Nothing was visible when she drew back the curtains but a billowing yellow cloud. Sukey, the Beestons' maid, came in as Bell stood watching.

"Oh, Friend Wiston, where's thy shawl?" the girl said, and picked it up to bring to her. "Thou will take cold, surely." As she draped the shawl over Bell's shoulders, she tut-tutted and then began to cough, a dry wheezy cough. She waved away Bell's concern, gasping, "No, no, it is nothing," but she was pale, and fighting for breath between coughs.

Bell made her sit on the bed. "Have you taken a cold yourself, Sukey?"

"No, thank'ee, 'tis only my old cough. I shall be well in a moment. I always do get the cough this time of year."

"No wonder, if these fogs are common here," said Bell.

"Fogs?" Sukey followed Bell's glance. "Oh, no, 'tis no fog. 'Tis the coking fires. Darbys started coking last night. The wind brings the smoke down the Dale."

Bell was amazed. No one in the house seemed either surprised or concerned to be enveloped in grimy smoke that darkened the windows and smelled of sulphur and soot. They shrugged; this coking would be over in a few days, they said, and then the fires would sometimes be put out; the wind would change soon; the smoke did no harm, except for dirtying the curtains and leaving smuts on the laundry. They assured her that Sukey had suffered with the cough all her life and it had nothing to do with the smoke; she always coughed in October.

"But if the fires make more smoke in October, Alistair, how can they say that?" she demanded, exasperated.

Her brother just smiled at her, his mind on some pumping experiment, and strode off into the fog.

Susannah smiled placatingly, and said that the Lord's work must be done, despite inconveniences.

Bell thought irritably that Susannah and her whole family did not always clearly distinguish between the Lord's work and the work of the Beestons. She did not say so, but there were moments when she could see the attractions of long, arduous journeys to testify to the Truth in cleaner, prettier places.

Over two weeks, Sukey's autumn cough developed into a continuous, wheezing struggle for breath. Bell wished she had thought to bring some of the cough mixture of coltsfoot and honey she made every summer. Then, one morning, carrying coals up to the parlour, Sukey dropped the pail and tumbled down after it herself. They had much ado to get her up to her bed, as she clutched desperately at helping hands and fought for air through blue lips.

Rebecca was sent for, and was clearly distressed when she saw the girl's condition. "I fear she has need of our good Friend Rachel Lewis. Run, Susannah, and ask her if she can come to our aid."

As Susannah grabbed up her hat and cloak and disappeared, Bell found herself, without thinking about it, taking charge of the bedside, calming the patient and fending off clumsy helpers.

"Is there hot water, ma'am?" she asked Rebecca Beeston. "Steaming hot, for we must let her breathe the steam to ease her. And a towel."

The steam, and Bell's calming voice, helped Sukey a little. Before long the healer came, a stout elderly Quaker dressed very plain and carrying a large bag. She nodded at Bell and her arrangements, and then took Sukey's hands for a moment. Intercepting the next fresh bowl of water, she uncorked a small glass bottle and tipped a few drops into the bowl. The biting odour of camphor flooded the room. Side by side, Bell and the healer stood watching while Sukey's gasping began to subside and her breathing steadied. She emerged damp and shaky from the tent of the towel, and clutched the old woman's hand.

Rachel smiled at her patient. "Thy thanks to the infinite mercy, friend, not to me who am but the poor instrument. Do thou stay abed here today and make thy restoration complete." She returned the bottle to her bag and turned to Bell. "I see thou has been favoured with a cool head and steady hand, friend."

Bell smiled. "I am often called upon in such matters when I am at home. It is a pleasure to be of use here, where I have felt always the receiver of kindness, not the giver."

The old woman looked searchingly at her. "The hand of providence is in the day's doing, then, for there is much work of this kind, and I grow no younger. Would thou be willing to help me again?"

"Why, certainly, I should be very glad," said Bell.

The healer smiled. "If Friend Rebecca can spare thee at this busy time, I will certainly call on thee. We may learn from each other."

Bell went down with her to the door, and watched the stout figure disappear into the fog. Once more she wished in vain for some of her stock of ointments and syrups from home, that might be useful to the healer. The thought of home reminded her of Hope, and she felt a pang of guilt as she imagined her, all alone at Brynsquilver, dealing as best she could with the various folk who came to the cottage for help. And no one to talk to but the cat, thought Bell. A great wave of love and longing and homesickness caught her by the throat. Blinking back tears, she started back upstairs.

Ten
Brynsquilver

Hope woke late to autumnal sunshine streaming across the bed; she stretched out lazily for Bell and found her gone. There were little noises down in the kitchen: still half-dreaming, she pictured Bell making the fire, sweeping the hearth, indulgent of her late sleeping. For a minute she dozed luxuriously, until she was shaken awake by the sound of the baby crying. Bell's space in the bed was cold; it was Lucy in the kitchen. Hope dragged herself out of bed to face another edgy, uncomfortable day.

She was beginning to think that even loneliness would be better than sharing her home with a morose and slatternly stranger. By the time Hope came down, Lucy had retired to bed again. She refused to get up till nearly noon, and then sat indoors, staring at the wall. The baby was fretful and sickly, its grizzling cries grating Hope's nerves until she could have strangled both of them.

A knock at the door was a welcome relief. Hope sprang to open it; Lucy retreated, as she always did when someone called, behind the curtain that screened her bed-place. To Hope's surprise, it was Mercy, breathless and beaming, carrying a covered basket. Once a frequent visitor, she rarely climbed the hill to Brynsquilver these days. Now she stood, panting, gazing out at the wide sweep of the hills.

"Oh, 'tis pretty. I had forgot how pretty it were up here."

Hope hugged her. "It's good to see you. Come indoors."

The basket was full of small garments.

"I've just brought these few things for the baby, the poor lass can have had nothing ready, and these will never be needed in our house now. So I said to William, that little fatherless child shall have them if he has nothing else."

She looked round, clearly wondering where the infant was.

"But how did you know?" asked Hope curiously.

"Bron Richards told me," said Mercy. Then, seeing Hope's frown, "But don't you worry, m'dear, I'm not one to gossip of the girl's troubles to anyone else. That's not my way, as you do know. When you keep an ale-house, you hear everyone's secrets some time or other, and you learn quick enough to keep mum about them."

From the basket she took fresh swaddling bands, clean and smelling of lavender, a tiny cap trimmed with lace and a baby's gown. "These were my little Mary's," she said, "and too small for Joey when he came, great ox that he was, even as a babe." Her eyes were bright with unshed tears. "They were worn but a few days, as you know, and may suit the little one here. Bron said he was naught but a tiny thing."

"Lucy, come out," Hope called, certain that Lucy would be listening to every word. "Here is a good friend of mine who would be a friend to you."

Lucy appeared, suspicious and frowning, the babe on her arm.

"Oh, he is a mite!" cried Mercy. "The dear pet! He will look like a little angel in that gown."

Lucy made no resistance as Mercy scooped up the baby and, sinking into the chair, began to unwind his blanket and stained breech-clout. Hope seized the opportunity to leave them together and escaped into the fresh air.

When she came back Lucy was sitting in the chair, the baby for once peacefully asleep in her lap.

"I mun make haste now back to the Crosses," said Mercy, "or I shall have hard words from William and Nance, for the house is full. God bless you, child, and the little one too." She enfolded Lucy in her large embrace.

To Hope's surprise, Lucy smiled and hugged her back. The smile transformed her – Hope realised again how pretty she was. For some reason it made her cross. It's a pity she doesn't smile more often, she thought uncharitably.

Lucy was pleased with Mercy's visit and talked cheerfully to the baby about his fine new clothes, but the next day she was low again, her eyes swollen with crying and her temper shorter than ever. In spite of a thin, drizzling rain, Hope decided she must escape, even if it was only into the garden. Pulling open the door, she found Bron looming on the step, crook in hand.

Bron ducked into the room, then, catching sight of Lucy, seemed almost ready to retreat again. Lucy seemed equally dumbstruck; Hope felt a huge impatience with both of them.

"Have you come to see the baby?" she enquired. "Lucy, let Bron see the baby."

A look of almost comical alarm crossed Bron's face as Lucy handed her the infant. She did not take it in her arms, as people will with babes, but dropping her crook into her elbow she held the child in her hands, as she might a small animal, turning it to and fro to examine it. She was gentle enough for all that, for the child stopped crying and gazed up at her, its unfocussed gaze seemingly fixed on her face. Hope became aware that Lucy was staring at Bron with something of the same round-eyed admiration. It made her fidgety.

"Now, Bron, how goes it with you?" she asked, a little over heartily. "Will you take a breath in the garden while it's still light?"

Giving the baby back to Lucy, she steered her slightly bewildered friend out of the door and away from the house. "Thank goodness you've come," she said. "I don't think I can stand another minute alone with the two of them. She either cries or says nothing all day, and when she's not crying, the baby is, poor little scrap, until I think I shall run mad. And I can't get her to wash. She seems to care nothing for herself, or the child."

She threw back her head, breathing deeply as she looked out across the valley.

Sighing, she let her eyes slide down the tree-clad slopes and rest on her own garden stile. A black and white sheepdog sat to attention on the spot where Bron had left it.

"You've brought Gwennie!" said Hope, delighted. "Come, Gwennie! Good girl!"

Bron whistled short, and the old bitch, given permission, came trotting eagerly to them. Hope noticed that she was limping slightly. She dropped on her haunches to greet her old friend. "Why, hello, Gwennie, hello!" She rubbed the greying ears and muzzle, and ran her hands down the dog's back. "How's that old leg, then? Giving you some trouble, old girl?" The dog was hot and tired; she whined a little as Hope felt the back leg that she had set a year ago, when Gwennie was caught in a keeper's trap on the edge of Waldon Forest.

"She's not ailing," said Bron, "just tired. You made a good job of the leg, and it healed well." She paused. "I brought her with me because she's been fretting, that's all."

Hope looked up at the note of strain in her friend's voice. Bron's tanned face was drawn, unsmiling. "Bron, I'm sorry – what's the matter? You look tired to death – come and sit down."

She led her up the path to the little seat under the high hedge, beside the bee skeps, where Hope and Bell sat on summer evenings to catch the westering sun. The row of overwintering hives were quiet now. Bron sat down heavily, standing her crook in front of her. Gwennie sat close to her, resting her head on her mistress's knee. Bron looked back towards the house, and then glanced sideways at Hope. She seemed burdened with something she wanted to say. Eventually she found her voice, talking with uncharacteristic speed and urgency.

"I told you Hamer's out to drive me off my land?"

Hope nodded.

"This morning – this morning I found my big fold'd been opened up in the night, and every one of my ewes was away into the hills. Except for six. They were bloody and dead, their throats bitten out." She flinched away as Hope involuntarily put out a hand.

"Took us past noon to round them up, Gwennie and Gelert running like mad things into every brake and briar bush on the hills. And just as we came in with the last, there he was, asking if I was having trouble with foxes. Foxes!" Bron struck her crook savagely into the ground between her feet. "What fox did you ever see lift a six-foot hurdle? Gloating, he was; and that great hound of his grinning at his side, full-fed to bursting. I nearly went to beat its brains out." She stopped, and drew a long breath. "But the beast is not to blame for what its master tells it to do."

"You must go to law," said Hope decisively. "You have to stop him!"

Bron only shrugged, and whistled through her teeth.

Hope took this for a no. "Why not? Bron, come – you've as much right to the law as the next. You must bring a complaint against him. Why won't you?"

Bron shook her head. "I got no rights," she muttered. "No one'll take my side. He says I got no right to my own farm. Justice'll say the same. I don't want more trouble."

"But Bron, that's foolish! Of course the farm is yours. It was your father's, and he left it you."

"He left me nothing," said Bron savagely. "He never meant me any good. He treated me worse than a beast. The farm was for Davy, that's what Da thought. If Davy hadn't died the very next week after Da went, I'd have been his drudge too, to this day."

Bron flung herself to her feet, almost knocking over the nearest skep, so that the bees roared inside it. She dropped her crook and steadied the hive, shushing them. Gwennie circled, whining.

They were both standing now, embarrassed. Bron said, "No offence, Hope, I know you mean friendly. Some can go to law, and others is like me. That's all."

They walked back to the house, stopping at the door. Hope said, "Well, you know best. But, Bron, you will call on me? Whatever there is to do? Only ask."

Bron nodded, "Thank'ee, Hope," and turned to go, Gwennie at her heels.

As they passed the cottage window, she stopped to look in. "The babe doesn't thrive," she said. "He's not right, is he?"

"No." Hope shook her head. "He feeds, but he's not growing. And you saw the shape of his head."

"Ah," said Bron. "He was frail from the first. Well, it may be for the best." She shook herself. "See you at market next week, maybe. Come, Gwennie." And she was gone, taking the stile as always at a leaping run.

Bron was right. The babe died, and it was best so. He lived for barely two more weeks, sucking less and less in spite of Lucy's frantic efforts. It was Hope who found him, quite still at last.

Lucy rushed to her side as she felt in vain for life in the cold morsel of flesh. Hope looked up at her, but Lucy spoke first.

"He's dead, then." She gave a great sigh, as if she had just put down a heavy load. Then she turned away towards the hearth and started to bang about, tending the fire.

Hope let her be. She went out to the little barn and made up some board ends there for a box, using up her precious stock of good nails, a last gift for the sad little boy. Or for his mother.

As the sun sank, she lifted the baby in its coffin to take it up the hill. At the door she looked back, waiting for Lucy. For a moment she thought the girl would not come. Reluctantly, Lucy got up from the stool by the hearth and followed Hope out into the darkening garden.

At the edge of the wood, Hope dug a deep enough hole for him beside the grave of Dame Marjoram, from whom she and Lucy had inherited the cottage. A few yards away an almost flattened mound marked the resting place of the Dame before her. Hope and Bell had always tended these graves, and the village and farm women sometimes came up with odd offerings of remembrance.

"No church would've had either one of 'em, and they'd have no dealings with parsons and such-like neither," Mercy had said, chuckling. "So I reckon they'm best here." It seemed a fitting place for Lucy's nameless, unbaptised baby.

Lucy stared down at the rough box, dry-eyed. Hope waited. Then she said gently, "You should speak to him, Lucy," but the girl showed no sign of hearing her.

As Hope reached for her spade again, Lucy finally spoke.

"Goodbye, little baby," was all she said.

Then she turned and ran into the wood.

Eleven

She went out often after that. Hope wondered if she visited the grave, but she did not ask, and Lucy did not say. One day she came back with a lapful of windfall apples, green and sharp; they ate them stewed with honey. Another afternoon she brought a few mushrooms, the last of the year. She seemed to be looking for things that would please Hope. Out of gratitude, Hope wondered, or because she feared being turned out to fend for herself? She did not cry much now, at least where Hope could see her, and she never mentioned the baby.

Towards the end of October the weather turned fair again and the sun, though low, seemed still full of warmth.

"Where do you wash clothes here?" asked Lucy suddenly.

The weather was still good enough to wash in the stream, Hope told her; the business of heating water and washing indoors was a chore for the winter.

Lucy disappeared with a small bundle under her arm.

She was a long time. Hope told herself impatiently that the girl was old enough to look after herself, but eventually she grew concerned, and walked slowly up towards the pool. The spring from which they carried water for the house fed into a small, deep basin and fell in a little waterfall over its rocky brim, down to the wide washing pool below. The fall always sparkled when the sun shone; Hope would often find Parsley sitting on the rocks, mesmerised by the tinkling movement. The cat was nowhere to be seen today. Neither, Hope realised with mounting concern, was there any noise of splashing or wringing coming from the pool. Quickening her pace, she rounded the bushes and saw Lucy lying full length in the water.

For a heart-stopping moment, she thought the girl was drowned. Lucy lay, eyes closed, her head resting on a rock, her hair combed by the falling sheet of water. She was perfectly still, and entirely naked.

Hope let out a shaky breath. Lucy was washing herself clean – not just of the dirt of the past weeks, but washing away the hideous past that had brought her here. Looking down at her, Hope saw how beautiful she was. Hope had seen one or two black people before – some travellers, once a chapman at the market – but she had known none as friends. Lucy's body amazed her. She was used to hands and feet reddened by dirt or by the sun; bodies, under the clothes, were soft and white, as if not meant to be uncovered. But Lucy was the same smooth, chestnut brown from top to toe.

Hope went on staring. Lucy's skin was the rich colour of a hedgerow nut. Her private hair was a crisp, jet-black bush, her legs, smooth and slender as the springing stems of hazel, the same clear and lovely brown. As Hope gazed at her, Lucy opened her eyes and looked back. She did not move but, meeting Hope's eyes, slowly smiled.

In the weeks that followed, Hope did try to send her on her way. Lucy seemed to sense when the subject of her leaving Brynsquilver was about to come up, and always found an urgent task to do, or a new story to tell Hope. She talked freely about life with her mother, about taking in washing for the farmers and gentry in a village many miles to the north. Sometimes she told stories of her life on the road; she spoke of her adventures with a studied carelessness, but it was clear that it had been a desperate time. One evening, as they sat by the fire, Lucy told Hope about her father.

"Mam had a place at a big house, and he belonged to the master there. They catched him in Africay, Mam said, and took him to the islands out west, where it's always hot. And then his master brought him home." She grinned. "And he was catched again by my Mam." Then, challenging Hope with a stare, "That's why I'm so ugly."

Hope, taken by surprise, said nothing.

Lucy stared moodily into the fire; memories chased across her face. "When I was little, I thought I could wash it off. I went in the wash-house one day, and scrubbed my face with the sand we used for the doorstep." She grinned, self-mocking. "Got blood on me clothes, and cried a lot. Mam didn't know whether to laugh or cry. She told me I was a fool, some people just were this colour and that was that. Like the black king in the picture with baby Jesus, in the church, you know? That was when she told me about my dad. She said he was a prince in his own country." Her voice roughened. "But that's rubbish. He was just a slave. I'll get some logs in." And she slammed out.

That night, Hope lay long awake. She tried to imagine the ugly life that had made Lucy so hate her beautiful face. The memory of Lucy's nakedness returned, insistent; she tried fruitlessly to wipe it away. Her loneliness for Bell was an urgent, aching void.

As the weather grew colder and they spent more time indoors, Hope found herself increasingly disturbed by Lucy's presence. Lucy restored to health was even harder to ignore than Lucy moping. Determined to earn her place in the household, she attacked any available chore with energy, chattering like a starling, her skirts tucked up to reveal a distracting length of brown leg.

She seemed to have no self-consciousness at all about her body. One morning Hope walked into the house to find her naked to the waist, contemplating her breasts with a concerned frown.

"I've still got milk, look," she said to Hope. "Why hasn't it stopped?"

Hope allowed her eyes to rest, as instructed, on the taut fullness of Lucy's breasts, still swollen with milk.

"You must bind them," she said as matter-of-factly as she could. "That will soon make it stop. Cover yourself up. I'll find you some cloth that will serve."

They tore an old shift of Hope's into long strips. Lucy unlaced her bodice again and turned to Hope. "Show me how?" she said.

Hope looked at her sharply. But Lucy's dark brown eyes appeared entirely innocent. She swallowed, and picked up the bandage.

The right moment to suggest that Lucy might move on never seemed to occur. Hope busied herself with the usual autumn tasks: readying the goat-sheds for winter, lifting and storing the remaining root-crops in the garden, cleaning tools, sorting and labelling her seeds. Lucy was an enthusiastic, if spasmodic, assistant: she would appear suddenly at Hope's elbow to ask, "What are you doing?" or, "Can I help?"

Hope had to admit that it was useful to have another pair of hands, but just as often she longed for the peace of solitude.

The darkening days brought fewer visitors to distract their attention from each other. One dull morning in early November, Hope looked up from labelling some packets of seed to see Lucy watching her closely.

"If you can write, that means you can read as well, doesn't it?"

Hope grunted assent.

"Was it hard to learn? Who taught you?"

Hope looked up, surprised. "My great-great-grandmother. I was very small. She wanted me to be able to read the Bible." She had a sudden clear memory of a beautiful hand, the freckled skin almost transparent with age, pointing to each black letter; and of her grandmother's voice reciting the verses.

"I can't remember learning, exactly. I don't think it was diffi-cult. She used to tell me the stories, and then show me where the words were on the page. Then I had to read them. Everyone in our house could read the Scriptures."

Lucy shrugged dismissively. "You don't need to read to take in washing. And anygates, I wouldn't be able to learn it. I'm not clever enough."

Hope turned on her, annoyed. Why did the wretched girl never have anything good to say about herself? "Don't be so foolish, Lucy," she said, more sharply than she had intended. "You are quick-witted and determined. I see no reason at all why you should not learn to do anything you set your mind to. You are no friend to yourself, to speak in that way." She turned back to her task.

Lucy was quiet for a while. Hope thought she was offended. Then she said, "Go on then. Teach me. You'll soon see how stupid I am."

As Hope had predicted, Lucy was a quick study. Hope sent her out to look for an old piece of slate and a sliver to write with. They started off with the letters of Lucy's name. When she had copied them until she had them by heart, she insisted on learning to write Hope's name, too. Though she would have died rather than admit it, she was clearly pleased with herself. Hope would come upon her, bent over the bit of slate, practising.

One morning she found their two names scrawled on the hearth with a piece of charcoal from last night's fire. It made her uncomfortable, in a way she was unwilling to examine. She had a fleeting picture of Bell, arriving home to find "Hope" and "Lucy" inscribed on the hearthstone.

"Time for you to learn all the other letters, now," she told Lucy briskly, scrubbing them out with her foot. "Then you can read what other people write, as well."

The writing on the hearth had set off an idea Hope had had in the back of her mind ever since William had bought Mercy her gift to mark twenty years. The next morning, before she blew up the fire, she fetched in a hammer and chisel, and after some thought began to cut two emblems, one for her and one for Bell, into the great black beam over the fireplace. She was no craftsman carver, such as might make birds and beasts to decorate a fine house; to cut their names would be too difficult for her. So at one side she carved out the shape of a bell, complete with clapper, and on the other the anchor which her grandmother had always taught her was the emblem of hope.

Lucy watched critically. "But why is hope an anchor?" she asked.

"It just is," said Hope irritably, wondering if she had made the two points of even size. She stepped back to look. Perhaps the two emblems were too far apart? She thought she might put a date in the middle, to bring the two together. It would take a few hours, but it was a good job for a cold wet day, and would be a gift for Bell when she came home.

Each afternoon, when their outdoor work was done and the dark coming on again, they would make up the fire for warmth and light, and Lucy would have her lesson. The only books in the house were an old book of receipts, which was much too difficult, being hand-written, and Bell's precious copy of Culpeper, which Hope did not want to risk. So she wrote out the alphabet on a piece of board, and Lucy copied it laboriously over and over again on to the slate. Once she grasped the idea that everything around her could be caught in this net of letters, she took to going about the house, naming things that began with the same letter.

"Wood and wall and water."

"Good," said Hope, who was trying to concentrate on cutting "1716" in the middle of the chimney-beam, for the year she and Bell had come here.

"Cat, and... cushion."

"Good."

"Fire." Lucy looked round, searching for inspiration. "Fire and..." Her gaze lighted on the shelf of medicine bottles. "Fire, and physic."

"Er, no."

Lucy stamped her foot. Her eyes kindled. "But why not?" she said angrily.

With a sigh, Hope put down her chisel.

Soon she was writing whole sentences on the slate for Lucy to read and copy. She would sit in her wooden chair by the fire with the cat on her lap, and Lucy would sit on the floor at her feet, so that Hope could see what she was doing. They were both pleased with Lucy's progress, and it made them better pleased with each other, Hope thought. She looked down at Lucy's dark head, bent over her writing, and felt an unexpected surge of affection for the girl. Demanding and infuriating as she might be, her presence had brightened the gloom of life without Bell in the last few weeks.

Lucy had also begun to take some care of her appearance. Today she had dressed her hair high on her head under her little white cap; the curve of her neck was young and soft in the fire-light. With some effort, Hope resisted a sudden impulse to reach out and touch it.

Twelve
Coalbrookdale, November

Alistair and Susannah were to be married in their local Meeting. Susannah explained to Bell, "We might go to Quarterly Meeting, if we chose, or have a special day of our choosing here; but Alistair and my father think it best to make no display, and they are very right. So we shall make our promises in First Day Meeting, five weeks from now. I am pleased it will be so."

Five weeks, thought Bell longingly. And then I will go home. She stood up to fetch another ball of thread, and to cover her selfish thoughts. She looked at Susannah, her dark head bent over her sewing, smiling quietly as she stitched a plain white bedgown. The more she saw of Susannah, the less Bell worried about her lack of years compared to Alistair. Indeed, her brother often seemed to Bell much younger in mind than his solemn little bride. But she was a good child, and could think clearly when she chose. Bell thought they would be happy. She took up her sewing again. Five weeks: that would be the third week in December. She thought again, I shall be home for Christmas, and the thought gave her comfort.

In the meantime, it seemed that there had begun to be a role for her here after all. Rachel Lewis had called for her assistance more than once since Sukey's attack, and Bell was seeing another side of life in the ironworks. Visiting in the cottages, she had begun to feel for the tough, silent people of the Dale. Their lives were as much a part of the works as the wooden cams in Alistair's wheels and mills, and they were just as frequently broken by the relentless strength of the machines.

Bell was used to treating pain and injury, but there was suffering here such as she had not imagined. Last week she had seen a girl whose spine was pulled into a curve by the weight of the cart she dragged on a chain behind her, as she crawled each day along a coal seam two feet high. Rachel had said that such women could rarely give birth, and those who did seldom survived. Almost all the men Bell met carried the marks of their labour: the burns and breaks and hammer blows she helped to treat were far worse than anything she had seen at home. The men who worked in the forges and the mines were strong and fine-looking, muscled like ploughmen, but their faces and bodies were stained blue with coaldust, or seamed and pitted by fire.

Bell thought of the visit she had made yesterday to Charles Butler, the man with the short leg whom she had seen at work in the finery. Two weeks ago, quite soon after Bell had seen him at work, Rachel had taken her to the foundry cottages, where the old man was laid up with a burn to his arm, a raw, weeping hole where the flesh had been pulled away by a cooling cinder.

"We can keep this clean, Friend, and as dry as we can, and pray God to do the rest," said Rachel cheerfully. To Bell she had said, "The dressing needs to be changed every day. Could thou come down to him, think'ee, and save my legs?"

He had endured the pain without complaint, grinning and making light of the hurt when Bell dressed the angry wound. He pretended to enjoy his enforced leisure, sitting with his Bible at the cottage hearth and stirring up the little fire to warm her when she came.

"I wonder you can touch the fire, Friend Butler," she had said to him yesterday.

"Nay, my dear!" he replied. "Where would we be without the fire? I keep this little one here to remind me of his big brother, yonder. No, don't 'ee speak hard of the fire. 'Tis God's beautiful gift to His children. Blessings on its fine and yellow face."

Bell put down her sewing and shook her head to clear the suffering people from her thoughts. She glanced out of the window up the valley. It was a dull day, darkening without having been truly light.

"Your father spoke last night of visitors. Will they come for the wedding?"

"Oh, yes. At least, cousin Richard will stay. He is on his way home, to Yorkshire – he has been to the West Indies, about his father's business, and then to Pennsylvania. He is travelling with a respected Friend, Thomas Goodwin, who is said to have a great gift in ministry. They came together from America; the minister is to visit several parts of England. I do not know whether Friend Goodwin will stay here long, but Richard has told my father that he will be at the wedding to support Alistair. Father had a letter from Bristol yesterday; we expect them within the week."

"America!" said Bell.

Susannah nodded, satisfied at her admiration.

The New World seemed extraordinarily far off for such round trips, but Bell was no longer surprised by the arduous journeys undertaken by the Friends for ministry and business. Alistair had enthused about the value of their connections abroad: news and ideas spread fast wherever they were numerous enough to set up a Meeting and offer the hospitality of their leading houses to sympathetic travellers. The town mansion in Ludlow where she had first seen Alistair had been such a known house; here in the Dale, visiting friends were received by the leading ironmasters, the Fords and Darbys whose names Bell heard daily in everybody's mouth.

"If Friend Goodwin stays, will it be here or with the Darbys?" she asked Susannah.

"Oh, Mother hopes he will stay with us. The Ford house is full, and young Friend Abraham has not been at home. You would have met him if he were in the Dale; he calls here. I think he will be back before – well, soon." She blushed a little.

Bell did not ask about this young potentate. Obviously he was a social connection of whom the Beestons were proud. They were perhaps straining a little, she thought, to move in the very weightiest circles.

As the arrival of the visitors came closer, she saw that she was right. It set all the household in a stir. The family was small; Samuel and Rebecca had no surviving children but Susannah, and they kept only two indoor servants. The house itself was modest, and already filled to the limit of comfort by the addition of Alistair and Bell. Rebecca became visibly more agitated, and Sukey more breathless, as the days passed. Bell and Susannah worked all day, helping to draw and pluck fowl and to make pies and puddings for the demands ahead. The crowded kitchen was hung about with drying linen as every bed in the house was aired and shaken up. Richard was to sleep with Alistair, and Bell found to her dismay that she must move in with Susannah, so that the American minister could have her room. The privacy of a room of her own had been one of the things that had helped to make her visit bearable; she heartily wished the esteemed Friend a short stay in the Dale.

In the event, she missed the arrival of the travellers. Trudging back from Charles Butler's cottage through sleety rain, she met John, the Beestons' outdoor servant, leading two tall horses. He nodded to her, and grunted, "Aye, they're come at last," before disappearing down to the foundry stable.

So Bell did not set eyes on the visitors until dinner-time; and then both of them surprised her. The much-heralded American minister was quite ordinary to look at – rather like Samuel Beeston, indeed. Grey-haired, solid, deliberate in manner, he showed no outward sign of his fabled gifts as a preacher. He spoke like a foreigner, certainly. Bell had not met an American before, and was struck by the lilt and tune in his tongue, like and yet unlike a West Country gentleman such as her own father. Otherwise, the awesome guest was largely unremarkable.

Cousin Richard, on the other hand, was much more striking than she had expected. He was taller by a head than Samuel, and his hair was the warm red of a squirrel's tail. He faced her across the laden table when they sat down to eat, and Bell studied him with some interest. He sat quietly enough, as all the Friends did, but otherwise he bore little resemblance to his kin. He had a mobile, intelligent face and dark brown eyes which seemed to miss nothing. In someone like Susannah the quietness seemed part of her character, but in Richard it seemed to Bell a conscious thing, a restraint on a naturally restless spirit. Catching her looking at him, he smiled, and she found herself smiling back.

Meals were usually taken in silence. Occasionally one of the family might be moved to pray aloud, or to testify to the truth of some Bible saying. Bell had been startled by this at first, but had already become accustomed to the combination of bodily and spiritual nourishment. This evening, though, there was little speech at table. Samuel had said a long grace, giving thanks for the deliverance of the travellers from storm and tempest, and for their safe arrival in Coalbrookdale, as well as for the food before them. After that no one spoke except to help a neighbour to food or drink, but there was a suppressed excitement among them. Bell felt the Beestons were tense and shy, while Friend Goodwin no doubt looked forward to a new audience for his legendary eloquence. She hoped he would not demand everybody's exclusive attention.

But when they rose from meat, the visiting minister excused himself and retired to his room. Disappointment and relief chased across Rebecca Beeston's face. Bell was annoyed that the man who had caused so much work and anxiety should calmly take himself off as soon as he was fed, giving nothing in return for the good-wife's labours. But she supposed he would testify at their next Meeting, when their neighbours could all approve Rebecca's hospitality.

Lamps were lit in the parlour and the family party settled comfortably for a catching-up. Cousin Richard was well known in the household, often coming down from Yorkshire about his father's business. He seemed to be the Friends' version of a lawyer, dealing with wills and disputes for them and raising money for their enterprises, though Bell was given to understand that the oath-taking involved in worldly law forbade his working outside the community. He had been on such work in the New World.

"Now, Richard – the matter of the inheritance? That went well?" Samuel Beeston asked as they sat down.

"Well enough, Uncle, thank'ee, though not without complications. Thou knows the Governor of Tortola is a Friend? John Pickering. He was helpful to me, and I left an agent, a worthy man, to see that my father's wishes are carried out. I hope it may be well."

"What is your father's business in the Indies?" asked Alistair.

"There is but one business in the Indies, Friend," said Richard, smiling a little grimly. "It is a sugar plantation. They grow cane, and ship sugar and molasses home. I think thou would be interested in the mills they have there, for crushing the cane."

"Water powered?" Alistair said eagerly.

"In winter, yes, for the streams come down from the mountains with some force. But the great heat of the summers dries them up."

He turned, to include Susannah and Bell in the conversation. "It is truly one of the most beautiful places in the world. You have heard it called an earthly paradise? I used to dismiss that as partiality in those who have chosen to make their homes and fortunes there. But it is just as one imagines Eden."

Bell had not heard any description of the Indies at all, indeed she was less than certain where the islands were. Richard began to describe the beauties of Tortola, its everlasting sunshine, its lush greenery and exotic fruits. Bell listened with increasing fascination.

Samuel Beeston snorted. "Adam fell from grace, even in such a place. And so have many since."

Richard nodded. "Thou might well say so, Uncle, if thou could see how some of the planters live, who have too much leisure and too little of grace to know what to do with it. But the Meeting grows apace, and the Friends are strongly guided. And so their works thrive."

Bell was still thinking about the sunny island, and of the cold and damp in some of the cottages she had visited that day. She said, "How much better a life the poor of that country must have than here! For they are at least warmed by the sun, and food is plentiful all the year round."

Richard looked at her rather oddly. "There are few poor in the islands." He hesitated. "Unless thou mean the bonded, and the slaves?"

Bell said nothing. She felt suddenly out of her depth. Slaves?

Richard said, "I think if thou saw them, thou would not think their life so easy."

Before Bell could speak her amazement, he turned quickly back to his uncle. "The matter of slave-holding is the only one on which the Friends there are not in unity. It was the cause of some of my difficulty. Of course there are those who are of a mind with us, and hold that no man may buy or sell his fellow man. But there are too many Friends who think their duty done if they treat their slaves well."

He gestured impatiently. "Even if they cannot see how wrong it is, they should be able to see with one eye that it simply cannot last. The islands are a keg of gunpowder waiting to blow. Men who are controlled by pain and fear will rise, sooner or later, and that is as true of the black man as the white. It happened in St. Croix last year – hideous bloodshed and even worse retribution. The Africans on my father's plantation talk of it – one of them even talked of it to me."

His eye caught Bell's, and he stopped. "I have distressed thee," he said. "Forgive me. I should not have spoken of such things."

"Oh no," said Bell, "It is not that at all. I wish to learn – I have known nothing of this." She smiled ruefully. "I had been thinking that the journey into Coalbrookdale has brought me into the great world of change and business, but now I see I have not yet travelled far enough."

Thirteen

Her voyage of discovery was about to begin. Quiet evenings of little conversation were transformed by the presence of Richard, who brought a new perspective to every topic. He was widely travelled, not only in Britain but in America and the Caribbean, and he had a natural gift for painting what he had seen in a few unexpected phrases. He talked with his hands and face as well as his voice. As the family hung on his words, Bell caught herself wondering if he spoke in their Meeting: she had not heard any of the Beestons mention it, if he did.

The visiting minister had stayed only a day or two, eager to travel north before the weather worsened, but Richard seemed in no hurry to go home. Every evening he devoted himself to entertaining his hosts, and particularly his aunt who, though slightly scandalised by the liveliness of his manners, clearly relished his company. Bell had never seen Rebecca Beeston laugh as she did at her nephew's stories, particularly when he imitated the way the Yankees spoke. He had wonderful things to show them, too; one night he brought down an Indian head-dress of rainbow feathers, and put it on, stalking about the parlour to demonstrate.

But more often the talk turned to serious topics. Samuel wanted to hear the news from abroad, and to discuss with Richard the moral questions which troubled so many of the Friends, so that Bell heard not only about the evils of slavery and the difficulties of trade, but also of how the Friends stood firm against war, refusing to bear arms themselves and arguing patiently with those who did. Older than either Richard or Susannah, she felt sometimes like a child as she listened. She had lived through war, and they had not, yet she had not thought about the things they were saying.

She watched with pleasure the friendship between Richard and Alistair. The two men spent their mornings striding about the Dale, talking excitedly, shouting like boys as they planned and argued. Bell watched them wistfully from the parlour window until one morning, as she waved them off, Alistair turned and called her down. "Our friend Dick is in the right," he said. "We shall not settle our difference about this new cauldron without expert advice. We need a woman's opinion. Could thou spare us an hour, sister?"

Bell needed no further urging, but caught up her hat and went down with them to the lower forge, where the new moulds were being put together in the black sand, ready for casting the great pots. The argument, it seemed, was about how large a cauldron could be achieved in this way. They talked of weights and stresses and the quality of pig-iron, and how the molten iron might be raised to fill the mould.

Bell listened with amused impatience. Finally she said, "Your pardon, brother, but what will be the usefulness of this monstrous vessel?"

They both looked at her.

"You have invented a pot which is taller than the cook. How will she stir the broth or lift the pudding out?" Straight-faced, she added, "Perhaps you could devise a great lifting engine for the purpose, and sell it with the pot? It would take some wit, of course, to determine whether to sink the cauldron or to raise the cook…"

Richard shouted with laughter. "Alistair, I shall make thee a wedding present of this same pot, and thou can work on the problem thyself."

To Bell he said, "Thy brother is an engineer, but no business-man. You two should go into partnership. No man could stand against you."

After that, Bell went out with them whenever she was not needed by Rachel. Alistair was showing Richard how he planned to improve the Beeston furnaces, picking his brains for mechanical ideas Richard might have seen abroad. One of their shared convictions was that, although workmen were conservative and cautious and guarded the secrets of their trades, a clever man might find out useful hints from their first-hand experience. So far, however, they had been remarkably unsuccessful in getting any of the men to talk to them.

Taking Bell with them, up to the Darby works or down to the foot of the Dale where the nailers and chain-makers laboured in their own back yards, they found she was already known to many of the families. The women and children spoke to her when they were afraid to answer the gentlemen, and Alistair made more progress with his fact-finding.

Almost everyone they met was marked or marred by their work and Bell could see that Richard was as moved as she had been by the crooked limbs and scarred faces. The condition of the poor quickly became another topic of debate between them. Alistair believed fervently in the power of machinery to lighten men's lot, but to Bell the machines seemed capable of more than human cruelty. Richard, though he shared Alistair's excitement about the innovations being made up and down the dale, tended to side with Bell.

"Thy sister is right, Alistair. The man who follows the plough may be cold and wet, but his labours move to the seasons of toil and rest. If it snows, he will stay in his cot; when the horse is weary he will bring it home and they will both rest. The crops obey the seasons, and so do man and beast. But here," his arm swept the valley below them, "the fire and the machine eat up all, and are never weary. Nay, friend," as Alistair tried to interrupt him, "there is work here that is like the tortures of the damned, endless, unceasing and ever renewed."

"Nonsense, man." Alistair was in high spirits and ready for an argument. "You spoil your case with overstating it. Wait till you see what we have climbed up all this way for. The Newcomen engine works for the miner's help and his safety, and drives no man mad!"

They were talking as they rode. It was a glorious sunny day, though bitingly cold, and they had ridden out to see the wonderful new fire engine of which Alistair had heard report. It had been set up at the Broseley mines, which lay over the ridge at the head of the dale. Setting out early, they had passed the trains of pack-horses on their way down to the Beestons' forge.

"There at least is a machine that still goes on legs," teased Richard, "and can carry only what the beast can bear. I am surprised thou has not fitted wheels to the ponies."

"Thou may jest," said Alistair eagerly, "but I was talking to a fellow yesterday who thought it possible to let a horse pull wagons over rough roads by setting down tracks, hollow rails that would hold the wheels..."

And they were off again, remaking the world. They had climbed now to the top of the ridge, and Bell could see down to the wooden scaffold that stood over the mineshaft. Beside it was a new brick building, smoking from a tall stack.

"That will be the new engine house, look!" Reckless of the steep, narrow track, Alistair put his horse into a trot. Bell and Richard, laughing at his eagerness, followed more carefully.

Even Bell had to admit that the pumping engine was impressive. The great beam nodded to and fro overhead; huge pistons – fat, oiled drums the colour of thick ice on a stream and just as slippery – slid up and down, hissing and gasping. Dirty water, gallon upon gallon, came rushing up from the mine workings and gushed away downhill. That was what Alistair was after: all that water, pulled upwards without the labour of horses or men. Not just to be spilled out on the ground, as here, but to drive the bellows and the hammers, summer and winter, non-stop as long as someone fed the fire.

He talked about the engine most of the way home. "You saw for yourselves, did you not, that no one suffers because of it? All the power comes from the fire and the steam: thou saw, Bell, the man hardly moved all the time we watched, and the two labourers down below were leaning on their shovels most of the time. I could make it work for us, I'm sure of it." He pulled out a notebook; his horse slowed to a near stop and started to graze at the side of the path.

Richard grinned at Bell. "He will not hear thee. Thou were going to ask what happens to the men in the forge, where the hammer never pauses. Thou must save the question for later. But this was a fine place to stop – look!"

Coming out this morning, they had laboured up the slope, seeing only the way ahead, but now they were at the very top of Jagger's Bank and looking down at the whole of Coalbrookdale laid out below. It was late and the works fires had burned high all day, but now in the frosty air the columns of smoke rose cleanly from the black chimneys.

"Like great grey-trunked trees," said Richard, "growing all down the valley."

Or like the ghosts of trees, thought Bell. They towered over the huddled buildings, spreading their pale canopies above the scenes of human life.

She said softly, "What are the fruits of such an orchard?"

As their mounts shifted, Richard's knee jostled hers. He backed his horse, then reached out and patted the neck of hers.

"Who knows, indeed?" he said quietly. He looked into her face; then raised his crop and pointed down the valley. "Is the new house we see there thy brother's?"

Bell looked. "Yes, on the hill, to the left of Beeston's works. Have you not been there?"

"Alistair has not so far thought to learn anything from plasterers and joiners, so I have not had that pleasure," said Richard.

"Oh, the plastering is long over. They will move in as soon as they are wed, and Rebecca would not let them live in a damp house! We have been sewing for the beds and curtains ever since I came; they are nearly all ready."

"And will thou move at the same time? Thou are to live there with them, as I heard?"

Bell was so surprised that she jerked her horse's head; the few moments of trampling and pulling covered her confusion.

"Why, no," she said when they were still again. "No, indeed, I shall go home as soon as the wedding is over. There is a party of Friends riding westwards the very next day, and I shall ride most of my way with them, as far as the Ludlow road."

"Oh." Richard frowned. "I am sure Alistair told me thou were to settle here, with him."

It was not until she thought of it again later that Bell wondered about the regret in his voice. At the time, she had been too put about by Alistair's assumption to think of anything else.

Fourteen

Bell was furious; but the more she thought about it, the more her anger gave way to indecision and even fear. Her first instinct had been to confront Alistair and ask how he dared to say such a thing to others without asking her what she intended but, before she had any opportunity to speak with him, she realised that there were no words in which she could explain why she was so offended and alarmed. She worried for several days before the moment came when she could no longer keep silent.

She and Susannah had arranged to meet Alistair at the new house, to inspect the work of the painters, which was just finished, and to admire the kitchen ironware, which had been brought and installed that very day. The fire basket, hooks and spits had all been made in the family forge. Only a fireback was missing, and that, said Susannah, was to be a wedding gift from the Darbys, who would have it cast with the date as a memento. While Susannah explored her new kitchen and used Alistair's tinderbox to light a fire of sticks to test the chimney, Alistair and Bell climbed the echoing stairs to look at the rest of the house.

Alistair offered every detail for his sister's admiration, which was not difficult to give, for the house was well made and pleasant to be in. Built higher on the slope than the Beestons' house, it had views all up and down the dale. It was meticulously finished, showing off the products of the Beeston forges from kitchen to attic: even the window catches were little iron hands, shaped to hold the casements open or shut.

As they stood gazing at the wintry dale from a curtainless window on the second floor, Alistair said thoughtfully, "I have been a wanderer so long, and in so many places. And now I shall put my roots down here, and make a family home at last." He turned to face her. "It is a blessing I had begun to think I should never have."

Bell reached for his hand. "And I wish you joy of it, Ali, from my heart."

He squeezed her fingers. "Come, I will show thee a thing."

Across the passage, he pushed open another chamber door. Pale afternoon sun filled the room with light. Built at the corner of the house, it had windows on two sides, looking over treetops to the distant hills. Bell exclaimed with pleasure.

Her brother beamed. "I knew this chamber would please thee," he said. "It is thine own."

Her heart clenched with fear. She took a step back, and said, as lightly as she could, "But Ali, you have not forgotten that I ride home in a week? It is a lovely room, but hardly worth my moving for a night or two." Seeing his face fall, she added, "Of course, I shall stay here whenever I visit you."

But she could see he was disappointed. He said stiffly, "Thou must be the judge, of course. But I had thought, once thou were here..." He did not go on.

"I have already been away too long," Bell said. "Now we have found each other, we shall not lose each other again. But I must go home."

Her brother shrugged, his face expressionless. "As thou will, of course. But there will always be a place for thee in this house." He turned away, and she followed him downstairs without speaking.

Back in the Beeston parlour, waiting for the lovebirds to say their farewells below stairs, Bell was angry with Alistair for not understanding, and angry with herself for failing to say what she meant. But how could he understand? What could she have said? I have my own family now, and they miss me as much as I miss them? Hardly. Her family were invisible to him. To him she was an unmarried sister, approaching middle age, with no fortune of her own to support her, and so he naturally offered her a home, a place in his household where she could make herself useful. How could he imagine the other ties that bound her?

It would only hurt and offend him more if she tried to explain that Hope, whom he remembered only as a servant, was the centre and meaning of her life. Nor could she explain that dear, simple Mercy and her William and silent Bron were like the closest kin to her; that the people of the Squilver valley were her work, their children hers; and the stone cottage she and Hope had made meant more to her than any number of sunny bedchambers in a new-built house with him. She sighed, and longed again for the wedding day to come and go.

The third Sunday in December was bitterly cold. A freezing wind bit their faces and knifed through their wraps as the family gathered outside their own front door. The sombre colours of the men's hats, their brown coats and the women's long grey cloaks echoed the dull greys and browns of the winter landscape. But their mood was merry. We are like a flock of sparrows, Bell thought – all good cheer and dowdy feathers.

As they set off to walk up the Dale to go to Meeting, they formed naturally into a small procession. Samuel and Rebecca led the way, followed by Susannah and Alistair. Richard fell in beside Bell, offering his arm when the path grew slippery, and the servants Sukey and John brought up the rear. They strode silently for the most part, but from time to time Susannah would turn and smile at Bell, her eyes shining. Bell felt her own spirits lift. She had not previously chosen to attend the weekly Meeting, and was interested to see how it would be. She was curious in a thoroughly worldly way about the inside of the magnificent Darby house. And under these thoughts she was warmed by her own private excitement: in three more days she would be riding home.

By the time they passed the Upper Forge Pool, Bell's nose and ears were on fire with the cold and a few flakes of snow were drifting down. She was grateful to see the imposing facade of the house looming up. At the top of a steep bank, they turned in through an elegant iron gate but, instead of making for the front door, Samuel led them round the side of the house.

"We meet in Brother Darby's laundry." Susannah turned to her, anxious that she should understand properly. "We are a large congregation – more than fifty – and we have no Meeting House, so we have need of a great room."

"Yes, I see," said Bell, smiling.

The elders of the Meeting greeted them courteously at the door. They already knew Richard, and Bell was pleased to find Rachel there to take her hand. The place was not imposing, despite Susannah's anxious justifications. A bare room, its plaster new but already stained with workaday splashes, was packed with uneven rows of motley chairs from drawing room and kitchen, with even a low bench at the back. The central passageway was narrow, and exposed a large drain in the centre of the floor. There were some dozens of people there already; a few came to press Alistair's hand or to embrace Susannah. Richard took Bell's elbow and steered her to a seat, pointing out with a whisper and a discreet nod the great ironmaster Richard Ford. As they passed down towards the front of the congregation, where Ford sat, Bell saw people from the works and cottages that she had visited. Truly a close community come together here, she thought.

When all were seated, a hush fell on the room, and heads bowed in prayer as the Meeting began. Bell knew of this curious way of worship, and had wondered whether sitting in silence with a large group of strangers would seem like a service to her, but she found it felt quite comfortable. Not all the Friends were praying. Rachel Lewis, sitting just across from Bell, was gazing calmly ahead, and smiled again when she caught her eye. Occasionally someone shifted in the creaking seats, or coughed. Bell allowed her eyes and mind to wander. From a high window she could see the leaden sky, and a little bird – a robin, perhaps – in the branches of a tree. She watched it busily flitting up and down, the feathers on its head blown into a tiny crest as it paused and pecked and then fluttered away. There were a pair of robins in her own garden at home. What was Hope doing now? Had she been lonely, all this time? Bell pictured her cutting and stacking logs for the fire, wrapped up against the cold.

She came back sharply to the present when Alistair's chair scraped as he rose to his feet. Faces turned towards him, some smiling and nodding encouragement. He coughed nervously.

"You all know, friends, that my affections have long gone out towards Susannah Beeston," he began.

Susannah looked up at him, intent.

He got into his stride. "It is three months since I made application to her parents, and, by the grace of God, she and I found ourselves in unity of affection."

How odd, thought Bell, to tell the story of your inmost life to all these people, as if it were everyone's to share.

At length Alistair came to the point. He turned to Susannah, who was still sitting at his side. "In the fear of the Lord, and before the Meeting gathered here, I take my Friend Susannah Beeston as my wife, promising with divine assistance to be unto her a loving and faithful husband, until death separate us."

He put out his hand, and Susannah took it, and stood up. She looked up into his face, and Bell saw that, in the midst of the crowd, for her at least the two of them were in a private place. When Susannah spoke, it was as if to him alone.

"In the fear of the Lord and before the Meeting, I take Friend

Alistair Wiston to be my husband. And I promise, with divine assistance," she smiled into his eyes, "to be a loving and obedient wife to him, till death shall separate us."

Bell looked away. The elderly man in front of her reached out and clasped his wife's hand. Bell felt her own eyes prick, and a surge of love for her brother washed through her. She hoped with all her heart he had found a resting place now, and the two would be as happy as she and Hope had been, these twenty years.

One of the elders, a woman of sixty or so, stood up and began to speak, talking of Adam and Eve and the duties of Christian men and women, and praying for a blessing upon Susannah and Alistair. This was the pattern for more speeches, more prayers and amens, even some soft cries of "Praise the Lord" and "Alleluiah".

Bell saw that the Meeting relished the chance to enjoy a little sentiment, a few tears of joy. They would remember today, setting this young pair among all the other wedding days and their own. Suddenly she had to struggle not to cry in earnest. It was not just that Hope was far away, but that, even together, they would be here alone. She drew breath, setting her feet firmly on the floor. She should think of her brother's happiness. She looked resolutely out of the window. But the redbreast had flown away and, as she watched, the branches of the tree were hidden by a whirling blizzard of white snow.

Fifteen
Brynsquilver, December

Lucy put down her slate and peered out of the window. It had begun to snow. The green hill beyond the garden was already seamed and spotted with the gathering flakes.

Hope came round the corner of the barn, carrying her axe. Lucy smiled. What's she up to now? she thought. Putting on a show for me? She settled to watch as Hope started to cleave logs. She worked quickly and without wasted effort, letting the weight of the axe head do the work. After each blow, she planted herself squarely again, judging the distance, bracing her legs for the up-swing, pausing to aim. She could be a man, Lucy thought, she has as much strength as a man, and somehow a man's way of being in her body. Lucy held her breath as the edge came down, biting with such force that the wood sprang open and the white pieces rolled away. Could Mr. Brown cut wood like that? she wondered.

Hope paused and straightened up, putting her hair out of her eyes. In the cold light, Hope's hair was still the colour of cut corn. It was only close up that the grey wings showed, where she tied it back. I shall call her Mr. Gray, Lucy thought. She wondered again how old Hope was.

And then, as so often, she wondered about Bron. She must be younger: her hair was still black. Lucy conjured up Bron's lean, weatherbeaten face and bright blue eyes. Her body was wide and flat, very strong. She was very tall, taller than Hope, but carried her head low as if she wanted not to be noticed. Lucy remembered the big hands, holding the baby.

She sighed irritably. What does it matter? They both treat me like a runaway child, she thought. It was probably just her fancy that Hope had looked at her differently, ever since the day at the pool. And Bron she could make nothing of at all, she was that awkward, blushing whenever she had to speak to anyone. Maybe there was nothing of Mr. Brown about either of them. Lucy bit off her thread. If I knew more about the one who's away, she thought. Maybe I could tell from that. She's due back this week.

The gate creaked and a huge man appeared in the garden. He was a head taller than Hope at least, and wore an old caped greatcoat, so that his shoulders were as wide as the window.

Hope rested on the axe. "William! Is all well?" Her welcome was loud and hearty.

"Weather's none too good, but all else thrives, I hope. I've brought this." He started to dig in his coat pocket. Lucy could not see much of his face under the pulled-down hat flecked with snow. His voice boomed across the yard.

"We're in for a skyful, I reckon." He nodded towards the logs. "You getting your fire in?"

Hope smiled. "I am. The wind's easterly, and getting colder."

He had disentangled a small packet, and held it out to her. "Thing is, a man left this for you. He came through from Wellington – said there's been bad snow over there – no one'd come that way for a week before him. That was two-three days back, and you've not been down, so Mercy says to me, if that snow be coming our way, you get up the bank while you still can."

Hope had the little packet now, holding it close against her as if it were alive. She thanked him, kindly enough, but not in a way that invited him to stay, Lucy thought.

William obviously thought the same. "I must be going," he said politely. "I've another errand before dark." He hesitated. "It'll be from our Dame, then?"

Hope had pushed the letter into her pocket, but still held it tight. "I expect it will. If there's news I'll be sure to let you know."

When he had gone, Hope glanced at the house, but walked off quickly towards the barn. Lucy stayed put. You know when you're not wanted, she thought. It had looked a fat letter, more than one sheet. She thought about reading and writing. It had a kind of uneasy magic, the idea of talking to someone who was not there. Lot of use it'll ever be to you, she mocked herself. Who would you write to? She pushed the slate away irritably.

Hope reappeared suddenly, walking very fast. She grabbed up the axe and brought it down on the nearest log, shouting something Lucy did not catch. She heard it the second time, though – a furious, sobbing "No!" Hope was laying into the logs as if they were rats coming to attack her. "No!" she roared, kicking the severed pieces aside in her rage to get to the next log. Chips flew; the axe rang against the stony ground; the snow fell more and more thickly on the shouting, sobbing figure outside the window. Lucy felt afraid, but she reckoned she knew now, about Mr. Gray.

Hope's Bell could not leave Coalbrookdale. The snow was deep there. It was still snowing hard when she wrote. She might not come home for weeks. This much Lucy managed to piece together from the few words that Hope flung her. She dared not ask more.

Hope was like a pent bull. Lucy kept out of her way as far as she could, terrified that her bad temper would end in her throwing Lucy out of the cottage. Squatting on her little bed in the lean-to off the kitchen, Lucy thought about what this Bell must be like, to provoke such need and such fury. Very beautiful, without doubt, and cruel – otherwise why had she gone away? She had made everyone miss her, and had hurt Hope very much. And she had made Lucy's life pretty uncomfortable besides. Lucy decided to hate her.

Sometimes the gloom was broken by a visitor. The usual neighbours calling by for cough syrup or ointment did not venture out
so much in the bad weather. "Amazing how well they can manage
without bothering us when it suits them," Hope grumbled. But
Bron's visits seemed to grow more frequent. Lucy thought perhaps
she came to keep Hope company in her trouble, but she had very
little to say for herself. On Christmas Eve it seemed that they all
sat round the fire without speaking for most of the evening. Lucy
tried to talk to her, but Bron became more tongue-tied at every
question. Lucy shrugged to herself. The pair of them were strange.
What do I care? she asked herself. Blue eyes and black hair are well
enough, but not much good without a tongue in your head. Bron
must have been getting something from her visits, though, since
she walked five or six miles to make them.

The snow in their valley had not lasted long, but there was a
biting frost. On Christmas morning, William appeared again, beating his hands together and breathing out steam, to bring greetings
and one of his wife's Christmas pies, and to remind Hope that she
was expected for Twelfth Night, as usual. It was a sad pity, he said,
the Dame could not be home, but Lucy was welcome, of course.
Hope grunted some reply. When he had gone, Lucy tried to find
out more. Who would be there? Would Bron go? Hope simply
shrugged, and stomped off to the barn.

When Bron came by next day, she was oddly cheerful. The
neighbour she so hated, John Hamer, had slipped on a patch of ice
in his own yard on Christmas morning and broken his arm. When
Hope expressed surprise that she'd not heard sooner, Bron snorted
scornfully.

"He's no time for healers. Besides, he wouldn't be beholden to
a woman," she said.

"Serve him right if his arm festers and drops off, then," said
Lucy with feeling, making Bron look at her and smile. Her face was
quite different when she smiled: little laugh lines appeared all

round her blue eyes. Lucy grinned. She crossed her eyes and began to howl, limping round the room with her shoulder hunched and one arm trailing, pretending it was dropping off. Bron laughed aloud, but Hope shook her head at the pair of them and walked away. Lucy stopped. Bron was still smiling.

As casually as she could, Lucy asked, "Do you go to the inn, Twelfth Night, Bron?"

Bron stood on one foot and looked at the floor. "I reckon I may," she said.

The room had learned the chorus by now; well-oiled voices hung lovingly on the last wailing line of its sad tune.

"Last night the queen had four Maries,
Tonight she'll have but three;
There was Mary Seton, and Mary Beaton,
And Mary Carmichael, and me."

Lucy had been having a wonderful time until now. She had danced with the boldest of the village boys, to the round-eyed envy of the rest; she had eaten rich fat mutton and hot figgy pudding until she felt she would burst. She had helped to clear the food away, and Mercy had hugged her and called her a good girl. Then the music had started, and she had tucked herself and her ale mug into the corner of a settle where she could see the whole of the room. She had been astonished when Hope was called on first, and played on a pipe, wonderful dancing tunes that set feet and fingers tapping. She had finished with a sad, complicated air that made Lucy want to cry and that the travelling fiddler applauded. Then William had sung a comic song in a rolling bass voice, and everyone had laughed and shouted out the missing rhymes.

From where she was sitting, Lucy could see Bron, leaning against the wall in the corner by the fizzing barrel. Her dark face was lit from below by the flickering tallow dip stuck on the wall for Joey to fill the jugs by. Her eyes gleamed in caves of shadow.

She had put herself where she would not be noticed, but Lucy watched her and was happy.

Until the spare, sandy-haired man with a foreign-sounding accent had started this terrifying song. It was about a girl who was lady-in-waiting to the queen.

Lucy listened with choking dread as the story unwound. The girl had some dreadful secret that would lead to her downfall: they all waited for the singer to let them in on the secret, but Lucy had guessed already.

"She rolled it in her apron,
And threw it in the sea,
Saying, sink ye, swim ye, bonny wee babe,
Ye'll get nae mair o' me."

Thirty voices bellowed out the chorus again, and the mother of the dead baby was hauled off to the gallows. Lucy began to cry, burying her face in her hands to stifle the sobs she could not stop. As the song ended, the woman beside her put a hand on her arm.

"What's the matter, child? Too much of ale, is it, poppet? Shall I find thy friend?" She started to push through the crowd towards Hope.

Lucy got up quickly and slipped round behind the high settle, heading for the door.

Outside it was damp: the frost had let up enough for snow to begin again and the huge, clammy flakes kissed Lucy's hot face. She crossed the yard quickly and took shelter in the open byre, smelling the grassy breath of cows. Leaning against a post, she let the sobs come. She cried for the little dead baby, and for herself, until her tears were spent. As she raised her head, wiping her eyes on her skirt and breathing hard to ease her throat, she heard the door open. She looked out. The moon was a pale smudge in a fuzz of cloud; it was a moment before she was able to see that it was not Hope, but Bron, who had followed her. She watched the tall figure lope across the yard and duck under the low roof of the byre, close to where she stood. For a moment neither of them spoke. Then Lucy put out her arms.

Afterwards she could not remember if Bron had walked into them or not. She remembered clinging on, her cheek against the roughness of Bron's jacket, remembered turning her face up, pressing her mouth to the silent lips. And then she was flung off, with a violence that sent her tumbling against the flank of the nearest cow. It bellowed in alarm as she scrabbled to stop herself falling into the stinking straw. When she looked up, Bron had vanished.

Sixteen

Hope stared miserably into her empty ale mug and wondered how she had ever found pleasure in this hot, rowdy crowd. Every year since Mercy and William had had the Two Crosses, she and Bell had kept Twelfth Night here with their neighbours, and gone home full of goodwill to the world. But tonight they all felt like strangers. She wondered what she had ever seen to like in any of them. Clearly they cared nothing for her – all they had asked about was Bell. How was she? When was she expected home? Was it true the snow in Coalbrookdale never melted until Whitsuntide?

Hope let Joey fill up her mug again. She had already had more than she usually took, and began to feel as if she were floating away from the rest of the world. Well, it was Bell's fault for not being here. Bell was my anchor, she thought self-pityingly, and now I shall drift and be lost. Tears tightened her throat. She drank again, and wondered uneasily if she should go and find Lucy. Bell would have known what to do about Lucy. But she chose to go off, thought Hope, and left me to deal with her. And her baby. And her moods. And her aching need to be loved.

Hope gripped the mug. The picture of sun-dappled water over long brown limbs, which she had tried so hard to put away, surfaced with unnerving clarity from the fog of ale. And she could have sworn these last few weeks that the girl was making sheep's eyes at her. She had studiously ignored it, most of the time. Only in her darkest moments, when anger and loneliness threatened to overwhelm her completely, she had thought, just fleetingly, that it would be Bell's fault if she had opened her arms to Lucy's need.

Well, there was no cause to worry about that any longer, she thought irritably. She was angry with herself for feeling so betrayed. What was it to her if Lucy had spent the whole evening throwing herself at one clumsy red-faced lout after another? And now Annie Shipton tells me she's gone off weeping over one of them. Again, Hope suppressed the urge to go and find Lucy and comfort her. The girl was none of her responsibility. And if she was breaking her heart tonight, it would mend soon enough. She'd soon find another swain – she was pretty enough, in all truth. Those big dark eyes. Smooth, brown skin. Hope closed her eyes to shut out the picture. The dark behind her eyelids would not keep still.

A small cold hand touched hers. "Hope? Are you ailing?"

Hope opened her eyes and focussed on Lucy. Her hair was dewed with raindrops, and the dark eyes fixing Hope with such concern were heavy from crying.

Poor little thing.

Hope put a protective arm around her.

The fiddler struck up again, and the dancing went on. The candles had guttered out one by one, until only the hanging lamp and the flickering flames of the fire illuminated the shining faces of the revellers. Hope went on drinking steadily, as Lucy dozed in the warmth of her arm.

It was long after midnight when William's voice boomed above the noise. "Now neighbours, a loving cup to warm us all before ye go, and Yuletide is over for another year!" He held up a great pewter tankard. Mercy, her face even rosier than usual from the fire, pulled the old iron poker from the flames and plunged it into the spiced ale. While it still hissed and fizzed, William drank and handed the mug to his wife, who drank in her turn and passed it to her neighbour.

Hope and Lucy watched the cup pass from hand to hand towards them.

Lucy said suddenly, "Thank you, Hope. For bringing me here."

Hope turned to look at her. Lucy's eyes were huge in the lamplight. "My pleasure," she said softly.

The loving cup came to the man on the other side of Lucy and she turned to drink with him. Then she turned back and held the cup to Hope's lips. Their eyes met over the steaming surface.

Almost roughly, Hope seized the cup and handed it away.

At that moment Mercy appeared beside them, wiping her glowing cheeks with her apron and smiling broadly. "That were a fine revel! Well, here's to next Yuletide, my dears, prosperity to us all, and a safe return for our Dame, eh?"

She threw her arms round Hope and kissed her cheek, then did the same to Lucy. "And good luck to you, child. Why, you'm worn out! Near asleep, I can see. Hope, must you walk all that long way tonight? There's a bed above you could have, and then set out fresh tomorrow."

Hope was giddy with ale, but not too far gone to see the perils of a shared bed. Avoiding Lucy's eye, she said heartily, "You are a kind friend, Mercy, but the night air will do us good after all your strong drink. Good night, and thank'ee!"

So Mercy made herself content with lending them extra shawls, and they pushed out of the door with all the other folk, calling farewells, one or two voices still singing in the rapidly clearing night.

As they began the long climb to Brynsquilver, Hope watched the stars spin overhead, and wondered how much ale she had drunk. The new fall of snow was freezing underfoot, and the air was biting. They plodded on in silence, their breath smoking in front of them. Before they had gone a mile, the snow had soaked through their boots, and the cold air knifed their lungs. Lucy, walking more and more slowly, finally stopped.

"Is it much further?" she said in a small voice.

Hope took her arm and pulled her close, as she so often had with Bell. "Nearly there," she lied. "Step out now, there's a brave girl, and keep warm."

They struggled on, clinging together, floundering through drifts and slipping on the frozen mud. An owl called eerily, and Hope felt Lucy shiver. At last they rounded the hill and saw the stile, black against the snow at the end of the little wood.

"Look," said Hope. "We're home."

Lucy raised her head and then, before she could speak, missed her footing, slithered a few steps and sat down suddenly in the snow. Hope bent and hauled her to her feet, and they stood for a moment clutched together. Hope could feel Lucy's heartbeat and the warmth of her breath. Suddenly, without warning, she was sick with desire. The prowling need which she had kept so resolutely at bay all evening had taken her off guard, and the force of it made her shake. She dropped Lucy's hands as if they burned, and turned quickly away, stumbling up the path towards the cottage.

She was getting the fire going again when Lucy came in, laughing with relief, stripping off sodden shawls and dropping them on the floor as she hurried towards the hearth. She flung her wet cloak on the chair and began to take off her dress.

"Ooh, look how wet I am. Even my shift is soaking. Blow up the fire, Hope, and I'll take that off too."

Hope looked round. She had a blurred impression of laughing lips, brown skin and wet linen. She tried to say something, to stop what was happening, but only made an inarticulate noise, as if she might be choking.

Lucy stopped, concerned. "Hope? What is it?" Then her face cleared. "Oh, poor thing! You are as wet as I am. Come here, let me help you." And she put out a hand to unlace Hope's bodice.

Hope said, "Lucy, please –" and then her arms were round Lucy in a fierce embrace. She had no strength left to resist, only the strength of her longing. She pulled Lucy against her, mouth and hands greedy at last. She kissed Lucy's hair, her eyes, crushing her close until the girl wriggled and whimpered with pain.

Alarmed, Hope loosened her grip. But instead of moving away, Lucy smiled and reached up to take Hope's face between her hands. Then, still smiling, she pulled Hope's head down until their lips came together.

And Hope's last defences were gone, swept away in the storm of her need as she pulled Lucy to the floor, pushing the cold wet linen from her warm breast.

It was fully light when Hope finally stirred. The first thing she knew was that her head hurt almost beyond bearing. The second was that something soft was brushing her face. She opened her eyes. It was Lucy's springy black hair, spread out on the pillow.

And then Hope was wide awake, with a jolt that made her sick to her stomach, out of bed, on her feet, staring down at Lucy. She remembered, with a clarity that made her shake, what they – what she – had done last night. Done, and done again; for the cold that crept into the flagstones before the fire had not stopped them, only driven them to bed. She had poured out all the pent-up passion of her nights without Bell on this girl's sweet and willing body. She groped blindly for her shift – the two of them were naked as babes. Lucy stirred, turned on her back and opened her eyes. When she saw Hope standing over her, she grinned and put out her arms.

Hope backed away, speechless: panic and horror filled her. She could not speak. Lucy was lying in the place where Bell had lain for twenty years and she, Hope, had brought her there, laid her down and – her mind flinched away from the memory.

She found her voice. "Get dressed," she said roughly. "And get out."

Seventeen
Coalbrookdale, January 1736

Bell shook her head. "I still say there's no harm in it. Folk need some reason to come together, to sit by the fire with their neighbours in the cold, dark days of the year, as we do now. And what if they tell tall stories and sing old tales? No one is hurt by such imaginings, surely?"

"But does thou think so?" Richard leaned forward eagerly, enjoying the argument. "I have seen whole villages in terror of some bugbear no Christian should believe in. Thou may say that fireside tales are harmless, but through them the evilly inclined can fright the weak and childish, and bend simple men to their will."

"Oh, come, Richard!" Alistair's voice was always the matter-of-fact one in these discussions. "We speak here of Twelfth Night, not of thy poor benighted Africans. Hast thou ever met decent English villagers, however simple, who still believe in magic and spells? Granted, I have seen the effect of popish superstition, but that was in France. Our people here are of too stolid a nature to be so easily misled."

Bell thought of old Charles Butler, who kept a little fire god in his modern cast-iron grate, and of her neighbours in the cottages up and down the valley at home.

"One moment, Ali. These are two different things. Perhaps

people are not so easily frightened, as you say, but they do very many of them believe in charms, I assure you."

She turned to Richard, who sat across the hearth from her in Susannah's new parlour, a book still open on his knees. They were supposed to be a sewing party, with him as their reader, but Alistair had come home early because there was more snow falling, and now the new bed-curtains lay neglected around Bell's feet. Even Susannah, who contributed little to these passionate and rambling discussions, was listening more than stitching. She sat close to her husband, smiling her agreement when he spoke.

"I am a healer, as you know," Bell said to Richard, "but most folk cannot quite believe that what I do is only herb-lore and careful watching. In the early days, they would ask me outright for a love charm, or a blessing on a babe I had helped bring into the world. They know better now than to ask me, but I believe most of them still hope that there is good luck in the bottle with the cough syrup, or a kissing spell in the box of balm." She smiled ruefully. "At least they do not look to me to curse their foes – they know me a little better than that."

"If they look to thee for aid in their troubles," said Susannah, "then thou art favoured with a great opportunity of grace, to pray with them, and turn them to the contemplation of their true health."

"I suppose I could," said Bell. She doubted her patients would return for more of such medicine, but it seemed unkind to say so. She turned back to Richard. "Was Ali in the right? Was it the superstitions of the slaves that you were meaning?"

Alistair groaned. "Oh please, sister, not again! I knew 'twas ill-advised to remind thee of these same Africans!"

Richard gave his characteristic shout of laughter. "Now, then, friend, thou art touchy because thou lost the argument last time."

"Oh, I am sure he did not," said Susannah quickly.

Alistair frowned. "'Tis not a matter of win or lose. Richard thinks that no man should be bound or beholden to another, and I think that it is misguided to suppose these poor creatures can survive unaided."

"And thou art right," said his wife loyally.

I am so glad that I found him again, thought Bell, and just at this happy moment in his life. There he sits, by his own fireside, with his adoring wife – who will soon learn not to agree quite so readily with everything he says – but for now, he can be a little spoiled, after all his troubles. He is growing bald, and a little fat, and his speeches that used to be all enthusiasm and fire will soon seem just a little pompous; but it is his time now for some good fortune. No doubt Susannah will soon give him another child, to keep him young – and this one he will be allowed to keep, please God.

"What does thou think, Bell?" Richard asked.

When did Richard start to call her Bell, she wondered, startled. "I think? About what?"

"Thou has never given thy opinion on this. Should men's bodies be bought and sold?"

"Of course not," she said at once. "And no more should women's."

"That is not the point," said Alistair.

"Why, do men and women differ in this? I am surprised to hear a good Friend say so," she teased, "who goes every Sunday to hear women preach."

"Women do not come into the question, particularly. That is all."

Susannah looked up. "Oh, are there no women slaves? I am so glad to hear it." Bell looked at her sharply, hoping for irony, but Susannah's head was bent again over her needle.

"No – yes – there are female slaves, of course. But that is not the point at debate. We talk of the obligations of one man to another. Whether the only good society is, as Friend Richard would have us believe, one where all men are governed solely by their own consciences; or whether, on the contrary, a good society can only exist, under God, where all men know their duties and their place, and carry out their mutual obligations."

"Under God," said Richard, "all men are created equal." He caught Bell's eye. "Yea, and all women also, friend."

"And their inequalities are of their own making, thou would say." Alistair was in full flight now. "But in this fallen world, we cannot presume to put that right; that must be for the life to come. Say that a man is born to wide acres and many servants; of course he is a bad man if he mistreats that estate and those servants which are his –"

"But do you make no distinction between the two, then?" Bell broke in. "The estate is his property, Ali, but the people are his trust."

"Yes – yes, that's right."

Susannah smiled to see them agree, but Bell went on, "So when there is conflict between the good of the estate and the good of the people, what then? What if an acre may be made to yield more sugar, by redoubling the efforts of the slaves? Or here in the Dale, a mill could be built that drives faster and faster, so that the workers are hurt and broken, or put out of work?"

"Then we see whether the people are indeed a sacred trust, or merely property by another name," Richard finished for her. He stretched his long frame and looked out of the window. "It has stopped snowing. This intellectual and spiritual exercise is very fine, but my limbs grow soft from sitting. Who will take the air with me for an hour before dark? Bell, will you?"

She smiled her thanks for stopping the argument before tempers were raised further. "I should call at the nailers' cottages; there are three children sick. You may go with me, if you please." She looked at Alistair and Susannah. "And these two may spend some moments alone, at last."

*

The bedded snow of the last three weeks was still hard under the new fall, and the sky was overcast, but it had, indeed, stopped snowing. The paths had been regularly cleared and with care, one could walk right down to the Severn, where Nailers' Row was. There had been some talk of the river freezing, but as they came round the high bank by the forge pool, Bell could see in the distance that it was flowing still, iron-grey and angry between its white banks. She shivered, and Richard offered her his arm. Her spirits rose. It was good to be out of doors in the bright snowlight.

Immediately she felt a little guilty that she could be enjoying herself here without Hope. But that was foolish: she had been wretched enough at first, and then, after the wedding when the snow came, she had been desperate with grief and disappointment. She had no sooner made her stand against Alistair, told him that she must go home, than the weather had given her the lie and forced her, after all, to take up residence in his house. She wondered again whether the letter she had sent had ever reached Brynsquilver, and how Hope was managing on her own.

Whenever she thought of home, she ached with impatience to be there. But she had to admit that the stay in Coalbrookdale had had its pleasures. Not only the company of her brother, restored to her after so many years, but all the new thoughts and ideas which living in this place had put into her mind, and which she would share and talk about with Hope.

And then there was Richard. She had not expected to find such a friend to enrich her stay. She glanced up at him as they walked. How would she describe him? A truly civilised man, she thought. His enormous physical energy and hard, acute mind were tempered by a passionate sympathy for other people and their points of view. He had shown her another kind of Quakerism from that of Susannah and her family, a kind of thoughtful courage which she found both attractive and admirable.

They had come to the steep grey steps which led down to the waterside cartway. Jumping down, Richard turned and offered her his hand to steady her on the icy stone. It was odd that he was a lawyer, she thought. She would have expected any profession but the grasping, scheming punctiliousness of the law, which had always seemed to her no more than a means for tricking people out of their belongings. It must have been different for him, of course. Denied the privilege of studying at university or reading for the Bar, and all the pomp that went with that way of life, he would have chosen the law simply for the service he could render to his own community. Certainly no other lawyer she had known would have been found on a raw January afternoon taking mutton broth and elderberry syrup to the children of the poor. She took his arm again as they turned into the teeth of the wind.

January turned to February, and the frost still held. At least while the river stayed open they were not cut off entirely from the world. Supplies for the works could still come by water, and occasionally letters and parcels were entrusted to the bargemen, so that business did not cease completely.

One afternoon as she walked home, Bell was stopped by a wharfinger who asked for Mr. Samuel Beeston's house. He had a letter to deliver, come all the way from Bristol. Since she had to pass the house on her way, she relieved him of the packet, and he turned gratefully back down the slope. She looked at the letter and saw that it was addressed not to Samuel, but to "Mr. Richard Farley, at Mr. Beeston's house in Coalbrookdale or at 6, Minster Close, York, England." It had clearly come from further away than Bristol.

Richard was at home, and she stayed while he opened the letter.

"It is from John Pickering, in Tortola," he said, "written soon after I left last autumn." He frowned with concentration, running one hand through his fiery hair as he read on. Then he threw the letter down on the table and looked at Bell.

"Well," he said at last, "I know not what to say to this. It is an honour, certainly, and shows a flattering trust in my abilities, from those who have known me but a short time. Still – I could have wished to be spared such a charge."

"What is it he wants you to do?"

"They are for building a road, it seems – and they certainly have need of one, for the way from the plantations to the seaport is narrow and perilous." He chuckled. "One must cross dizzying chasms on bridges of rough rope, like a spider on a web. 'Tis no way to do business. But to build a road, they need an Act of Parliament and that, seemingly, is where my assistance is called for. They have a man in London already, but Friend Pickering writes that he does not speed. He has met with obstructions." He barked with laughter. "I have no doubt he has – the brethren of the quill will be wringing their profits from him to the last drop." He folded the letter and tapped it edgewise in his hand, staring out of the window. "I had no thought to go to London. I am halfway home here, and my father will be waiting for me. And the snow has delayed me a month already."

But it was clear he would go; it was not in his nature to refuse a challenge. So now, thought Bell, we are both waiting for the thaw, he perhaps less eagerly than I.

As if in answer to her thought, the weather grew suddenly milder. The wind swung into the south-west, and by dusk of the following day the eaves were dripping.

"We shall be awash by tomorrow morning," said Alistair, and so it proved. Two days after that, the first mail coach from Shrewsbury came through, and the following afternoon Richard came to say his farewells.

Bell was alone in the parlour when he came in. She eagerly told him her news: she had just heard of a party of Friends who would be riding westwards in a week's time, in whose company she could make most of her journey home. They spoke for a while about the route Richard would take to London, and laughed together about the difficulties of packing.

"Who can account for it?" Richard laughed. "I give away mementoes from my journeys at each place I stay – and I buy nothing, that I can think of, but still the trunk lids close with more difficulty each time I try to lock them up."

"I have only packed this once, and I have the same trouble exactly," Bell agreed. Then she added, "But to speak seriously, Richard – I take away some things from here, lightly and easily carried, that will be most valued possessions. You have given me so many new things to think on, these past weeks, I shall be busy for months yet, pondering them. So you must take with you my most hearty thanks."

He looked intently at her for a moment, and then down at the floor, as if weighing something in his mind. When he raised his head his face was serious, and he spoke carefully, as if choosing each word.

"Friend Isabella – Bell – it warms my heart to know that thou values my company, as I do thine. I thank the providence that shut us up fast here, since it brought me to the pleasure of knowing thee." He paused. "Since we are to part now, I must risk thy displeasure by asking thee a thing I should better perhaps have left longer."

Bell met his eyes, and the smile died on her lips. *No!* How had she not seen this coming? She was filled with horror, but it was too late to stop him.

"I know thou art not a Friend, but thou hast much sympathy with our way of life and thinking. And thou and I have found a unity of thought and feeling beyond the common, have we not?"

She nodded, dumbly.

He went on, urgently. "Forgive me if I speak unmannerly, but we are neither of us children. Such a discovery of like minds is precious, not to be missed or mistaken – I had not expected ever to find –" He stopped, and started over again before she could intervene. "Bell, I should ride from here a happy man if I thought –" And then at last he broke off, searching her face, and there was silence in the room.

Bell was wretched. How had she let this happen? Was it her fault? She would not knowingly have hurt him, for the world. She forced herself to speak, choosing each word with care.

"Richard, I have never known a man, apart from my brother Alistair, whom I esteemed more than I do you, or whose friendship I valued more. I had hoped, when we both went from here, that we might stay friends, and write to each other sometimes of the matters we have discussed so freely and pleasurably. But I see now that was a foolish thought. And I am very afraid that I am going to lose your friendship, because –" she hesitated. "Because I cannot say what you want to hear."

With an inarticulate sound in his throat, he put up a hand to stop her. Then he turned away, and stood for a long minute with his back to her, head down, looking into the fire.

Finally he said, "We will not speak of this again." He turned towards her and put out a hand. He was smiling, but the pain was still in his eyes.

"Come, let us be friends still, in spite of all. Wilt thou shake hands on it and wish me a safe journey?"

Bell took the proffered hand. "With all my heart, friend," she said.

Eighteen
February

"Lucy, the lady and ge'man in the upstairs front are calling for their morning ale in their chamber. Will you take it up? You'm a dear girl." Mercy waded into the kitchen clutching a huge feather bed to her bosom. Her round face above the billowing lumps reminded Lucy of a meat pudding on mashed potatoes. She laughed to herself as she wiped out two pint pots and filled them from the creaking wooden spigot.

She played the demure serving-maid for the flushed, self-satisfied couple in the best bedroom. The man frowned as she emptied their chamber pot into her bucket.

"Will there be anything else, sir?" she asked brightly.

He grunted. The woman avoided looking at her by gazing into his eyes.

Bouncing back downstairs, Lucy stopped by the little dark window on the corner of the staircase and plonked down the slop bucket to run her hands through her hair and retie her apron. A great wrap-round tapster's apron, it was, that Mercy had given her when she took her in. She picked up the bucket and ran out to the privy in the yard to empty the slops. It was one of those bright February days that seem to give early promise of the spring; the air was cold still, but the snow was all gone. Lucy felt restless and disturbed. The stupid couple in the best chamber annoyed her. So smug to have been abed together, so pleased with each other.

Sorry for yourself because you're alone? she mocked herself bitterly. Well you're that, right enough, and only yourself to blame, my girl. It was her mother's voice in her head. But Mam was gone.

Lucy banged the bucket miserably on the stones. And now Hope was gone, too. She fought down the memory of the morning after Twelfth Night – the older woman's rage, and her own bewildered fury. They had both shouted and cried and blamed each other, and then Hope had turned her out with nothing but the clothes she stood up in. Mercy and William had taken her in, with no questions asked. She was making sure to earn her keep here at the Two Crosses.

Dumping the bucket by the privy wall, she wandered over to the wainhouse. The postchaise that had brought the guests in last night was standing there; the postboy must still be at his breakfast. He'd better hurry, she thought, they're bound to be impatient to be gone, now they're up. It wasn't her job to go and tell him, she decided. Instead she walked out into the lane. The first flowers were showing in the banks: little yellow ones with round petals, some gone pale and thin where the snow had damaged them. It was good to be on her own for a while.

It was all very well here, but so many people coming and going was strange – tiresome. You needed to get away sometimes. She was sharing a bed with William's youngest sister, Nance, who chattered endlessly about people Lucy didn't know; and all day long the people who came in wanted to ask her some fool question or another, or crack their favourite joke for a new pair of ears. Mostly they were regulars, like that John Hamer. He lived right up in the hills, but he seemed to find some errand to bring his old waggon down by the Crosses nearly every mortal day. Then he'd come in for his mug of ale and his mean, complaining conversation with anyone who would listen. Quite often there were strangers, too, passing trade from the Ludlow road like the pair she had waited on that morning. Market days were busiest, but even on other days the parlour rarely stood empty.

I like to be alone sometimes, she thought. Perhaps some people do, more than others. Like Bron. Somewhere far up in the hills, all on her own.

Lucy lifted her head and looked at the high horizon crested with trees, imagining the tall, loping figure, dark hair flying, alone in the hills.Where was Bron's farm? Cloudborry, it was called. A house up near the sky. The thought of Bron brought back the moment in the barn. She felt hot and confused at the memory. She wondered if she would ever see Bron again.

She stopped to look over a gate. A big fallow field sloped down to a line of willows. There was a little river there, she knew, but she did not know its name. A long dark tunnel gaped in her mind, leading to her mam's cottage on the wide grassy bank of her childhood. She flinched from the lurking horror – quick, think of something good.

She stared hard at the willows. Mr. Brown?

Mr. Gray.

Damn.

She sighed again. How could she have known Hope would be like that about it? She remembered the hot, wild hands, the urgent tongue, and the fierce cry when she came, thrashing and sobbing. Mr. Brown had not been a bit like that. She had been wicked; smooth, sliding, with magic hands and a cool whisper in Lucy's ear. It was me that thrashed and screamed that time, she thought, grinning.

She could feel herself getting wet. Gritting her teeth, she set off back to the inn.

It was at dusk that the nightmare began. Lucy was doing nothing for a moment, sprawled warm and comfortable by the great kitchen hearth, half listening to Nance's chatter and watching the winter afternoon gloom into night.

Then William came in. "Will one of you lasses go into the parlour? I've Waldon's man here about the oats and dung, and can't leave him. Some gent, a stranger, just come in, is calling for ale and marrow bones."

Lucy always reckoned to jump before she was told. She bounced to her feet, shook down her petticoats and seized a napkin off the horse.

The long kitchen passage, lined with black oak, was already dark, but she knew her footing there. The second panel from the far end was an opening which let through some dim light from the parlour and the murmur of voices. She recognised John Hamer's grumbling tones before she could hear his words. The man practically lived here – had he no home fire of his own? Then, a step from the squint, she froze. Another voice. Hideously familiar. Her heart hammered in her chest so that she thought she would stifle.

His voice.

It echoed in her head as if from the bottom of a well.

"Did you indeed, sir?" he was saying. "Well, to my mind you had a lucky escape, if you take my meaning. I fear it could have been much the worse. Perhaps you carry some holy charm for your protection, whereby providence has saved you thus far?"

Lucy's blood drained down to her feet. She was icy cold and faint. She staggered against the wall, clutching the ledge, and saw him. He had his back to her, his chair drawn up to the parlour fire and his muddy boots on the hearth, leaning forward, talking earnestly. She could only see the back of his head, the wispy grey pigtail twitching on the deep collar of his old black coat, but she knew without doubt it was him. Noll Wethered.

It was an hour before she stopped running. Out of the front door, up the lane, with the frosty air biting her lungs, until she saw someone up ahead. Over the ditch, through the hedge and away, up the hillside, stumbling and gasping, into the gathering dark.

She was running blind, at the end of her strength, when her foot plunged through a crust of ice into a deep hole and she fell headlong into the gnarled black hands of the dead heather. Its spiky fingers were hard as iron and one of them gouged her cheek as she fell. She lay panting, gulping in blades of icy air, until she had breath to scream and then to cry. The yammering panic shaped itself into words that beat, over and over, in her head. He had come: Wethered had come. He had found her. He must not catch her. He had come to get her.

For months, when she knew she was carrying his baby, she had believed he was after her, was out to track her down. She had run before him like a wounded bird doubling and turning, zig-zag, to throw off the hunter's dog, and she thought she had succeeded. After the baby, she had even thought she had been mistaken, wrong in the head, and that he had never been following her at all. But he had. And now he had come. The heat of her running drained away quickly into the wet ground. She felt nothing – not cold, or pain – nothing but despair. She could die here. If she lived, he would get her. Today, tomorrow, somehow he would find her again.

There was a sound in the darkness. Red panic surged through her and she clutched the ground. It came again: an animal noise, she realised, not a person. She raised her head.

It was pitch dark, the heather only knowable by its cruel spiky fingers in her face. The only light was a change of black for slate grey, a jagged line where the hills above her met the muffled sky.

Above the sighing wind, the sound came again – a little, heart-rending voice. And quite near. Lucy raised herself to her knees, then dropped again with a cry, as pain shot up the leg that had plunged through the ice. Hearing her, the animal set up a feeble stream of bleating.

"What are you?" She rolled on to her back and sat up. "Little lamb, are you? Little lost lamb?" There was some kind of comfort in talking to another living thing, even if she couldn't see it.

"You and me both," she went on grimly. She felt her leg: the ankle was hot and swelling. She peered about: black nothingness. Then the wind whipped a gap in the cloud and a gleam of moonlight showed her where she was. She had been climbing up a gully, where a stream ran between boulders. To her left there seemed to be a low cliff, broken away sheer. And at the foot of it, only a few yards away, a splodge of white.

Kneeling cautiously, she crawled towards it. It was a sheep – a dead one. Good and dead, with its thin sticks of legs in the air like an overturned stool. Something small and fast scuttled away from its head as Lucy approached. Where was the lamb? She could not see it at first, until it cried again, even more faintly, and there was a suggestion of movement in the darkness beside the dead ewe. It was not white, as she had expected, but a little black thing, pressing itself to its dead mother's belly. It was too weak to struggle; when she had it in her arms, it gave a final, feeble bleat and lay still.

"You an' me both," Lucy repeated, hugging the tiny creature to her.

Behind the fallen ewe there was a hollow under the bank, smoothed out by the stream in spring flood. Still clutching the lamb, Lucy edged herself into the gap and lay down.

Nineteen

Hope moved the wooden spoon carefully, scraping the thickening syrup from the smooth side of the little pot. There was not enough daylight to see how the reduction was coming on, and the morning fire was low. Gingerly, gripping the outside edge of the hot brass boiler with a rag, she used the spoon to tilt the inner pot. It slipped, splashing oily liquid into the fire. Smoky flame spurted up and she grabbed her hand away, catching the rag in the brass handle. Quite neatly, the whole thing up-ended. Boiling water and nearly made cough mixture – a whole bag of herbs and some precious sweet oil, and four hours of pot-watching – poured into the heart of the fire.

In a cloud of smoke and steam, Hope dropped into the chair. A red lump of tears swelled in her throat. Everything she touched went wrong. She was never going to be any good at this. When would Bell come home? She scrubbed her forehead with a grubby hand. She could not be both of them, she just couldn't.

The people kept on coming. At first they had been interested to have the story of Bell's journey to take away along with their cures, but now they glared at Hope, as if she had Bell hidden away somewhere, as if it was her fault that the Dame was not here when they wanted her. She had never expected Bell to be away this long. All the stock of cough syrup and most of the ointments were used up already. She knew what went into the cough stuff, but she'd not made it before – not on her own. And now it was all spoiled, lost. The tears spilled. She put her head in her hands and sobbed.

Parsley came butting her knee, purring. Hope reached out but the cat, alarmed by her suddenness, slipped aside, out of reach, head cocked.

"Even you don't want me, do you?" Hope asked it. "I'm no good to anyone, Parsley, I'm not surprised no one wants me."

As if in answer, Lucy sprang into her mind. Warm and eager, brown and sweet as a hazelnut. Lucy had wanted her. And, if she was honest, she had wanted it too. She still did. Self-pity curdled into self-contempt. Bleakly she got up and lifted the pots from the smoking mess on the hearth, regardless of hot soot on her hands. She carried the little cauldron to the door.

As she elbowed it open, she saw Mercy toiling up the path, all out of breath, her shawl fallen from her shoulders and her hair dripping frosty mist. Seeing Hope, she stopped, then came on at a run.

"Where's Lucy? You got her here, Hope, safe and sound? She'm here with you?"

Hope stepped back. Before she could answer, Mercy was inside.

"Lucy! Where are you, girl?" Still panting with exertion, she scanned the smoky kitchen. "I've a bone to pick with her, running off like she did, and us all afeared for her. Lucy!" She drew back the curtain screening the little alcove where Lucy had slept.

Hope finally found her voice. "She's not here. She has not been here since... since she came to you."

Mercy stood quite still, quite at a loss, one hand to her mouth. "Oh, Hope. Oh my dear, where can she be gone to?"

Hope helped her friend to sit down and brought her a cup of small beer. "Now tell me," she said gently.

Mercy wiped her face with her shawl. "I thought she would come to you. I'd have run from him myself in her place, nasty old man he is, and sitting in my parlour like a lord. But I said to

William, she'll be up the bank at our Dame's house, surely she will, so we'll fret no more tonight, and I'll go up there tomorrow."

Lucy had gone? Hope's heart was thumping. She could not tell if she was glad or sorry. She turned to the hearth and began to tend the ruined fire, her back to Mercy as she said, "Run off, has she? Bound to go, I suppose, sooner or later. She was a bolter, wasn't she? Not likely to stay in one place long?"

"Oh, no," said Mercy, "she didn't mean to go far, I'm sure. Why, she never took nothing with her, left all her things, such as they were, never even took the good shawl I gave her against the weather. Nance says she was afeared of him, and I do believe her, for he do make a body shudder just to look at him."

Hope turned to face her. "Who do you mean?"

"I'm telling you. This fellow come in yesterday, off the high road. Grim-faced, he were, and had a way of staring at you, you know? He looked respectable enough by his clothes – good black coat and hat, dirty boots but then the roads be dirty enough – but he'd not been in our parlour five minutes before he was thick as thieves with that John Hamer, talking a lot of nonsense about witches and I know not what."

"Witches?" Hope was still mystified, but suddenly uneasy.

"Oh, he'm your man for witches, seemingly," said Mercy scornfully. "What he don't know of 'em's not worth knowing, by his account. So Hamer calls for more ale and soon this stranger's telling him he was most likely witched into falling over and breaking his arm."

"Nonsense!" Hope banged down the poker and turned to face Mercy. "He slipped on the sheet of ice that ran out of his own midden."

"I know that, my dear, but he'm a daft old bugger that John Hamer, would believe any old tale. And then," she leaned forward earnestly, "our Nance hears this stranger telling him of a witch he knew himself. He said he knew for a fact she laid with the devil and had a child as black as sin – says this girl child was an evil spirit sent by Satan to witch men's hearts and corrupt their bodies. Nance says by now they were all like men turned to stone, harkening to his mad nonsense, when he says, he's heard the girl was in these parts, and had they seen the black slut?" She paused, her face troubled. "And then he said, she had a baby of her own though she was not wed, and that was another way they would know her."

Hope was up and pacing the floor. "What did they tell him?"

"Well, you can be sure no one knows about the babe but you and me. And William," she added honestly, "but he'll hold dumb as a stone. Our Nance was away from harvest time to Christmas at her granny's house – who died, rest her soul – and we did never tell her about the child, nor anyone else at the Crosses. No need for gossip as well as grief, my William said. So the stranger had no joy of that. But Hamer and the others were that ready to tell all they know, they soon made sure it were our Lucy he meant.

"Nance tried to throw them off the scent – she've a quick wit, our Nance – said Lucy'd left the house, and no one knew where, but she could tell they didn't believe her. So she come running to me, and then we found it were true – she were really gone. Oh Hope, I'm that afeared for her! Where can she be?"

Hope looked out of the little window. Pale sun shone on frost-white twigs. It was no season to be astray on the hills or on the road.

"I wish I knew," she said.

Lucy drifted between nightmare and waking pain. Noll glared at her, the flames of burning cottages in his eyes. Voices in the wind wailed down the gulley, calling her name. When she woke to their call, pain gripped her and she heard herself whimper and cry. But each time she woke and reached out for the lamb, it was there, warm under its hard-caked curls. It did not struggle, except to nestle nearer. They waited together for the dawn.

As grey light like dirty dishwater trickled into the little valley, Lucy woke and saw that she was lying with her face to the crumbling black soil of the cliff. The fleece of the dead ewe was warm at her back. Its lamb still lay in Lucy's lap, its face stretched up close to hers. The next time she stirred, they both woke and it cried feebly, nudging her as if for food. She found she could not move, she had no strength left. The pain was much less, but only because both her legs were numb, dead as logs. Trying to heave herself up with her arms, she knocked head and shoulder against the bank, filling her mouth with grit. She slumped back, defeated.

The lamb, having seen daylight, was even more sure it was hungry. Kicking her with its sharp little feet, it struggled out past her face and on to its legs. It butted feebly at its mother, and set up a wailing cry that sounded like despair. Lucy shut her eyes. Tears of pity squeezed out between her eyelids and ran into the cold earth.

In her dream a dog was barking wildly, excited. Then she heard it scrabbling and whining close by.

"Lie down!" a voice called in the distance. "Gelert, down!"

The scrabbling gave way to a panting growl. Lucy opened her eyes, but it was still dark. She tried to move, and the dog barked again in the real, waking world, close to her ear.

There was the crunch of boots coming nearer and Lucy's heart came into her mouth. She tried to scream, but no sound came.

She heard the voice again. "Good dog. Leave, now!"

Then she felt the dead ewe pulled away, and heaved herself over, falling out into the splintering light. The dog's warm tongue was rough on her face, licking and whining all at once. She flung up her arms to hold on to him, but he bounced away, barking. She felt her head and shoulders lifted. A hand wiped the hair from her eyes and there, leaning over her, was Bron. Lucy closed her eyes again, but it was not a dream.

The lamb bleated. Bron said, "Fetch, Gelert! Good dog!"

Lucy heard him spring away. Then she was lifted bodily, her face pressed against another fleece, dry and warm this time and smelling of smoke and humanity. She opened her eyes and met a steady blue gaze.

"Poor lambkin," said Bron.

Lucy woke indoors, the play of firelight on her face. At first she thought she was back home: the great flat hearth, the little unlighted room, were like her mother's cottage. She was lying in front of the fire, her face close to a familiar, dark, moist floor of beaten earth. But there was a quilt over her which she did not recognise – she inched out a hand to touch it – an old quilt of many pieces, some washed thin as cobwebs, its faded colours comfortable together. She tried to lift her head to look round.

"Be still. You must rest awhile more."

It was Bron, in an old wooden armchair drawn up to the fire, the lamb between her knees. Its tail waved vigorously as it sucked on a rag in the neck of a bottle. Two dogs lay on either side of their mistress, heads on paws, tongues lolling. Their bright eyes met Lucy's. One of them – the one who had found her, Lucy thought – thumped his plumy tail in greeting.

Bron dropped a hand to fondle his ears. "Yes, yes, good boy for finding. Went looking for one little lost lamb and found two, eh?" The dog grinned and wriggled with pleasure.

Lucy eyelids drooped again. She spoke with an effort, her voice creaking and painful. "Is this your house?"

Bron's sounded amused. "It is."

"Can I... can I stay here?"

Bron and the dog regarded each other seriously. Then Bron said, "Gelert will not let you out of his sight for a while yet."

Twenty

It was morning again when Lucy woke properly. She was lying on a mattress of sack and straw. There was no sign of Bron. She felt rested all right – until she tried to get up. Then she found her leg was still useless, swollen and tight round the ankle; she could not put her weight on it without shooting pains. She sank back into the rustling bed.

The glow of the embers in the fireplace and the light from a small window showed her the rest of the room. There was little enough to see: the chair Bron had sat in last night, a couple of benches by the wall, a black oak cupboard, a plate rack. At the far end of the room a ladder led to an attic or loft. Everything was very clean and neat, Lucy thought, but bare. Even Mam had had her one or two ornaments – a blue and white jug with no handle that she sometimes put flowers in, before she got so tired; a china cow that was meant for a cream jug, that one of her men had won at a fair. Here, there was nothing but what was useful – Lucy thought it was more like a workshop than a home.

Bron was a puzzle to her, but one she liked to think about. Hope had said that Bron had always lived here, looking after her father and brother. Her father had died, and soon after that her brother had been killed by a falling tree. Bron had stayed on, alone. With no one to talk to, Lucy thought, except the dogs. Lucy had not understood until now about the dogs. Gwennie and

Gelert were like Bron's family. She lived and worked with them and they were company for her. Perhaps that was why she did not talk much to people. Lucy wondered too about Bron's mother and how old Bron had been when she died. Perhaps she had made the quilt. Did Bron remember her? Lucy could not imagine asking.

The door let in an icy blast and Bron came in from the yard, preceded by Gelert and followed by the black lamb, which tottered purposefully towards Lucy and collapsed in a heap on the quilt. Lucy gathered it into her arms.

Seeing that Lucy was back in the world, Bron brought her bread and milk, and a steaming cup of something brown and strongly scented.

Lucy wrinkled her nose.

"That's sovereign against cold and pain. Our Dame made it," said Bron firmly. "Drink it all."

While Lucy ate her breakfast – she was very hungry, she found – Bron reached up to release a catch on the wall. What Lucy had taken for a piece of panelling fell slowly outwards and became a bed. Bron gathered up the quilt and spread it over the feather mattress, then helped Lucy towards it.

"No need to sleep on the floor tonight," she said gruffly.

Lucy thought about this for a minute. "Where do you sleep?"

Bron's face closed. She jerked her head towards the ladder. "Above."

She took away the cup and bowl and gave Lucy the bottle for the lamb, then stood for a minute, watching while Lucy fed it.

"Reckon you owe her," she said finally. "I'd not have found you but for Gelert seeking after her noise." She walked to the door and pulled on her old jacket. "I'll be away a while. Stay here and rest your leg." Then she disappeared.

She was out most of the time, off on the hill with the sheep. It was coming up to lambing now – the little black cade lamb had been the first – and still bitterly cold. Sometimes Bron was about in the yard, and then Lucy would watch through the little casement window as she dragged hurdles into the barn ready for the lambing, her boots crunching the icy mud and her breath steaming. Lucy never tired of watching the tall loping figure, but she took care that Bron did not see her.

The two dogs worked with her, or even alone, fetching sheep when she told them and keeping them in the shed or in a corner of the yard. Lucy loved to watch them. They lay, tongues out and eyes gleaming at the terrified sheep, which stood stock still until Bron came to deal with them. Both dogs could work that way, though Gelert was noisier and sometimes he would snap and worry the silly creatures until they lost their heads and bolted. Gwennie spared her steps; she was Gelert's mother, Bron said, and the wisest dog anywhere on the hills. Her pups fetched a great price, but she was getting on now, and Bron would not make her breed again. Bron talked to the dogs in their own private language of whistles and calls, and fed them scraps from her pocket. She treated them like her friends, her equals; watching them, Lucy sometimes felt like an intruder in their harsh, hard-working world.

As her ankle grew stronger and she could move around more freely, she felt Bron withdraw again into her old, private self, silent and awkward as she had been at Brynsquilver. It was as if she wanted to push you away, Lucy thought. The more friendly you were, the more she put up her guard. Like she did on Twelfth Night.

When Lucy was quite small, a bony little cat had come to the cottage door, driven by hunger but too wild to be touched. It had flattened its ears and hissed at Lucy's mother, showing all its teeth, when she pushed a dish of milk and water towards it. Lucy had tried to catch it and it had scratched her so she bled. Her mother showed her how to win it.

"It's fierce because it's frightened," she said. "It's got no reason to trust you. Don't jump at it, our Luce, and don't look it in the eye. Just feed it and sit still. It'll come to you in the end."

It had worked with the cat, but Bron would be a tougher job altogether. Although Lucy would have scorned such behaviour in anyone else, she found herself looking for small ways to please, putting Bron's stockings to dry by the fire, or making broth ready for her return from the fields. She could never tell whether her gift would be accepted; whether Bron would shy off, stomping wordlessly out to some urgent task, or reward her with that sudden, transforming smile. The easiest time was in the evenings. Bron usually had some task of mending or making, and they sat companionably enough by the fire, the dogs between them and the black lamb curled in Lucy's lap. For the first time in a very long while, Lucy felt safe.

By the fourth day, her ankle was much better and she was heartily sick of her own company and her imprisonment in the house. It was too cold to be out of doors without working, but there was little enough to do inside, once she had made up the fire and tidied her bed. Bron was on her own in the yard, Gwennie and Gelert were away up the hill after a strayed ewe. Lucy wondered wistfully if there was some task Bron would let her join in. As she limped towards the window, the lamb following as always, she heard the noise of wheels in the yard and a man's voice shouting.

Lucy rubbed a peephole in the frosty pane and peered through. Bron had come out of the byre and was standing, dung-fork in hand, staring at the intruders. John Hamer, one arm still in a scarf, held the horse's head; two other men sat in the cart, muffled against the weather.

Then Bron spoke, harsh and loud. "You're not welcome here, John Hamer. I've no business with you."

Hamer made no reply, but one of the others climbed down and came across the yard. He was a short, rusty-haired man, wearing the tricorn hat of a bailiff. Bron said nothing, only lifted the dung-fork and held it like a weapon across her chest.

The bailiff thrust his face close to Bron's, so that their smoking breaths mingled in the air. "Bronwen Richards, you'm arrested," he said.

Then, as Bron gazed uncomprehendingly at him, "Put that thing down, missus, and come with me. I'm to arrest you, see? On the deposition of this man" – he gestured importantly towards Hamer – "on a charge of witchcraft."

Lucy gasped, but Bron gave a bark of disbelieving laughter. "Witchcraft? You gone daft, Ned Gilroy?" She pointed the fork at Hamer. "If there's a witch in this parish it's more likely him," she said scornfully. "Gets boundary stones walking about in the night, he does!" She turned away as if to go back into the byre.

"Hark'ee, woman." Gilroy grabbed her by the arm.

With a violence that sent him reeling, Bron threw him off, lowering the dung-fork to keep him at bay.

As the bailiff found his feet and reached out for her again, Hamer tossed the reins into the cart and started towards them.

"No! No!" Regardless of the pain in her ankle, Lucy hurled herself at the door and out into the yard, shouting. She had no idea what she intended to do, only that she must help Bron. At the sound of her voice, everyone stopped and turned towards her. There was a moment when no one moved or spoke. Then the man in the cart stood up. His hand shook as he pointed at her.

Lucy did not need to hear his voice to know him. Terror made her dizzy. She swayed and fell against the wall, fighting for breath.

"Look, look!" cried Wethered. "The devil's whore! Quick, catch her! Leave the other – catch the black slut!" The horse shied as he leapt down into the mud and strode towards her.

She wanted to run, but her legs were like water. Whimpering, she slid down the wall, cowering in the mud as Noll stood over her.

"Where are you hiding it, slut?" His voice cracked with excitement. "Where have you put the brat, devil-spawn?" His eyes held her.

Lucy licked dry lips. "He – he's dead," she whispered.

Wethered gave a cry of triumph. "I have you now, whore!" He turned to Ned Gilroy. "Take her up, bailiff! She has murdered her own child! She has sucked its life away!"

Hamer and the bailiff looked at each other, hesitating.

"My warrant is for this one," said Gilroy. "No baby in it, was there?"

At that moment the black lamb appeared in the doorway. Bleating for its bottle, it trotted up to Lucy.

"See, see!" screamed Wethered. "Their familiar! Their evil spirit! Filthy spawn of the evil one!" He swooped on the lamb, lifted it bleating into the air, and hurled it against the wall.

All hell broke loose. Lucy screamed, and Bron ran towards her. The bailiff stepped forward to stop her and she swung the heavy dung-fork, catching him on the shoulder. He swore and staggered. Then Hamer flung himself bodily at Bron, pinning her against the wall of the byre. Before she could throw him off, Gilroy was on his feet again and had hold of her.

Noll, ignoring the battle behind him, seized hold of Lucy, catching her round the neck and dragging her across the cobbles. She choked and squirmed, trying to bite him. She heard a cry from Bron, suddenly cut off. Then Noll's boot caught her sprained ankle and a wave of pain wiped out the light.

The next thing she knew was the motion of the cart over stones. Lucy opened her eyes. Bron, her hands tied, lay beside her in the bottom of the cart. There was blood on her face, and her eyes were closed.

Twenty-one

The spaniel bitch could not keep all five puppies in the basket. Each time she settled to feed them, they kicked and yelped, and one fell head first over the side on to the smooth stone floor. The smallest got pushed out most. Lucy watched it land on its back, all belly and waving paws, then scramble into the basket on top of its brothers and set them squabbling and pushing again. The basket lay under a huge old black cupboard with carved legs. It was a horrible room, cold and narrow and dark with a window like a church. Like Noll's church. Lucy tried to concentrate on the puppies, so that she did not have to look at Noll, or at any of the other men in the room. The men talked. Noll talked a lot. Lucy watched the little spaniel and her litter.

Suddenly she heard her name, loud. She put her head down. Someone shook her arm, roughly.

The gentleman spoke again. "You are called Lucy Weaver?"

Lucy dragged her gaze away from the puppies. The gentleman faced her across a scarred black table strewn with bundles of old papers. His face under the flowing brown wig was pale, the heavy eyes pouched and hooded.

"Stand forward, wench, and make your duty to Sir John." That was the bailiff, Gilroy, who had kept hold of her ever since he had dragged her from his cart at the door of Waldon Hall, and tied her hands to stop her clawing him.

151

Lucy gritted her teeth. They should not know she was afraid. She pulled away from him and stepped up to the table. Staring at Sir John, she dropped a curtsy and waited.

Sir John Waldon looked her over, slowly; she felt as if the eyes of all the men in the room were on her, too. She could not keep her head up. Looking at the floor, she wound her hands in her skirt to stop them shaking.

When Sir John finally spoke it was to the bailiff.

"Does she understand the charge?" His voice sounded weary and rather distant.

Gilroy considered. "She do seem to have her wits, my lord, even though she did fight like a mad 'un when we fetched her in."

Sir John turned to Lucy. "You know this man?" he asked, indicating Noll Wethered. Noll and Hamer stood together, away in the shadows. Lucy glanced up quickly, and away, nodding.

"Ah, a response," the gentleman said. Now he was speaking to the other man, the one with the pen who sat at the end of his table, under the light from the window. "Really, Jenkins, I do wonder about the in-breeding of these people. Most of them are near-idiots. But look at the colour of this one!"

The penpusher nodded, staring at her. "Quite extraordinary, my lord. I suppose it could be dirt? Here is the deposition." He handed a sheet of paper down the table.

Lucy hated them all. It helped. Her hands stopped shaking, and she held up her chin.

"This man," the justice said, reaching for the paper and holding it up to show her, "brings the charge against you of killing your own child. That is a charge of murder. Do you understand? It is a hanging charge."

Lucy, aghast, stared at him. She opened her mouth, and tried to say no. She could only utter a strangled sob. The room went suddenly still.

Leaning towards her he went on. "If you had a child that soon died, and if it can be shown that before its birth you concealed your condition from the world, so that it was not known you were with child, then by law you stand guilty of that child's death. So it is important that you tell me the truth. Now, did you have a baby?"

She thought of the little boy, lying wailing in her arms at Brynsquilver, of how it had looked like Noll, and of the day they had buried it. Her breath felt tight in her chest. No words came.

"She cannot deny it!" Noll broke in suddenly. "She must be examined by a midwife. She cannot deny it!"

Sir John looked at him briefly, then back at Lucy. "Well?"

Her voice was a whisper. "I did have him, sir." She licked dry lips. "It was a boy."

Out of the corner of her eye she saw Noll twitch, as if to speak again, but the justice went on, "Where did you live while you were carrying the child? Who tended you? You are very young. Surely your mother knew of your condition?"

"My mother is dead," said Lucy flatly. She could feel Noll's eyes on her. She thought for a moment, what if she told this lord about Noll, and the cottage and the fire and… she could not. He would kill her.

She spoke carefully. "When I knew I was with child, I left the place where I had lived. I tramped mostly, and found work where I could…" She could see in Sir John's face that this was not good enough. She stopped.

"And you told no one of your condition?"

She swallowed, avoiding Noll's eye. "No, sir."

"Jenkins, what did our canting friend here tell us? No, wait, I have it here." He picked up the paper and sighed, flipping his fingers impatiently along the edge of the sheet.

"Mr. Wethered says that when he asked after you in Chester and other places, those who remembered you made a shrewd guess that you were carrying, but, he says, no one heard you speak of it. So it was kept secret, he says. But such rumours and negatives are not enough for the law – on either side." He frowned at Noll, quellingly.

There was a silence. Then he leaned forward, his elbows on the table. For the first time, something like concern showed in his face as he spoke to Lucy. "The babe was surely baptised before it died? Which churchyard is it buried in? A clergyman's word is a strong defence in such a case."

Lucy shook her head numbly. Tears gathered in her throat. "He is buried in the wood."

Noll gave a crow of triumph. "She could not bring the devil's brat to the holy font!" he cried.

Sir John sat back with a sigh. He gestured wearily to his clerk. "Write it down, Jenkins. The Sheriff will need it. Good God, what barbarians we live among. I know not which is worse, the rabid witch-finder or the wretched witch."

He snapped his fingers unexpectedly. "Here, Artemis," he said, in quite a different voice. The little spaniel heaved herself out of the basket, scattering squealing pups, and came to his boots. He scooped her up into his lap, and began to pull her silky ears through his fingers. Then he raised his long face and spoke to Lucy. "I fear there is a case against you after all. Let us be clear on the matter. You had a child, and the child died."

Lucy nodded.

"It was never baptised."

She nodded again.

"And it is buried – you say – somewhere in a wood."

The scratching quill was loud in the silence. Tears began to spill down Lucy's face.

"You had told no one you were with child. There is no one who can testify that they knew. No one who saw the baby alive –"

Lucy looked up, startled. "Oh, yes," she said, "Hope saw it. I was in her house. And Bro–" She bit her tongue. Bron was in enough trouble already. She would not draw her in to this.

There was a general stir in the room. Sir John looked enquiringly at the bailiff.

"Hope Bishop, My lord. A cunning woman of these parts, or so some do believe, begging your lordship's pardon."

Noll burst out, "The word of a witch to save a witch? She raves, my lord. The case is clear against her."

Lucy kept her eyes on the gentleman. "And Mercy Jones," she said urgently. "She knew about him. She gave me a little cap and a gown for him..."

"Wife of William Jones keeps the Two Crosses," supplied Ned Gilroy.

Sir John passed a hand across his brow. Then without warning, he rose to his feet. "I will dine," he announced, "while these... persons... are fetched. Jenkins, write up the depositions. Bailiff, bring the girl back in an hour, and the other accused woman with her. This business has taken enough of the day already." Dropping the spaniel on the floor, he left the room.

Twenty-two

And then, of course, he made everybody wait. Hope and Mercy and William – Mercy would not come without William, summoned or no – kicked their heels for an hour in a slimy corridor hung with rotting embroideries.

Mercy sat on the only bench. Pictured over her head, a boy with one blue leg and one red one held a horse's head. Hope stared at it, and the horse stared back out of large brown eyes with ridiculous curly lashes. William stamped and fumed. He did not like Sir John, who taxed the inn heavily and still gave sundry cottagers permission to sell beer whenever it suited him. And Sir John certainly did not fit Hope's idea of a squire, which had been formed by her experience of Bell's father, who was also something like the father of his people.

Sir John, on the other hand, held no harvest suppers for his tenants; he had no wife or daughters to send soup and charity into their cottages; he collected his rents through his bailiffs. Hope did not know him even by sight. The only time she had been to the hall – she had remembered it vividly as they hurried up the long lime-tree avenue at Ned Gilroy's heels – was twenty years ago when she and Bell had sought refuge there in vain, on the run from King George's troops. This had been a Jacobite house then, and some said it was so still. People liked to think their remote lord harboured hidden Catholic priests and traitorous Scotsmen.

Hope thought he was probably merely selfish and bad tempered.

And so am I, she thought, with a flash of irritated insight. Here we are, come to speak up for this unfortunate, infuriating child, who seems to plunge wildly from crisis to crisis, bowling over everyone she touches as she passes by.

Her feelings about Lucy were still complicated and painful, but more than anything her heart misgave her for Bron, dragged into this latest broil and carried off from her farm – with some violence, from what Gilroy had told them – just at the start of her lambing season. And kept locked up, perhaps. She rubbed her face, distressed. Dear Bron, so strong and sure in her own place, but least able of any of them to cope with the unfamiliar and threatening world of justice, clerk and bailiff. To hold Bron prisoner would be like caging a hawk.

And when they finally got inside, it was worse than she had imagined. She was shocked at the sight of Bron. Standing beside Daniel, the Clun bailiff, a great butcher of a man, she seemed caved in upon herself, forlorn as a scarecrow. Her old jerkin had been torn half off her shoulders, and bits of straw were sticking in long daubs of mud all down her skirts. But it was her face that frightened Hope. Not so much the bruises, already blue and purple under her tan, but the look of dumb panic in her deep blue eyes. And her hair: Bron always wore her long hair in a solid plait, out of the way, off her face, but it had been torn loose, and spread everywhere round her shoulders and half across her cheek. She could do nothing to help herself, because her hands were tied in front of her with a rough length of hempen rope. Hope had to stop herself from rushing to her friend's aid.

Lucy stood the other side of Daniel and was in the same state as Bron. She was tumbled and battered. Her hair was uncovered, like Bron's, and stood out in a huge tangled bush that made her head look too big for her slight body. Hope was pierced with pity and anger for both women.

At the other end of the room, John Hamer and a pallid man in black – this Wethered, she supposed – were standing side by side; Sir John sat with his clerk in his official seat to be their judge. Hope set her jaw. Sometimes her mother's Puritan, independent blood spoke out in her against the pomps and vanities of the wicked world and such potentates as these. She would have to be careful not to make things worse. Gilroy ushered her and the Joneses to stand before the justice.

Sir John settled himself and looked them over.

"William Jones?"

William touched his forelock. "Sir?" He sounded startled.

"Step forward, man, and tell us what you know about this to-do."

The colour came up in William's face, and he swallowed. Hope could feel his confusion. He had not, after all, been called for to the court, and words did not come easily to him at the best of times. She supposed that Sir John had had enough of talking to women for the time being.

"William, do you know these two women?"

"Aye, sir. I've known Bronwen Richards since a child, sir."

Gilroy helped him out, officiously knowledgeable. "Keeps her father's holding, my lord – since her brother died – at Cloudborry beyond Mardu."

William nodded, encouraged. "I've never known ill of her, to this day," he said firmly, "nor has my wife."

Mercy, alarmed to hear herself mentioned, took her husband's hand.

"And the other?" asked Sir John.

"An incomer, sir," William replied, "but a good girl I do believe. Works hard, sir, and civil to the customers. Before she come to us she was up at Brynsquilver, at our Dame's," he added, as if this were a guarantee of Lucy's goodness.

Sir John's gaze flickered in Hope's direction, but he continued to talk to William.

"What do you know of the girl's past life, before she came into this parish?"

"Nothing, sir, before she came here."

"And when was that?"

William scratched his head. "Last back end, sir, after harvest time, as far as I can call to mind."

"She had a baby with her?"

"No, sir, she had the baby soon after."

The man standing with John Hamer began to mutter to himself. The justice sat up.

"Mr. Wethered," he said in a voice of steel, "I have heard your testimony at some length. Now I wish to hear this man's evidence."

"Let him say where the child is, then!" cried Wethered. His pale face gleamed with perspiration, and he clenched and unclenched his hands as he spoke.

"Silence!" Sir John's voice cracked across the room. Wethered subsided, his lips still moving silently.

William said, "It was Mis'ess Bishop here delivered the child, so please you, sir, and kept the girl some weeks after."

Sir John spoke to his clerk. "Take down this woman's deposition," he said. Then he turned to Hope.

I must say this right, Hope thought, but I do not know what will help and what will do harm. She breathed out, and met Sir John's eye as calmly as she could.

"Now, mistress. Did this girl at any time try to conceal from you that she was with child?"

"How could she, sir?" said Hope, surprised. "She was far gone in travail with the child when I found her. No woman could have concealed it."

"You found her, you say. Where?"

"In my goat-house. She had taken shelter there in her pain."

"It would have been better for her to have sought out some

inn, or indeed any cottage, rather than to hide herself in a shed. That looks like concealment, does it not?"

Hope hesitated. "I think she was hiding, indeed, but not to conceal her state from the world." She looked at Lucy, desperately trying to judge whether this was the right thing to say. The black eyes stared back, fiercely urgent, but Hope could not read them. She plunged on. "She had been ill-treated, sir – misused indeed, by a man who left her for dead – and I think she was always in fear that her attacker would find her."

Sir John looked at Lucy, and then back at Hope. "If she told you the child was the fruit of a rape, she lied," he said calmly. "It is a fact well known to those who deal in such cases that no conception is possible, unless the woman is willing."

Hope felt Mercy stir beside her, and took her hand to warn her to be quiet.

"So you took her in," Sir John continued, "and the babe was born in your house. You delivered it?"

"With help from Bron Richards, I did, yes." Hope remembered that long night. "It was a hard birth," she said softly, "and I thought at first that neither of them would live. The babe was but weak from the first, and did not thrive."

Wethered gave a shout of triumph. "No wonder, when it had been overlooked by two witches! The mother ill-wished it, and then the hag who overlooked John Hamer put the evil eye on the child!"

Hope looked at him, horrified. Bron had saved Lucy's life. Surely this madman could not use that to harm her?

"We will come to that matter in due course," said the justice irritably. "Mistress Bishop, you have delivered other children, I am told. You are held by some to be a cunning woman, and must have knowledge of children's ailments. You say the child was sickly. Did its mother seek its death? In your opinion was she in any way to blame for it?"

"Indeed she was not," Hope said. "She tended and fed him as best she could for six weeks, until he died. And she did not try to conceal him in my house, either. Mercy Jones and her husband knew of the baby. Mercy can tell you – she brought him baby clothes." She looked at Mercy, and added gently, "Mercy Jones is tender of such sad infants, sir."

William touched his forehead again. "If you please, sir, we have had four of our own die."

Suddenly Mercy found her voice. "'Twas God's will," she said stoutly, "so 'twas, and no witchcraft. 'Tis mortal hard to bear, sir, as I do know. But He as gives do also take away, so they say." Her dark eyes flashed at Noll Wethered. "And it is naught but wickedness to say otherwise."

Unexpectedly, Sir John smiled. "Well, Jenkins, we have a Christian among us at last. Set it down that Mistress Jones vouches for the naturalness of the infant's death." He looked at each of them, and then at Lucy. "I think we can dismiss this deposition here and now."

Wethered sprang forward and grabbed at the papers on the table, "No, no you cannot – I have my deposition against her, that I gave in Chester – your man had it – where is it? Let me have it! I have sworn she is a witch!"

Sir John batted at his scrabbling hands among the papers, and Gilroy stepped forward to haul the gibbering creature off.

"Behave yourself, sir!" Sir John bellowed at him. Wethered cowered back. "I will hear no more from you about this young woman. She is dismissed into the charge of Mistress Jones here, and you will refrain from molesting her from now on. Jenkins –" He began to get up, but the clerk shook his head.

"What about the other one, sir?"

Sir John slumped into his chair, threw back his head and closed his eyes. "Mother of God! I will not hear another word from this man!" he said.

Wethered turned and pulled John Hamer forward. "It is not my complaint. It is Mr. Hamer – one of your own tenants, sir!" he said, triumphant. He prodded Hamer, who flinched ostentatiously and held on to his bad arm.

"I see," said Sir John. "Well, Hamer?"

And John Hamer stood there, not looking at Bron, and reeled off his story. How she had ill-wished him many a time, and frightened him by her looks and evil words. How his stock had not thriven, when hers did, and how at Christmas he had wished her the joys of the season and she had given him back ill looks, and that very day he had felt her evil wishes come upon him, hot as the devil's breath, so that his legs had given way under him in his own yard and he had fallen and broken his arm. And now, only this week, his dog that he was so fond of had walked across her field, innocently like, and come straight home and died.

He stopped and at once, before any of them could deny this tissue of nonsense, Wethered broke in. "And now we learn, before your own face they admit it, that she overlooked this baby and it died. She is surely a black witch, my lord, evil as sin, damned to hell with unbelievers and papists."

There was a moment's total silence. Sir John looked pale, like a wounded man, or rather like an angry corpse. His voice, when he finally spoke, was controlled almost to a whisper.

"Jenkins – take down this deposition. Witchcraft is a felony I am not empowered to hear. Commit her to Shrewsbury Gaol, until the next Assize."

Twenty-three

Free at last of the close, damp crush of the coach, Bell stood by the road and breathed deeply. A cold wind swept down the hill track, bending the ragged wayside bushes and whipping her heavy skirts against her legs. Cold, but clean. She gave a great sigh, emptying her body not only of the stale stink of the coach but of the soot from a thousand Coalbrookdale fires. All winter she had felt as if her lungs were being slowly and painfully smoked by the dirty air of the Dale, until her very soul had begun to dry out and turn leathery. Now she gazed up at the hills of home, almost laughing with relief and pleasure. She grabbed up her bag and sprang on to the first stile.

As she climbed the familiar track, she was glad that she had made the final leg of the journey alone. Alistair had been concerned that the riding party of Friends had to leave her at Ludlow, but the coach, slow and stuffy as it was, demanded no intimacy or farewells. She was burning to be off, to get home at last, and she had no time for feigned expressions of regret. Making a big stride over a puddle, she hefted her old bag into the other hand. It was heavier than when she had packed it five months earlier, but even so it did not contain half the things she was bringing home. The coachman had promised to drop her smart new box at the Two Crosses. Later Hope would help her to fetch it home and unpack all the treasures that her new family had pressed on her as she left.

The Friends had proved unexpectedly demonstrative at parting. Bell twitched her mind away from the memory of Alistair, standing at her stirrup, his puzzled face closed and rigid as he bade her godspeed. But Rebecca Beeston had cried over her as she put up food for the journey. She had made Bell a present of a good woollen dress-length and a pincushion with her initials on. Even Rachel Lewis had come to see Bell off, bringing a precious package of some of the remedies they had discussed together. That was in the box with the other presents. Brushes from Alistair, spare and elegant, mounted in fine chased silver – French, of course; Bell had not asked where they had come from. Susannah, too busy with the novelties of housekeeping to sew anything for her new sister, but eager to be remembered, had given her a bundle of pamphlets on the latest phases of the non-juring controversy. Bell had dutifully tried one in the coach, but it was wearisome stuff when one had other things to think about, like home and Hope.

Some of the things Bell had bought as presents for Hope were in the bag she carried. And that's why it's so heavy, she thought, heaving it on to the top of the gate that led to their lower pasture, I'm carrying five pounds of nails. For some reason this made her want to laugh out loud.

She surveyed the little enclosure. No goats – they would be back up in the near field long since. And Hope had probably fixed the leaking roof on their shed months ago. Bell pulled herself up on to the gate, swinging legs and skirts clear over, and sat there, resting for a moment. Beside her face the goat-willow was already budding: soft, slippy paws of grey down, tipped with yellow that set the dull afternoon alight. Bell stroked one with a cold fingertip. Then she kilted her skirts and set off up the wet fields, home.

The barely contained tension that had been with her throughout the journey mounted again: her heart was hammering with excitement as she came to the stile leading into the garden. The cottage was just the same, utterly familiar, yet for an instant it looked smaller than she remembered. The garden was winter bare, only a row of leeks standing blue against the cold. Hope must be indoors, by the fire: Bell could picture her, cat on lap, at some task of making or mending, humming a little nameless tune. For a moment she felt unexpectedly nervous, as if they were newly acquainted, newly in love. She smiled and pushed open the door.

The house was dark, the fire low. Bell looked round, non-plussed. She called Hope's name. There was no answer.

It was ridiculous to feel so disappointed. Of course there was no reason Hope should be waiting there for her. After all, she had not known Bell was coming today. Bell shrugged off her cloak and went to blow up the fire and feed it from the stack of logs by the hearth. The wood was dry and soon the leaping flames were brightening the winter afternoon. Bell straightened up and looked round the room. It was deeply untidy. She smiled as she started to move about, touching familiar objects, noting how much of her herb-store had been used, straightening the pots and jars into her own order. On the table which she had always taken such care to keep clean, a small garden fork with a split handle lay in a mess of twine beside a cooled glue-pot. Hope had clearly been in the middle of mending it when she was called away. Bell's irritation gave way to a stab of fear. Where was Hope?

Telling herself that her fears were foolish, Bell picked up her travelling bag. She laid the packet of new-made iron nails on the table, then crossed to the ladder which led to their sleeping-loft and began to climb. She smiled to think of the fine new staircase in her brother's house, and the chamber she had slept in, almost as big as this whole cottage. The narrow space under the eaves where she and Hope slept held far more comfort.

Parsley, curled warmly into the feather bed, opened one eye as Bell reached the top of the ladder and gazed at her warily.

"Parsley! There you are! Good girl." Bell put out a hand, but several months' desertion was not so easily forgiven. With an accusing yellow stare, the cat unfolded herself and slid to the floor, avoiding Bell's hand. Bell sank down on the bed and gazed out through the low window. Dark was already falling, hiding the hills, and the wind was getting up. To stop herself fretting, she let her mind wander over the adventures of the last few months: Alistair's wedding, the wonders and horrors of the ironworks, the passionate conversations about ideas and beliefs. She had seen and learned more than she could have imagined; how much she would have to tell Hope! The thought of Hope made her worried again; she stood and moved towards the ladder.

As she did so, she heard the door open and Hope came in. Her head was down, shoulders hunched. There was a defeated air about her: Bell was shocked by how old she looked. Then Parsley dashed past Bell's legs and down the ladder, calling out in greeting. Hope looked up and saw Bell. Her face registered blank shock, then disbelief, and then she put out her arms and Bell, scrambling anyhow down the ladder, was in them.

She found that she was crying and laughing at the same time. "I'm home now," she heard herself saying over and over again, as she clung to Hope. "I'm really home now. Oh, I'm so glad!"

Hope was holding her so tightly she could hardly breathe. "I wanted you," she muttered into Bell's hair, "I wanted you so much."

Bell hugged her back. "I wanted you, too. And now all will be well."

Hope was still clutching her as if to save herself from drowning. "I needed you," she groaned. "Why didn't you come?"

Bell drew back and looked into her face. It was pale and drawn. "What is it? What's wrong?"

Hope said, "They've taken Bron away. I've just come from Waldon. They've taken Bron to Shewsbury gaol." And she began to cry.

It was hardly the homecoming she had dreamed of, Bell thought ruefully as they sat close together by the fire, exhausted by the events of the day. They had talked fitfully, sometimes both at once, about things they had done since they parted. Now they sat in silence, holding hands, staring into the flames. Bell struggled to make sense of what Hope had told her about the events leading to Bron's arrest. Someone called Lucy, whom Bell had never met, figured greatly in the story. Hope spoke of her casually, as if she knew her well, and this more than anything else made Bell feel keenly what a long time she had been away.

Beyond this, Hope was not inclined to be talkative. She kept one arm round Bell's shoulders, as if afraid she might suddenly disappear again, but she was preoccupied and showed little curiosity about Bell's travels. What had happened to Bron hung on them both like a great weight.

Finally, Bell said, "Perhaps we shall be able to think better in the morning," and they climbed wearily up to bed.

It was selfish to be so disappointed, Bell told herself as she pulled off her shoes in the darkness. She was home, that was all that mattered, and there would be other opportunities for the passionate reunion she had so often imagined during her lonely winter nights in Coalbrookdale. She smiled ruefully to herself. There had been a time, when they were young, when they had been able to work all day and make love all night. When had that youthful energy slipped away? Automatically she unpinned her hair and braided it, then took off her gown and petticoats and slipped into the cold bed beside Hope.

Hope turned to her, reaching round to pull her in. Their bodies touched, belly and thigh, and Bell drew a sharp breath, moving urgently to seek Hope's lips with hers. The force of her longing was at once shocking and utterly familiar. It was as if the two halves of one body reunited, locking, fitting, healing into place. Desire flowed like life-blood between them, warm and sure, sweeping away tiredness, carrying Bell away on a tide of joy. She fought to free herself from her shift, hungry for the touch of skin on skin.

They made love again and again, as the moon climbed across the little window frosted by their warm breath. In between, they lay snug in the comfort of their bed, laughing, teasing, talking in broken fragments of conversation, finishing each other's sentences; saying the things that people say, Bell thought, who need not say anything at all. She wondered idly if Alistair and Susannah would ever feel this rightness, this total ease, but she could not imagine it. Hope's fingers stroked her hair back behind one ear, and Bell turned to kiss her palm. Why not? Because her brother and his wife were newly wed? Because of the differences in their ages? Or because they were man and woman? She drew her hand down Hope's back, feeling the wide swell of her hip, the rounded backside. It felt good, she tightened her grip. Hope pressed her knee gently between Bell's legs.

Then she stopped, quite still. Bell was straining to see her in the dark, to see what was wrong, when Hope spoke.

"I had forgot Bron's sheep. What are we to do?"

"Her sheep!" Bell frowned. "They must be ready for lambing."

Hope flopped down on her back, still holding Bell's hand. "More than ready – the first have come. They can't be left on the hill without watching. The losses would be too great. "

"Oh, Hope! Gwennie and Gelert, too – where are they?"

"We must bring the flock down," said Hope decisively. "We'll go up there at first light. Do you see yourself as a shepherdess, my love?" She gathered Bell close, dropped a sleepy kiss on her forehead, and pulled the quilt over them both.

Twenty-four

Loose scarves of mist rolled away from valley after valley as they climbed up to Cloudborry. They were still warm with their night of coming home to each other, and slightly light-headed from lack of sleep.

"I'm too old for this life of debauchery," Hope grumbled happily as she panted up the steepest part of the bank.

"Then it must stop at once," replied Bell, straight-faced. "And you shall sit by the fire of an evening with your stick and your spectacles, and I shall fetch you a posset as I used to do for my father, to aid your poor old frame in sleeping."

Hope grinned. "There's but one thing I need before sleeping, mistress, and 'tis not a posset." She was in high spirits; she felt as if she had suddenly come back to life, or walked out of a cave into the sun. The sky was brighter, the wind keener, and the world was full of reasons for living. No, just one reason: Bell. Under all the worry about Bron, about what they would find at the farm and whether they could do anything with Bron's flock, flowed a stream of pure joy which was swirled and sweetened by every movement Bell made. She warded off a bramble from the hedge, and Hope found herself smiling; she tucked up a stray lock of hair, and Hope wanted to reach out and stroke it; she caught Hope's eye and held it, and Hope's inside turned to water. All the events of the past few months seemed unreal, a dream from which she had woken again to the real world. Bell need never know about her night with Lucy. It was over and it meant nothing any more.

Without breath for more conversation, they pulled each other over gates and stiles and hurried on across wet pasture. They covered the six miles uphill in less than two hours. Bron's holding was on the top of the world, with views all across Wales. As they emerged from the end of a high-banked green lane on to close-bitten turf, they expected to see the usual scatter of ewes. But the field was empty. They looked at each other in alarm. Then they heard barking – it sounded like Gelert, urgent and excited. They began to run down the muddy track to the steading tucked under the brow of the hill.

The sheep were all in the yard. Crammed in to the open square of the buildings where the low wall of an old pigsty joined the house to the facing barn, a dirty sea of fleeces, crested with cocked black ears, twitched slightly as it stood. The mad yellow eyes of forty sheep were turned, not on Hope and Bell, but on Gwennie, sitting up tall and still, eyeball to eyeball with the first row of ewes. Only the three or four lambs scrambling and nudging under the bellies of the flock made any movement. Gelert doubled to and fro behind his mother, barking short, as if daring the sheep to move. He turned as Hope and Bell appeared and bounced towards them, grinning, telling them as clearly as if he had spoken that he, Gelert, had done this fine thing, and had everything under control.

"Well, look at that!" said Hope. "Now what shall we do?"

"Whatever they will let us do, I think!"

"Gwennie!" Hope called, and the bitch's ears flicked in reponse, but she did not take her eye off the sheep. Gelert, crouching low, returned to his job.

"We are in no danger of losing the sheep, at any rate," said Bell. "We should look first to see all is well in the house."

It did not take long. The fire was out; there was no food about save a hardening loaf on the table and a few turnips in a bucket by the door. The side of bacon hanging over the chimney was carved away to the rind and up to the string: this was the hungriest time of the year. Bell folded away the old quilt, and between them they lifted the bed back into its place in the wall. Then they left. There was no way of securing the door from outside, but as Hope took a last look back into the room, she knew there was little harm that Hamer or any intruder could do to the meagre possessions that made up Bron's home. She went quickly across to the barn and collected her friend's real treasures, a sheep-crook and a few iron tools, which she wrapped in a sack and swung over her shoulder before joining Bell in the yard.

They stood together in the mud, surveying the sheep.

"Do you have any idea what to do next?" Bell asked doubtfully. "I've watched so many people herding sheep, but I still don't know how Bron tells the dogs what to do. Is it words, or whistling?"

"A bit of both, usually. I know the words, but I think most of it is in the voice."

"So you have to pretend to be Bron? Is this going to work?"

It has to work, Hope thought. Assuming a confidence she did not feel, she said, "Don't worry. The dogs will do most of the work once we start to move." She looked across at Gwennie, still at her station. Gwennie looked back levelly. She had brought the sheep into a safe corner, she seemed to say; she expected Bron back any minute, and until then she knew her duty.

Hope bit her lip. The first thing to do was to break the sheep out of the yard. Gwennie and Gelert would soon gather them together again outside. She was looking round for a way to distract the dogs when Bell suddenly gave a cry.

"Oh, look, one lamb has died already!"

It lay in a crumpled heap against the barn wall. Hope bent to inspect it. "It's not a newborn," she said, puzzled. "And its neck is broken, but not bitten." She shrugged. "But it will do."

She carried the body of the black lamb to the battered mount-ing block by the barn door and pulled out her old hunting knife. Gelert whined as she sliced and flicked, turning some of the offal out on to the flagstones at her feet.

"Come, Gelert. Yours – good dog."

He leapt, wolfing down his share. The sea of ewes trembled in incipient panic as the smell of blood reached them.

"Best not to feed sheep-meat to dogs," said Hope, watching the flock, "but desperate measures... Bell, take the crook and try to hold them till I tell you, while I call Gwennie off. The dogs can't have eaten since the day before yesterday."

Bell, frowning with determination, held out the crook to block off any breakaway from the corner of the yard. Gelert jumped up at Hope, yapping hopefully.

"Lie down!"

He dropped automatically into guard position, licking the last traces of meat from his jaws, his eyes swivelling back to the sheep. Hope went back to her impromptu table and picked up a bloody titbit. She moved near enough to Gwennie to let her see and smell the meat.

Gwennie's ears went to and fro. Her tail thumped. She looked at Gelert, who showed his teeth and kept his place. Then she stood up and turned her back on the flock, and walked stiffly up to Hope, who backed away a dozen paces before she threw down the food and Gwennie bent her head to eat.

"Now!" Hope shouted, waving her arms. Bell lowered the crook, Gelert started to bark madly, and the sheep, in panic, bolted for the gap.

After that, as Hope had predicted, the dogs knew better than she did what was to be done, galloping in wide circles on the open hill, rounding up stragglers, and snapping at the heels of the ewes along the lanes. Bell marched ahead, carrying the sack of tools, and Hope brought up the rear, with a day-old lamb round her neck and its mother bleating at her knees.

Halfway home, their way led through Mardu Farm. The sheep poured out of the lane and flowed into every corner of the farm-yard. Fortunately both the Wayland boys were in the yard and Joshua kept hold of their dogs while little Will ran to head off ewes that tried to bolt into the barn. Finally he and Gelert stampeded a gang of stragglers back through the muddy pond, and they got the flock penned in the green lane beyond the farm gate.

Bell went in briefly to speak to Mrs. Wayland, who had borne a third son since Bell had last seen her. Panting, she caught up with Hope and the sheep a few minutes later. "Some things don't change," she said, smiling. "Mary Wayland can still talk enough for two women, and John Hamer is still as much disliked as ever he was. The Waylands were truly shocked to hear about Bron, and will go up now and then to keep an eye on her house and yard. Hamer will know of it, and not try any mischief, I hope."

It was well into the afternoon before they had Bron's sheep eat-ing hungrily in the lower pasture at Brynsquilver. By the time they had run about with hurdles and faggots and anything else they could find to stop up holes in the hedges, they were tired beyond speaking. Hope fed the dogs again, in the shed where they could also sleep. She knew there was a chance they would try to go back home, but with the flock here, and food to be had, perhaps they would have the sense to stay?

The smell of wood-smoke floated out to her: Bell had got the fire going. Gratefully, she trudged into the house.

"Oh, look!" said Bell as Hope shut the door behind her. She was standing at the window. Outside, Gwennie and Gelert sat on the threshold, gazing expectantly at the closed door. Gelert, catching sight of them at the window, raised a begging paw, and barked once. At that, Parsley shot up the ladder, spitting. Hope and Bell looked at each other.

"Bron keeps them indoors with her."

"She does, clearly."

"Parsley would never forgive us."

"But the dogs do need to know they live here. Or they might set off up the hill again, looking for Bron?"

There was a moment's pause. Then Hope gave in, and opened the door.

"Will you walk down to the road with me to see Mercy and fetch my box?" Bell asked the next morning. "They must know I'm home – I expect all the valley does by now! – and I do want to see them again. And we can ask for news of Bron. The Shrewsbury carrier will have been by."

"Not today," said Hope, more brusquely than she intended. "I must finish looking to the fences in the lower pasture, and the old goat-shed needs work at once if it is to be fit for the lambing. Surely it can wait a day or two?" Picking up her axe, she fled from Bell's disappointment.

Coward! she told herself bitterly as she pleached a couple of ash saplings to fill a lamb-sized hole in the hedge. Bell and Lucy must meet sooner or later. Putting it off would solve nothing. Even so, she found one excuse after another to delay their visit to the inn.

On the third morning, Bell lost her patience. "Is this what months of solitude have done to you?" she cried, exasperated. "You think life is for labour only, and good company consists of talking to the cat! It's a beautiful morning: fetch your hat and come and see our friends!"

"I will, I promise. Later on. We'll go this evening. It is a pity to waste the good weather when there are jobs to do out of doors."

It was just the weather for hedging, calm and dry. Mending the boundary of the lower field for the sheep had made Hope realise how neglected and straggly all their hedges were, and she had moved on to the one round the garden. It was heavy work, driving in posts, then slashing and bending the stems of sycamore and ash, weaving them into a living fence that would keep both sheep and goats out of the vegetable plot. As she paused to straighten her back, Hope saw that they had a visitor.

It was Joey Jones, with a heavily laden donkey. Since the only way into the garden was by a stile, he had tied the beast to the stile-post and was struggling, red-faced with effort, to unload a roped trunk from its back. Bell's box, without doubt. Hope felt guilt and relief in equal measure, as she pulled off the thick leather hedging glove and hurried to help him.

Bell came out of the cottage at the same moment. She embraced Joey, who grinned widely and reddened even further.

"We knowed you were here," he explained earnestly, "because of the box. But this was the first chance I had to bring it, we'm that busy. Mam says to give you her best greetings and please excuse her not coming up herself, on account of business being brisk, but she do have a good side o' salt pork soaking and she say, will you come and help us eat it one day soon? She'm doing it with prune sauce," he added encouragingly.

"We shall indeed," said Bell, smiling. "Hope was saying to me only this morning how she longs for a little company, were you not, Hope? But now you must come in, Joey, and have something to stay you before you go back down."

She led the way indoors, still talking over her shoulder. "So what has befallen in the world to make you so busy at the inn?"

"Oh, nothing of account. 'Tis only that we'm short-handed now Lucy's gone, so Mam has to help our Nance wait on the gentlemen, and then she don't get her other things done."

"Lucy's gone?" repeated Hope.

Joey clapped a hand to his head. "Oh, lord! I forgot. That was the other thing Mam said I should tell you. Lucy's gone off again, only this time she've taken all her things with her. She went at first light the day before yesterday, seemingly. Leastways, she weren't there first thing when Nance got up to light the fire."

"But why?" Hope heard the urgency in her own voice and saw Bell look at her curiously. She struggled to keep her voice calm. "Where has she gone?"

Joey shrugged. "No one knows. Don't know where she come from, did we? And we don't know where she'm gone."

Twenty-five
Shrewsbury

Shrewsbury was huge and dark, and it stank. None of these things surprised Lucy. Before she left home – in another life, it seemed now – she had gone sometimes to the market in Chester. The tall houses there leaned together over the streets, blocking out the light. But here the maze of buildings seemed to go on for ever, bewildering and black. And a bad smell was common enough. Some of the places she had tramped through with Henri and the boys had their own particular stink, like Wem with its horrible burnt-earth smell, and Welshpool which was perfumed by its cattle market. It seemed that any village bigger than a dozen houses buried itself to the knees in mud and horse-shit, like a great baby that could not keep itself clean. So the dark and the filth were only to be expected in a town so big. What startled her was the noise: Shrewsbury was the loudest place she had ever been in.

She had slept overnight at a place called Frankwell, on the other side of the Severn, and even there she had been woken before first light by shouts and singing. Shivering in her riverside attic, in a tiny truckle bed that cost full three farthings of her rapidly dwindling purse, she had wondered what kind of carnival was going on. But as she turned out cold and hungry into the gloomy dawn, she had realised it was no feast day, but work.

Men were shouting and laughing as they unloaded coal sacks

from a long black barge sitting low against an echoing wharf on the far bank of the river. Crossing the bridge behind a high, swaying waggon that rumbled over the cobbles like stony thunder, Lucy was engulfed in a wave of noise. Thumps, shouts, rattling wheels; the ringing of pattens and clogs on the cobbles of echoing alleys; a cow somewhere in the back of a shop, moaning to be milked. Boys yelled to each other as they ran to work; spruce young men clattered and crashed as they unshuttered wide shop-windows on to paved walks. Lucy pressed herself against a wall as a great waggon filled the whole of the way, ten wheels each as broad as her back grinding into the flinty mud. Her heart thumped, but with excitement as well as fear. It had taken her two days and nights, but she was here: she had reached her mark.

Another waggon loomed up, filling the passage so that its covered load nudged the overhanging buildings on either side. Lucy pressed herself back into the doorway of a tall black and white house with latticed windows. She felt faint suddenly and rather sick. Sinking down on to the doorstep, she drew in her skirts and pressed back into the shelter of the porch. Up to now she had been so sure about what she must do: she must come to Shrewsbury, must find Bron and stay by her in her trouble, help Bron as Bron had helped her. But now for the first time her courage failed.

The image of Bron had been with her all the way, spurring her on. She must get to Shrewsbury, must find Bron, must do whatever could be done to help her. She was vague about what that might be, but unwavering in her determination – her need – to find the woman who had twice saved her life. But now she was here, she saw suddenly how hard it would be. Lucy bit her lip, and wound herself more tightly into Nance's cloak. She could ask the way to the gaol, but when she got there, what had made her think she would be let in? Or would be allowed to see Bron? She saw now that the picture in her head had been of some village pound, where friends and family came and went with jokes and food for the poor drunkard of the night before. She looked up at the finely carved oak door behind her with its iron knocker shaped like a fist. Shrewsbury Gaol would be one of these great forbidding houses, its prisoners locked away behind high walls, its keeper too grand to speak to a muddy tramping girl from nowhere. She had no money and no friends. How had she thought she could do anything?

The people passing took no notice of her at all, far too busy with their own concerns. That was another thing about towns, she thought, I could die here in this doorway, and no one would care. A pretty girl of about her own age, carrying a covered basket, clicked past on high pattens. A maid-servant, Lucy decided, smartly dressed in her mistress's leavings, a warm hood lined with pink and a dark blue petticoat. As she hurried by there was the unmistakable smell of fresh bread, reminding Lucy how hungry she was.

She stood up. If Mam had been here she would have made short shrift of doubt and self-pity. "There's no one'll help you but yourself, our Luce, so you can leave moping and get on with it." And Mam would have been right. She was cold because her clothes were still wet from yesterday, and faint because she had not eaten. She still had three ha'pence in her pocket, and she would be no good to Bron if she starved on a doorstep. First things first. She shouldered her bundle and set off to look for breakfast.

There was no shortage of cook-shops and taverns. From the amount of food on offer, it seemed as if the people of Shrewsbury must spend their whole time eating and drinking. Lucy passed by the windows of several elegant pastry-cooks, knowing from the mouth-watering dainties on display that they would be too dear. The coffee-houses, with their strange strong smell, were still empty at this early hour; the ale-shops were either still closed, or full of men taking their morning ale on the way to work, which made Lucy feel shy of going in. Finally she found a little open-fronted shop in an alley, where she bought a hot pie and a mug of spiced ale. Even so she was horrified at the price: the leering man in the greasy apron demanded a whole penny for her breakfast. She drank the ale under his eye, and gave back the mug, then fled into the street, warming her hands on the pie. A thin, cold rain began to fall as she emerged from the alley. There was a church across the street and Lucy took shelter in the porch. Out of the rain and the wind, she ate slowly, making the food last as long as she could, and tried to think.

No one knew where she was. She had known, almost from the moment they took Bron away, that she would go after her, but she had not told anyone else, and had left the Crosses without any farewell. She felt bad about not bidding goodbye to Mercy, and about taking Nance's cloak without asking, but she knew they would have tried to stop her. So she had risen before dawn and put on all the clothes she owned – her old green gown, three petticoats and a shawl – for warmth, and to save carrying the weight. She had a little money of her own, odd coins given her by customers, which was good, for she had not wanted to rob Mercy and William. As it was she had taken bread and cheese and a scrap of bacon from the kitchen, tying them into a bundle with her little knife and an old cup. If Nance could read, she could have left her a message about the cloak. But then they might have sent after her, or told people where she was. Noll Wethered might have found out. Lucy pushed that thought away. So she was on her own, and must think what to do.

She must find the prison and try to see Bron, then bring her food or anything she lacked. And she must find lodgings for herself. All these things needed money, and hers was all but spent. It was frightening how costly everything was in a town. Clearly she must find work, and quickly. She felt warmer now. She scavenged the pastry crumbs that had fallen on her clothes, then stood up and set off through the rain.

*

There were a hundred ways of getting money on the streets of a town without actually begging. But it seemed that Shrewsbury had all it needed of boys holding horses' heads or carrying parcels; coach-fetchers and luggage porters stood three deep round every grand house. To be given errands to run you needed to be known and trusted in the shops and taverns. By noon Lucy had been sneered at and ignored, pushed aside and, eventually, warned off by every doorman, tout and running footboy in the city. An old lady in face-paint and a big hooped petticoat had smiled absently and given her a farthing for opening a church gate, and that was it.

As darkness began to gather in the shadowy streets she decided that, money or no money, she must find her way to the gaol. A crippled sweeper working outside the fine houses on Dogpole directed her: "Right at the cross, and up School Lane – you'll not miss it." Walking now past rows of shops, she peered into their doorways, wondering if she had the courage to go inside and ask for work; but seeing the aproned shop-keepers in their neat wigs and respectable waistcoats, and the snowy caps of their wives, she knew there was no point. Even if she could find nothing out of doors, she would have to look lower than that.

The butter cross stood abandoned at this hour: the dairy maids and farmers' wives had long since sold their milk and cheese and gone home to their warm fires. Picking her way through the littered remains of the day's trading, Lucy spotted a hunk of bread, dropped by someone into the mud and missed, for a wonder, by both cartwheels and scavenging dogs. She wiped it on her skirt and, munching hungrily, turned into the broad expanse of Castle Street. There were more fine houses here, stretching away downhill, and a prosperous-looking inn. Its swinging sign showed a black bird in a golden collar. Lucy spelled out the name: the Raven. Candles were already lit in the parlours and the windows glowed like lanterns in the darkening afternoon. The wide doors, up three broad steps, were painted a rich red. A few steps down the hill was the carriage entrance; Lucy glimpsed a paved yard and more lights. It was very different from the Two Crosses. She had not the courage to go in, but it gave her an idea. She could try for tavern work again. She had passed so many inns and ale-houses; why had she not thought of it? She would try her luck as soon as she came from the gaol – but in a place less well-found than this.

If she had not been taking note of all the taverns as she walked, she would have missed the prison completely. She found the lane that led to the school – a splendid building like a church – but saw no prison house. She turned back. At the bend in the lane she was gazing doubtfully at an ugly brick house with a drinking den in its front room, crowded with glum-looking men and smelling strongly of sour ale and old cheese, when she saw the sign on the door right next to it. County Gaol. She spelled it over twice, then stepped up to the closed door. She gave it a tentative push. Locked. There was no handle. She looked around. Beside the door, in a kind of dent in the wall, was a hanging bell. It looked quite terrifying. But what was there to lose? She had to get in here, whatever trouble it took. Lucy took hold of the rope and jerked the clapper twice against the side of the bell. The clanging echoed up and down the lane.

Nothing happened.

Clearly, she had come too late in the day.

Stepping back, she looked again at the drinkers in the ale-house next door. Two men smoking long pipes were seated by a small fire which struggled in vain to brighten the room. The landlord, a hard-faced man, listened unsmiling to their conversation. Lucy could not bring herself to ask that stony face for help – or for work, though this might be the ideal place, so close to the gaol. She looked up: no windows were lit above the closed door. Pulling her cloak up round her ears, she turned and walked slowly back up the hill.

Twenty-six

Even when she got into the prison, Lucy was afraid she would not find Bron. At first light she had been back outside the door with no handle, standing in the pouring rain jangling the bell until she heard the scrape and rattle of bolts. A surly boy had stuck his head out, stared at her and disappeared again, leaving the door ajar. She stepped into a gloomy passage, faintly lit by the glimmer of a candle behind a steamed-up glass window. The casement opened a crack and a man looked down at her; Lucy recognised the hard-faced innkeeper of the tavern next door.

"Well?"

"Please, I've come to see Bron Richards." She had kept the little parcel behind her, under her cloak.

"Have you now?" He thrust the window back further to look her up and down, but after a few moments seemed to decide there was nothing to be got out of her. Grunting, he sank back into his chair and slammed the window. Seeing Lucy still staring at him, he jerked his head, telling her to go on down the passage.

It led into a streaming yard, its wet brick walls pierced by barred windows – dark holes like the empty sockets of a row of skulls. The rain hammered down like rods of iron, beating on a pair of rotting benches backed against the walls and three skittles capsized in a spreading puddle. Lucy tried two locked doors before a third opened grudgingly to admit her to a low, stuffy room crowded with people.

She closed the door behind her and leant back against it, trying not to be noticed while she got her bearings. She need not have bothered: one or two faces turned towards her but soon turned away, not interested in her. As her eyes adjusted to the dim light, she saw a long narrow room, scarcely six paces across but dwindling away into the distance under a low ceiling darkened with smoke and grease. It was almost completely bare of furniture. One table stood under the small barred window nearest the door. Four men – gentry, in figured waistcoats and trim wigs – sat round it playing cards, with a single mug between them. Everyone else was gathered round the fireplace halfway down the room. Lucy could not see the fire for the press of backs, but the fatty smoke told her they were cooking their breakfast bacon. Her stomach cramped and her mouth filled with water at the smell. She peered about anxiously, but she could not see Bron.

The crowd round the fire were a mixed crew, mostly men without coats and ragged women, with a fringe of dirty children. One infant wore nothing but a scrap of shoddy blanket for a shawl; none of them had shoes. Bron was not among them. At length Lucy ventured to walk up to a girl who stood a little apart with a child clutching her skirts. Both she and the child were sucking their thumbs.

"Your pardon, mistress. Do you know if a Bron Richards is here?"

The girl took her hand from her wet mouth and stared silently at Lucy, then heaved the baby into her arms and turned away.

Lucy gritted her teeth. Still clasping the precious present under her cloak, she shouldered her way through the fringe of the crowd. The room stretched away into shadow, lit only by a second window at the far end. At the window stood Bron, all alone.

She was standing with one shoulder propped against the wall, her eyes far away, exactly as she had stood in the parlour at the Two Crosses on Twelfth Night. She did not see Lucy; she was gazing up through the window at the grey sky over the rooftops. The bruises on her face had darkened to yellow and purple now, but under them she was pale, her eyes puffy. Lucy could feel from ten paces away the freezing draught that streamed in through the barred window, blowing gusts of rain across Bron's face. But Bron seemed not to notice; she looked as if she was in a different world.

Lucy stretched out a soft hand to touch her arm. Bron swung round, throwing up her fists before her face. Lucy saw with a shock that she was fettered. Bands of rusty iron two inches wide were locked round her wrists, and rigid bars hinged her hands together. There was blood on the bands, some of it quite new. Lucy gasped, her own hands flying to her mouth.

Bron dropped her guard, seeing it was only a girl – and then she recognised her, and disbelief and then horror flooded her face.

"Lucy! But you was let go! The filth – why have they sent you here? You done no wrong!"

"No – no one sent me – it's all right. I just came to see you. I've brought food." Triumphantly she brought out her present, the big slice of cheese and two red herrings still wrapped in the shopman's paper. She had not taken so much as a single bite, though she had craved for a taste ever since she saw her chance in the morning market, and lifted the packet from the basket of a gossiping housewife. If she still could find no work today, she would have to feed herself in the same way. But this was all for Bron. She moved closer, so no one would see, and held out the food.

But Bron ignored it. She stepped back, her eyes on Lucy's face. She shook her head as if to clear it. Eventually she said roughly, "How did you come here?"

Lucy's hand dropped. She twitched her cloak over her offering. "On my feet. And a cold wet journey it was. I thought, maybe you would be pleased to see me. I thought you would need a friend." She stopped. Bron still stared at her. "You need a friend," Lucy repeated, "when you're in prison."

There was a silence. Then Bron nodded. Slowly, she held out her hand, and Lucy gave her the food. But she did not eat it, or even look, just thrust it into her pocket.

"What do they give you here?" Lucy asked.

"Bread and ale." Bron shrugged, expressionless. "When they remember. But 'tis not fit for swine. I do not eat it."

Her blue eyes were as grey and lifeless as the low sky over the prison roof. She had a look of defeat, of despair about her that frightened Lucy. Together they turned from the window, and Bron sank down with her back to the wall, but still where she could look up at the sky. Lucy squatted beside her.

They sat for a moment, the silence between them lengthening.

Suddenly Bron turned and met Lucy's eyes. "What has become of Gwennie and Gelert?" she asked roughly. "Have you heard tell? Or of my flock? They will all be lambing now."

Lucy looked at her helplessly. She had no idea what had become of the dogs or the sheep: her only concern had been for Bron herself.

The iron bar that joined her fettered wrists rattled as Bron dropped her head into her hands. "They will not work for John Hamer," she muttered. "The scab will have my ewes, I doubt not. But my Gwennie will not come to his call, though she starve first." She turned her head away, and Lucy knew it was to hide her tears.

Out in the street the rain had begun to let up. Lucy drew her hood close round her face to keep out the cold drizzle. She felt deeply disappointed and angry. Bron didn't want her there. She had not even eaten the food – good food, anyone would be glad of it, and Lucy had risked being set upon in the streets of the city to snatch it for her. Bron had not seemed to care. I should have kept it for myself, she thought. Ungrateful bitch. But her heart was heavy, and the pain was not just her own hunger and dismay. She was afraid of the change that had come over Bron. She had a sharp-edged memory of her, standing alone in the lashing rain by the window, her eyes empty, longing to be gone.

Leaving the gaol she walked at random, but fast, as if she had somewhere to go. Now the morning crowds had thinned, there were few people about the streets and they all hurried through the wet with their heads down. Lucy kept up, so as not to be noticed. But as she passed the end of a crooked lane, she was stopped in her tracks by a gaggle of boys exploding around her, whooping and laughing, almost knocking her over. The last one dragged something behind him through the mud, tangling it round a post outside a closed-up tavern. He stopped, giggling and cursing, tugging at the thing – it was some sort of cloth, a rich dark blue figured with paintings.

"Leave it, Jack – come on! What do you want with her dirty baggages, you clown?" The biggest lad ran back and grabbed his friend's arm. With a final tug the boy dropped the cloth.

"Teach the old witch!" another shouted. Still laughing, they swerved down the hill and out of sight.

Lucy picked up the draggled thing and held it out. It was worn in places, and dirty, but wonderful. The cloth was fine, with a deep pile on it such as Lucy had never seen. It was light and soft; the silk pictures – for it was not paint, but stitching, wild embroidery – ran all over it in loops and bursts, flower faces and strange signs hanging in swags of leaves and glittering ribands. She held it to her face, and it smelled strange: thick and sharp like the smells of the medicines Hope brewed, but again not like, for it had an edge of dry, bright heat. Spices, she thought, it smells of spices.

Her first impulse had been that she might get something for it in the market, but she would be suspected of theft, most likely, if she tried. And holding it against her, she could not help thinking of the woman they had already robbed – the "old witch". She turned quickly into the lane.

She had not far to go. Under the jutting windows where the

houses almost met overhead, an old woman was on her knees on the stones. She knelt upright in the central gutter, still and tense, leaning on a black walking-stick. Lucy could not see her face. Beyond her was an overturned table and, all around, spilt or broken bottles had tumbled into the mud. As Lucy approached, she leant more heavily on her stick and tried to heave herself to her feet.

Lucy ran to help, but the hand she put under the old woman's elbow was knocked away.

"Poxy dunghill farts – leave an old woman alone!" Then she was on her back, capsized by her convulsive start away from the hand upon her. Lucy stared down into a dark face, deeply lined, with glittering sunken eyes set in black caverns. A stream of curses drew back her thin lips like a spitting cat. She had lost her hat in the tussle and wisps of grey hair escaped from a yellowed lace cap topped with improbable silk flowers.

When she saw it was not the 'prentices come back again, her fury closed down into an impassive mask. For a second she and Lucy stared at each other. Then Lucy held out her hand and the old woman seized it in a bony claw and heaved herself up. Lucy bent and retrieved the bone-handled stick and the old woman took it, swaying as she rested her twisted body on its shiny head.

"Bless you, child." With a sharp nod, she took the cloth that Lucy held out. "East India goods," she said proudly, "worth a king's ransom." She wrapped it round her, shawl-wise, and then turned to her fallen wares.

Lucy moved quickly, righted the table, and began to gather up the bottles that had rolled unbroken into the gutter.

"There is a box," the old woman said. Swinging herself along on the stick, she moved with surprising speed to a passage between houses and hooked out a shabby lidless chest that ran on wooden wheels.

Lucy began to pack. Soon, under the old woman's instructions, she had the box laden, the cloth cushioning the bottles, and the table slotted down on to the base as a lid. There was a handle to pull the thing along. They looked at each other again.

"You need victuals, and drink," the old woman announced. "Do you not? Bring the box." And she set off towards the market place, Lucy at her heels.

She was Mrs. Mountain, and she was famous for her cures. Lucy listened as she ate the good manchet bread and the slice of Cheshire cheese the old woman bought her. It seemed Lucy was at fault, not to know of Mrs. Mountain's cures. Mountain's Elixir was famous through the land; it had saved the life of princes. Lucy nodded and drank her ale. But youth today were heedless, as Mrs. Mountain knew too well. She had had three boys one after another since last Michaelmas, and they would not stay with her long enough to learn the work. It was delicate work, selling the Elixir, explaining its powers, and guiding the right customers in to Mrs. Mountain, to hear their fortunes.

Lucy put down the pot of ale. "I have done that kind of work," she said, "and I took no time at all to learn my lines."

Mrs. Mountain cocked an eye, considering.

Lucy went on quickly. "I have skill in it. I brought my master good crowds and plenty of ha'pence, everywhere we stopped."

Mrs. Mountain looked Lucy over. Her gaze was calculating. "Dark mysteries of the Orient," she said thoughtfully. "Secret receipts of the Indies. Different head-dress, some earrings... you might do something."

"And I could push the cart," said Lucy. She paused, a thought striking her. "You aren't travelling, though, are you? I mean, are you working the roads, or here in Shrewsbury?"

The old woman looked affronted. "Travelling?" she said scornfully. "What can the girl mean? I am no highway tramp, child. I have my own residence, here in the city."

Lucy was relieved. "Then I will work for you, if you will have me," she said. "But there is one thing." She finished the bread and the last gulp of ale. "I have to have money."

Mrs. Mountain laughed. "Money? You'll get no money from me, girl. I will give you a bed – to guard the stock, and help me to make up the Elixir. But you get your money for yourself." Seeing Lucy hesitate, she leaned forward and added, "From the crowds, my girl, from the passing throng."

Lucy looked her in the eye. "Half and half. I won't work for less."

Twenty-seven
Brynsquilver

Hope scraped the last spoonful of oatmeal from her bowl. "That was good!" She smiled up at Bell. "Everything is more comfortable when you are here – even porridge tastes better. You must promise never to go away again."

Bell bent to kiss her. "I promise, as long as you don't take to sheep-herding for life – I never see you."

"A few more days and the worst will be past, I think, though they will need watching still." She rose and started to pull on her extra jacket. "Will you look to that lamb? It will need to stay by the fire a day and night more. We can try to put it to one of the ewes tomorrow."

Bell bent to stroke the tiny creature curled on the hearthstone. "Trust me. I shall feed it every time it opens its eyes."

Outside, frost still sparkled in the lee of the hedge, but there was warmth in the March sunshine, and the sky was patched with bright blue. Bell watched Hope out of sight down the field, heard Gelert's bark of welcome, then stood a moment breathing in the promise of spring. A pair of buzzards wheeled and mewed above her. Along the cottage wall, the daffodils had bent their heads, buds ready to open. With a sigh of content, she turned back indoors.

She would take her turn with the sheep later, but she had work to do first. Tying on a long apron, she raised the lid of her bread trough and lifted out the dough she had set to rise the night before. In their early days at Brynsquilver they had made all their bread on a bakestone over the fire, and still made barley-cakes like that most days, but since they had built the little brick oven by the side of the hearth, Bell could bake good yeast bread every week or so, and it was work she enjoyed.

Later she might make a pie crust to put over some of their dwindling store of root vegetables, and use the last heat of the oven when the loaves were out. This was a lean time of year, and anything that varied the unending vegetable broth was welcome. Then, while the bread was baking, she must check her store of dried herbs for spring tonics. It would be some weeks still before she could gather the fresh leaves of nettles and other greens that her winter-weakened neighbours needed, but meanwhile she would do what she could with dried ones.

The lamb stirred and made a small cry. Parsley, curled on the log stack by the fire, opened one disapproving eye. Bell dipped a rag in milk and stooped to let the little creature suck. It was very small, its trembling body still yellow and greasy from its birth, but it raised its wobbling head and sucked with surprising strength. Twin lambs were rare in these parts, as the pasture was thin and the ewes lean, and when twins did come, their mothers could rarely raise both. If this one lived, it might be fostered on a ewe whose lamb had died, and stand a better chance of surviving to swell the little flock.

When Bell took the rag away, it cried for more, its head swaying on its thin neck. It made her think, as she so often did, about the human baby who had lain here while she was away, the child who had died, and his mother, hardly more than a child herself. It had been a shock, after months of imagining Hope all alone in the cottage, to find she had had a lodger. What was she like, this girl who had kept Hope company in the dark winter days? The story snagged at Bell's mind. She had pressed Hope for details, trying to picture Lucy and her baby, to imagine them here, in this house. But Hope soon grew impatient with her asking and Bell, unable to put her real question into words, had let the subject drop.

She wiped her hands on her apron and went back to her bread. The low sun struck in at the window and fell across the table as she shaped the loaves. Her hands moved in the pattern of habit, leaving her mind free to wander. Her unease about Lucy was simple jealousy, she had to admit. It was foolish, she knew. In any case, whatever had passed, the girl was gone now.

Bell knew that she had been changed by her stay in Coalbrookdale. It would be strange if the events of those months had not made an impression on Hope, too. The important thing, Bell told herself again, was that none of it could change the love and trust between them, now so joyfully renewed. There was no more need to be jealous of Lucy than there was for Hope to worry about Richard.

Not that that had stopped her, Bell thought ruefully. She paused from making the long cuts in the tops of the loaves and stood, knife in hand, thinking. She had been taken aback by the hostility Hope had showed to the very idea of Richard – as if she knew, without Bell's saying so, how important he had been to her. In the end Bell had stopped mentioning him at all; she had never told Hope of his proposal. There was no need, she told herself again: it was a thing in the past.

The thought of Richard was always a troubling one, complicated by embarrassment and self-reproach. She would have liked above all things to keep him as a friend, but such a friendship was not possible, in his world or in hers. She beat the flour from her hands and went to open the oven. Heat blasted out. Quickly raking out the ashes which were all that remained of the fire she had set before breakfast, she put in the bread, stopping the door tight.

As she cleaned the table there was the sound of footsteps outside and a bang on the door.

It was little Will Wayland from the Mardu, clutching a basin and a stoneware bottle.

"Our mam says to wish you a very good day," he said. "She do hope you are well and could she have a drop more of the colic water for our Georgie? She've sent you some dripping." He proffered the basin.

While she refilled the bottle and asked after the baby, Bell looked at the little boy. The sores round his mouth were no better, a clear sign of the scurvy.

"How are your teeth, Will? Still sore in the gums?"

The child opened his mouth trustingly; his breath was strong.

"If I give you a remedy specially for you, will you be a good boy and take it every day until it is gone?"

He nodded, though his look was doubtful. Bell smiled, and poured out a small spoonful of blackcurrant syrup. A grin spread over his thin features as he swallowed it, and he nodded again with more conviction.

Once again Bell regretted her long absence. Rosehip would have been best, and would have eked out her store, but she had not been here at gathering time.

"Thank'ee kindly, Dame," the child said politely, stowing the colic mixture and the last of her blackcurrant syrup in his coat pockets. "Oh, and my da say to tell you all be well at Cloudborry farm. No sign of the old fox, he say."

She stood quiet for a moment after he had gone, thinking about the empty hill farm, and about Bron. On a morning like this, she had often looked up from her work to find Bron looming in the doorway, stopping by on her way down the hill. She had a sudden clear picture of their old friend, one shoulder propped against the door jamb, watching as Bell busied herself at the table.

Bron rarely came right in or sat down. She didn't say much either, letting Bell do the talking for both of them, but they enjoyed each other's company. Then, when it was time to go, Bron would whistle up the dogs and her eyes would crinkle in that wonderful smile – Bell found herself smiling in return at the memory.

But Bron would not be by today. Maybe never again. People were transported from the Assizes – and worse. The horror of what had happened swept over her again and she sat down at the table, clasping her hands to stop them shaking. Bron in prison, on a charge of witchcraft. Witchcraft. At first Bell had hardly believed it – had not wanted to believe it. Only weeks ago she had sat in Susannah's parlour, coolly discussing folklore and superstition, while here... it was horrible.

And anxiety was made worse by their ignorance: she and Hope had so little idea of what might happen. Hope spoke of keeping the sheep until Bron came home, but both of them feared, though they did not say so, that she would never return. Neither of them had even seen a prison. They did not know how or when the Assize trial would be conducted, or what the outcome might be.

Bell's father had been a magistrate, of course, but try as she might she could not recall him ever committing anyone to trial by jury. He had administered summary justice to the villages of Wiston Bassett and Bassett Moor; always the same few local villains being reprimanded and fined, or sent to labour on the Frome road. As Bell remembered it, he had sat in the court-room patiently sorting out squabbles over strayed cattle and neglected hedges. The miller's doubtful weights and measures were the cause of more passion and fury than any other issue in either village. Sometimes he had ridden to Taunton, and stayed a week or two – perhaps to attend the Grand Jury?

Bell had no real idea of how it all worked. What would the trial be like? Would anyone speak in Bron's defence? Even if that were allowed, she was far away from any friend who might speak for her. Bell wished suddenly that she could ask Richard – he would surely know all these things.

But asking Richard was out of the question. Who else would know? Ned Gilroy might have some idea, but he always put on an air of more wisdom than he had, building great castles of self-importance out of the small pebbles of knowledge he picked up working as bailiff at Waldon Hall. Sir John, who had committed Bron to trial, was probably the only one who knew what it was he had sent her to – and Bell could hardly ask him.

"But why should I not?" she said suddenly, out loud.

The cat pricked its ears at the sound of her voice and opened one eye.

"Why should I not go and ask him, Parsley? When I was no more than a girl, I was not afraid to ask for refuge at his house. I could surely ask for an audience now."

The cat regarded her disdainfully. Bell looked down at her worn gown and old apron. Isabella Wiston, the pretty young daughter of a Jacobite baronet, might well have been a welcome visitor at Waldon Hall, but a dowdy cottager of middle years was a less acceptable neighbour. Particularly if she was known locally as a cunning woman. It was a foolish idea.

But she could at least try. She thought of Susannah, standing unafraid in Ludlow market. The Friends spoke fearlessly to all manner of people, high and low, calling all men and women simply by their names, however high their rank. Bell had found the custom strange at first, impolite, until she had understood that it was because they spoke to the human being, their equal before God, not to rank or position. Susannah would have gone to see Sir John, or the king himself, had she felt called to do so.

Bell stood up, considering, pushing back her hair, absently settling her cap. Parsley, curled tight on top of the wood stack again, had given up on her. The lamb slept peacefully on the hearthstone. Before she could lose her resolution, she headed for the ladder, untying her apron as she went. From the clothes chest by the bed she pulled a clean cap and kerchief and her blue wool gown. Her Coalbrookdale gown. This was all she could do to help Bron. As soon as the bread was out, she would go to Waldon Hall.

Hope stamped to bring the life back into her feet. Spring it might be, or nearly so, but the grass was still frosted where the low sun could not reach, and lambing was cold work. It was past noon already, and she was beginning to feel hungry. Where had Bell got to? It was unlikely that she would be admitted to the Hall, but Hope understood her need to do something for Bron and had not tried to stop her. It was a bad business.

Hope's own helplessness more often took the form of impotent rage – when she thought of Bron penned up in Shrewsbury gaol she wanted quite simply to kill the men who had put her there. Her hands clenched now on the sheep-crook as she remembered the look of triumph on Noll Wethered's face. If there was any justice, it would be Wethered who was rotting in gaol, not Bron. She kicked savagely at a small rock. Gelert whined, alarmed, and she bent to rub his ears. "Good boy. Not you I'm angry with."

It was another half hour before she heard Bell's call and saw her coming over the far stile. Her step was weary as she climbed the long field. Hope walked to meet her and put an arm about her shoulders.

"What cheer, sweetheart?"

"Both good and bad, I think." Bell frowned. "I'll tell you all about it. Can you come up for some dinner now? I'm famished after all that walking."

"I could eat an ox. So you did speak with Sir John? I was sure he would not see you."

"I feared it. But I think he was curious to see this lowly woman of high birth he'd heard tell about." Bell smiled. "He was courteous, but I think I puzzled him. And he is clearly not in good health – he says he is troubled with the stone. I shall send him something for it."

Hope shook her head in disbelief. "Sir John talked to you of his ailments? You had better not tell anyone, or they'll be calling you the witch next!"

The cottage smelled of fresh bread. As Bell ladled out broth, Hope asked, "So what did you discover?"

"A good deal." Bell looked serious. "The Assize judges arrive at Shrewsbury at the end of March – the day before Lady Day, he says – and all the people waiting in the gaol are brought to trial then, all in a couple of days."

"But that's not far off – three weeks from now. Did he say how he thought Bron would fare?"

Bell hesitated. "He said it was in the hands of the judges. But the penalty for those found guilty of sorcery and witchcraft," her voice shook slightly, "is death."

Hope reached out and took her hand. Neither spoke for a moment.

Bell went on, "I asked him about the trial itself, how it would be. He said that Hamer is committed to appear, because he brings the charge against Bron, and the other man – the one you said knew Lucy –"

"Noll Wethered, yes."

"He will be called as a witness against her, in Hamer's support."

"I don't understand – these two will speak against her, but who will speak for her?"

"No one, apparently, unless she herself calls friends to witness to her good character."

They looked at each other.

"But she has no friends within thirty miles of there."

"That is why we must go there, Hope. We must go to Shrewsbury and speak for her."

"We? Go to Shrewsbury?"

"We can. I've been thinking as I walked back." Bell spoke urgently. "Someone surely will mind the sheep, for Bron's sake. And I think Mercy has a kinswoman in the town, where we might get a lodging. It is not more than five and twenty miles – not much more than a day's walk if we set out early and in fair weather – and who else can speak for her, Hope?"

Hope thought about it, frowning. "We lack skill in these matters. Even if we go there, how can we be sure to be called as witnesses?" Then her brow cleared. "Your Quaker friend – did you not say he was a lawyer? Could you not ask advice of him?"

"Richard. Yes, he is a lawyer." Bell hesitated. "But I do not know where he is. I believe he has gone to London. But I could write to Alistair. He may have some help or advice to offer. I have not written since I came home, and I promised Susannah that I would. I will write this afternoon."

Twenty-eight
Shrewsbury

"Rat me, Sal, what can I do with these?" Lucy brandished the blue glass bottles. "This one's got a crest on it – Lord Muck's own! Do you want me taken up by the Watch? Where did you lift them?" Then, as the girl opened her mouth, "No – don't tell me. I don't want to know."

"But I never! Please you, miss, I found 'em in the mud. Down by the Welsh bridge. Truly I did. I washed 'em off for you, but the mud's still inside." She grabbed one and up-ended it, desperate to prove her point. Her thin finger drew out a dark smear. "See! They was in the river!" She sniffed and rubbed her eyes, transferring the smear to her face. "I thought you'd be pleased with 'em. I don't want no more for 'em than for common bottles, though they's twice as big. Please, miss, just a farthing. I've had nought to eat these two days, almost."

Lucy rolled up her eyes. "This is a business, Sal, not a poxy charity. I buy no bottles I can't use." She looked more closely at the child's thin face. She really was very pale, the red scurvy spots standing out round her mouth. She sighed.

"You'll be the ruin of me. I'll give you a halfpenny on account. Get yourself a drink and a bite, then go back down the strand before it gets dark and fetch me some proper bottles. Common stone bottles, small – and I want four at least." She put two farthings into the eager palm. "Today, mind! Or you'll answer to Herself."

She watched the draggletail girl disappear into the shut, and shook her head. How had she come to be keeper of this horde of pitiful little city rats? she wondered. Bottles! When she'd driven her bargain with Madam, agreeing to find the bottles for the Elixir, she had no idea what a task it would be. Now she turned back to the bucket of water where those she had bought that day were steeping. Already she had learned the properties of every kind of bottle, which came clean and which did not, which necks broke when you scoured them, which would leak and which held a stopper best.

But getting to know the scavengers who brought them to her was going to take longer. So far she must have met twenty or thirty children, all sizes and sorts. Some came in gangs, with a loud-mouthed leader: there was a notable group of very small fry captained by a big girl of twelve or so, dressed in dirty flounces and with a lush, leering face. Lucy suspected she was with child already. Others came alone, like little Sal, thin and shrinking, bearing the marks of hunger and, very often, of blows.

It was hard to bargain with them: those who were not intent on cheating her were so wretchedly needy that she was forever on the edge of cheating herself, to bring a smile to their drawn faces. She would have lost money daily, but for their superstitious fear they would be witched: they were mortally afraid of Mrs. Mountain. She stooped and began to shake and scrape the bottles as clean as she could.

A gleam of sun cheered up the yard, striking colours from the shiny brown earthenware. When it wasn't raining, Lucy did her bottle-washing out of doors, drawing water from the well in the yard behind the Plough. She spent as little time as possible in the dank cellar in Plough Alley which was Mrs. Mountain's "residence in town". The airless room with its soggy plaster depressed her, and made her think of the dungeon where Bron was kept at night, chained to stone walls and floor. She had been going to the prison three or four days before she found out that the cold smoky room she visited was only for the daytime. The crowd huddled together there included both debtors, who had somehow to pay for their sleeping rooms in the house above, and felons, like Bron, who were herded down the dark steps in the yard and shut up in the bowels of the earth overnight. Bron would not talk about it.

She was mainly unwilling to talk at all. Every afternoon when marketing was over, Madam counted the takings, gave Lucy her share, and settled herself in the back parlour of the Plough with a hot gin and water. Before going back to Plough Alley to her bottles, Lucy would take herself off to the gaol for an hour. She went there doggedly day after day, though each visit was as hard as the first. She had thought at the beginning that Bron would come round, cheer up at the sight of her, or at least thank her for coming. But no. Her face stayed closed, the bruised lids drooping over dull eyes, and day by day she seemed more like a wild thing dying in a trap.

Lucy was not even sure she ate the food she brought her. It was as good food as you could get these hungry lenten weeks. Shrewsbury did itself well – better food than you would see on tables in villages or in the countryside was thrown away in its gutters. Out of her earnings Lucy bought whatever could be eaten without cooking: a pie or a slice of cold roast meat, some carrots sweet from storing, even a few apples that had survived the winter, day-old raisin bread that the baker sold cheap.

The food cost her a good deal; and so did getting it past the gate. When he saw that she came regularly, Wilding the gaoler – the slab-faced tavern-keeper was the keeper of the gaol himself – demanded garnish for every visit. He would have taken a kiss, or a quick grope in the passage, but Lucy put her money down. She could afford to keep herself to herself now. To her great surprise, the Elixir sold well. Lucy sold most of it from the table, where she sang its praises more fancifully every day; and then Mrs. Mountain sent her private patients back from their ten minutes behind the curtain to buy the "Special" – which was the same thing at twice the price. Lucy shook her head and picked up the bucket. These would have to do; it was getting late.

It was dark by the time she dumped her basket of bottles by the vat on the sloppy floor of the cellar.

Reaching for her stick, Mrs. Mountain prised herself off the settle where she slept off the gin. "Good girl. It's cool already, you can fill them up. Do as much as you have bottles for. It's Thursday tomorrow."

The Thursday cloth market was the biggest of the week, with the town full of strangers, and they should do good business. They must be up early to set up the table and hang the blue flowery curtain before anyone could invade Madam's chosen space. Lucy peered carefully into the thin green brew, stopping her nose. It smelled of leaves in ditches, with some sort of dark gagging catch in the back of it that made her retch. The customers told her it tasted bad, too, and she believed them; she certainly had no intention of tasting the stuff herself. Mrs. Mountain maintained it was the foul taste that made them think it did them good.

"And does it?" Lucy had asked once.

The old woman had opened her eyes in a blank, unwinking stare. "I have told you, miss. They believe in it. Of course it does them good."

"Now, young miss, do you attend on the healing woman?"

Lucy bobbed politely. "Indeed, sir. Would you have speech with her?"

Another solid citizen – the second this morning, all black hat and self-importance – had come to consult Mrs. Mountain about a little private problem. Lucy knew the gull's stool behind the blue curtain was free, but she made him wait while she stuck her head in and mouthed, "Another grand'un. Cure for the itch, I'll wager."

Madam frowned at her and arranged her head-dress. "Let him approach," she said loudly.

There was barely room for his well-fed bulk in the little recess, but Lucy saw the man bow humbly as she let the curtain fall to. She shrugged and turned back to the bottles on the table.

She had learned a lot in Shrewsbury, including the fact that the rich and lofty suffered as much as anyone else from old age and illness, embarrassment and fear. And they were as eager as their humbler neighbours to believe in the magical properties of the Elixir. Lucy sighed, and looked up again at the imposing front of Drapers' Hall. Below the stiff figure of a knight in armour was a tablet carved with writing. Shrewsbury was full of writing, and Lucy had plenty of chances to practise her reading. She particularly liked this bit, which told the names of the town bailiffs who had built the place, because one of them was called William Jones. If she ever saw the Two Crosses again, she would tell William that his name was written up in Shrewsbury market. The last part of the inscription was lost in the chalky dribble from an old martins' nest under the eaves. Lucy gave up trying to read it, and turned her attention back to business.

Trade was slowing down now. The gent behind the curtain had waited for the crowd to slacken before he ventured across to their pitch. It was past noon and the Welshmen were beginning to leave. Some rode the hairy ponies that had come to town laden with bales of rough woollen cloth from the hill farms. Others, who had spent their money on market goods, were setting off to walk home, leading a beast that carried sacks of flour or peas or, in one case, a huge black cooking pot.

Lucy shifted her weight from one foot to the other. She did not like the Thursday market, however rich the pickings: it was such hard work. The frieze-coated, wrinkle-stockinged weavers spoke little English. They stood in groups between the heavy pillars of the Drapers' Hall, twittering like hedge-sparrows, staring out under matted hair, round-eyed and distrustful as their shy, shaggy ponies.

When the bolder spirits ventured out to make their bargains around the square, Lucy began her patter, smiling and dancing, holding up a bottle of the Elixir. Once she had their attention, she had to act out her story. Shivering and groaning, miming agonies of the back and belly, she pretended to uncork the bottle and take a swig. Her recovery was miraculous and instant: she grinned, she danced, she offered the bottle to the crowd. Whatever ailed them, the Elixir was the remedy. By the time the last Welshman left the market, she was exhausted.

Weighing her purse in her hand, she glanced at the flowery curtain, hoping Mrs. Mountain was ready to shut up shop. The gent was taking his time. When he came out she would suggest a gin and water. A tempting smell of roasting meat came from the door of the Plough every time it opened. The smell of food made Lucy think of Bron. What should she get for her today? A nice pie, perhaps. Across the square the pie-men were strung out along the arcade of the Guildhall, a huge black and white building that cut off the market place from the High Street. Their trays were emptying rapidly as the market wound down. In the windows above them, usually dark, Lucy noticed people moving about. A door stood open at the head of the outside stair, and clerkly young fellows were coming and going with papers. Some doings of the Drapers' Company, no doubt – they seemed to have a hand in all the town's business.

A serving-maid came and bought a bottle. She swore by Mountain's Elixir for her ankles, she said. Lucy nodded, straight-faced, mentally adding yet another part of the human body to the list of the Elixir's triumphs. As she gave the woman her change, Sal appeared, grinning, with her apron clinking.

"I got 'em, miss!" She had four bottles, as Lucy had asked: she lined them up on the table, wiping each with a dirty hand as she set it down.

"You're a good little squib," said Lucy, pushing them into a sack under the table.

Sal grinned, and hung about, as if hoping Lucy might have forgotten she had already paid for the bottles. She gazed with frank interest at the man who emerged from behind the blue curtain. He hurried away, coughing nervously.

"If you've no other business, you can make yourself useful," said Lucy in a voice she recognised as her mother's. Sal, pleased to be needed for any reason, helped her to pack away the Elixir and stow everything in the cart.

"What goes on yonder?" Lucy asked her, nodding across at the Guildhall, where the clerks still came and went.

Sal looked up, her face closed in a scowl. "Don't you have nothing to do with that place," she said, and spat. "That's the courthouse, where they sends poor wretches to the gallows."

Twenty-nine

The coming Assizes might be a hanging matter for some, but for others they were a holiday. Over the next few days Shrewsbury filled up with county families and their people – especially their people. Stewards and footboys and sweepers and maids and cooks arrived in town to spruce up the grand houses, take down the shutters, shake out the mats, and greet their old friends who spent the rest of the year stuck out on country estates. Lucy saw two girls – as like as peas, they must be sisters – run the length of Fish Street into each other's arms to kiss and exclaim and hug tight.

There were other kisses, just as passionate but less open, when brisk young shopmen greeted their old customers, or footmen and maids parted since the Michaelmas hiring-fair met quietly in the low coffee-houses round the market square. The sun came out, glinting in the rainbow puddles of the streets, and a chilly wind blew holes in the clouds. It was springtime in the city.

But no sunshine penetrated the gloom of the county gaol, and the tilting slide towards judgement day brought blind panic to the inmates. One boy, a poor half-witted runt with no friends that Lucy had ever seen, cut his throat with a broken plate, for fear of the red-robed judge and what might happen in court. The day-room was full to bursting: petty lawyers in greasy black, with quills behind their ears and inkwells in their button-holes, flocked round the greater villains, and well-meaning lady visitors with Bibles in their hands bothered everybody. One of these ladies spoke to Lucy.

"Save thee, friend. Art thou companion to the countrywoman yonder?"

Lucy stared. What business is it of yours, madam? she thought.

The lady plunged on. "I am greatly concerned for her. I fear she may be sickening – there was a low fever in this place last year, which will doubtless return – or worse, she may be tempted to despair. Prithee, what is her crime?"

"She ain't done no crime," snapped Lucy. She did not need this busybody in a dowdy grey gown to tell her that Bron was in low spirits – a child with one eye could see as much. "She's been shut up because a poxy lying scab of a cowkeeper wants her off her farm, so he says she witched him. And because that whey-face Sir John ain't got the tripes to see him off."

The lady blinked at the violence in Lucy's tone. Then she said unexpectedly, "I am sorry to have vexed thee."

Lucy looked at her.

"She is accused of witchcraft?"

Lucy nodded.

"But that is barbarous!" The lady glanced round the room, as if looking for someone to tell about it, but Lucy had had enough, and with a bob she turned away and pushed through the crowd towards Bron.

As usual she was hunched by the far window. She barely looked up when Lucy approached. She listened without speaking – or perhaps did not even listen – as Lucy forced herself to chatter brightly about the strange lady, about her day at the market and about the spring sunshine outside the prison walls. Eventually she gave up. She closed Bron's unresisting hand round her food parcel and got up to leave. Bron did not move.

"Shall I come again the same time tomorrow?" Lucy asked, as she always did.

Bron did not look up. At last she said, "If you like."
And Lucy had to be satisfied with that.

So the coming of spring brought Lucy no joy. She worried about Bron and she hated everyone else – Noll Wethered, Hamer, Sir John Waldon, Wilding the gaolkeeper, the sinister lawyers and the stupid visiting-lady with her talk of sickness and despair. She hated her customers for believing in the Elixir, and the crowds of happy people in the streets for being happy. The crowds were increasing; the market at the Buttercross was busier every day. Pedlars came into town and opened their packs of ribbons and laces, caps and buttons; stationers pinned ballads to the woodwork of shops and houses. There were girls in from the villages with packed, velvety baskets of violets that filled the air with a musky sweetness, and bright daffodils that shouted back at the sunshine. Lucy scowled miserably at them all.

Mrs. Mountain did not do private consultations at the Buttercross, there being no suitable place, but sat behind the table selling the Elixir while Lucy did the barking. Sometimes, indeed, she did not come out to the early market at all, trusting Lucy to work alone. Lucy did not care either way. She was giving the work less and less of her attention as she fretted about Bron.

This morning she was working alone, the now familiar patter coming almost without thought. "Step up now, ladies and gentlemen! 'Tis time for a spring tonic – Mountain's Elixir will put the bounce back in your step, ladies, and the sparkle in your eyes. 'Tis good for a sweet breath and a strong grip, my lads – you'd not have your sweetheart disappointed, now, would you?"

A passing trio of apprentices giggled and pushed each other, but did not stop. Lucy paused to listen to a shy girl in a new pink hood, blushing and whispering her question.

She was new-married, and wanted to know if the Elixir would help to get her with child. Mrs. Mountain's rule was to say yes to everything. But the girl was so young – about Lucy's own age – and so full of longing, that Lucy's heart softened towards her. Whatever else it might do, the Elixir was some kind of purge – that, too, made people believe in it, according to its inventor – and Lucy had a strong feeling that it was likely to put a swift end to pregnancy, rather than encourage it.

She said as much to the girl, who looked disappointed. Lucy put on a wise face. "Better to take green tea fasting of a morning, and elderberry syrup before bed," she improvised wildly. "Then I'd not be surprised if you had good news before the month is out."

The girl thanked her earnestly, but could not be stopped from buying a bottle of the Elixir for her husband. Lucy dropped the money into the purse she had set on the table, and cast an eye over her stock. It was well down; she would soon need to bring out some more bottles. She raised her voice again.

"Mountain's Elixir! Renowned throughout the Marches for its wonderful properties! Proven good for all ills – sovereign remedy for the gout, the quinsy, for apoplexies and agues. Good for falling hair, flat feet and stinking breath. Mrs. Mountain's secret ingredients have been brought from the far Indies, here to you! Mountain's Elixir cures the gripes, the toothache, the bellyache and the screws! Taken on a fasting stomach daily, it protects against the wandering mother, cracking of the skin, hardening of the veins and mortification of the tripes!"

The crowd was thick, but not very interested in her wares. She needed to stir them up to the point of buying. She took a deep breath, but before she could start again she became aware of music coming up the hill. The crowd heard it too, and Lucy cursed under her breath. A gaggle of boys pushed into the cramped space, and behind them came a troupe of pipes and tabors, making for the steps of the Buttercross. Lucy's crowd wavered and started to drift that way, while she hurried to serve the three or four who were ready to buy. As she dropped their money into her purse she wondered if it was time to finish for the day. But the music might bring a fresh crowd that she could share: she would stay a little longer. She ducked down behind the draped table to stock up while there was a lull.

She was on her knees behind the table when she heard a bloodcurdling yell. Flinging the cloth aside, she snapped her head up. As her eyes came level with the edge of the table she saw two hands poised over her open purse. A grubby paw was plunged into the coins and held there. Its owner had clearly been about to lift her takings. But his wrist was clamped in the grip of a larger, stronger set of fingers, a hand that had caught him in the very act. The hand was black. As dark as – no, darker than Lucy's own.

Her eyes travelled slowly from the hand to the snowy ruffles at its wrist; from the ruffles to a deep, buttoned cuff, a cuff of canary yellow that extended almost to the elbow of an elegant yellow silk coat. And on up, to a black face smiling at her over more snowy linen. Lucy felt a surge of excitement, followed by shyness that made her face hot.

"Now, miss," said her saviour, "what would you have me do with this wretch? Shall I call the Watch?"

The would-be thief began to whine and struggle.

"Oh, no, sir! Please – please to let him go," Lucy stammered.

The thief's head snapped round to goggle at her. He began to babble thanks and apologies.

"Stop your noise, codshead," said the young black man scornfully. He shook the limp hand he still held, like someone flicking water from a cloth, to make sure there was no money in it, before he thrust the man away.

Lucy hardly spared the fellow a glance. She could not take her eyes from her rescuer. "Thank you, sir. It was my whole morning's take," she said.

His smile widened. "Faith, little sister, you need not call me sir!

Benjamin will answer nicely – or even Ben, when we are better acquainted. Your servant, ma'am!" With a flourish of his hat, he made her an elaborate, courtly bow. Several people in the crowd laughed and clapped.

As he straightened up, Lucy saw the gleam of the silver slave collar nestling in the lace at his throat.

But his eyes shone with fun. "And now, ma'am, if your la'ship pleases, I shall convey you to dine at the best eating-house in this town."

Dazzled, Lucy let herself be swept along, her mind whirling, confused. He was a slave, like her father, but he dressed like a lord. And behaved like one, too, with his airs and graces and his confident smile: the poulterer on the corner of Butcher Row had agreed at once to Ben's suggestion that he keep Lucy's stock safe for an hour or two. She followed her new friend through the maze of streets until the bustle of shops and markets was left behind. Ben stopped in front of a tall and beautiful brick house.

He waved an arm at it and grinned. "My humble abode, ma'am," he said. "Welcome."

He led her through the carriage entrance at the side of the house, and down some steps to a basement door. They hurried along a flagged passage with many doors, some standing open. Lucy caught glimpses of huge painted cupboards, of a girl sewing, of two men in yellow suits like Ben's, playing cards. It was like a dream.

They came at last to a kitchen that would have swallowed her mother's cottage whole – or even Hope's cottage, Lucy thought. A long, warm room, lined with shelves where bright brown pans were ranged, each larger than the one before. Ham and poultry hung from the ceiling; there were bowls of eggs and China oranges, buckets of fish and baskets of vegetables. A small girl in a large mob-cap was working at one end of the long kitchen table; she looked up as they came in, but did not speak. At the fire a great joint of meat, half an ox at least, twirled solemnly to and fro by itself amid a forest of gleaming metal hooks and bars. The dripping pan swam with fat juices whose smell made Lucy feel faint with hunger.

The queen of this paradise, she found, was called Mistress Rundle. She was a fierce, stringy woman with a red face and a sharp tongue for anyone who came into her kitchen – except for Benjamin, who had clearly charmed her, as Lucy suspected he charmed everyone. It seemed he had been at the market on an errand for Mistress Rundle, and now he flicked three little papers from his huge yellow cuff. She was pleased, tapping the ground spices out at once into the bowl where the kitchen-maid was pounding something with a heavy blunt stick. The girl still stared at Lucy, but did not stop working.

"Little sister, indeed!" said Mrs. Rundle scornfully. "Black she may be, but green I am not. You're a shameful young rascal, Benjamin, and I hope the girl knows it."

"What she knows, Mistress Peg my darling, because I told her, is that you make the best mutton pies in England. Look how thin she is! You'd not turn her away, now, would you, and you a good Christian woman as you are?"

For answer the cook slapped Benjamin's behind as if he were a small boy, and showed Lucy a seat at the corner of her huge table.

"There's no guest goes hungry from this kitchen, lassie," she said, putting a large plate of broken meats on the scrubbed white wood in front of her. "Though the Lord knows 'tis not what I call a kitchen! Nasty, mean, low place – miles of stairs to the dining room and a day's walk to the pump. And will you look at this poor wee fireplace with its nasty iron contrivances? Modern improvements, indeed! You'll wait all day for the meat to warm through merely, and there's no room at all for a dog to turn the spit or a boy to do the basting. Bet, what are you at? Put some go into it, lassie, you're not stroking your bairn's bottom there!"

She pushed the little maid aside and stirred the stuff in the bowl about, sniffing at it. Ben caught Lucy's eye and winked. Lucy went on eating the wonderful food.

"Ah, the mace has done the trick – at least, it smells a good deal better," the cook continued. "I canna abide this coming up to town. The meat does not travel, and there's who knows how many strangers to feed." She turned back to Lucy. "I'm glad to see you've a good stomach for your meat. Whose household are you from?"

Benjamin saved her from answering, saying that he thought the town far better than the country, and where would you send out for spices at home, he'd like to know?

Mrs. Rundle retorted sharply that at home she'd have no need to send out for anything, since she'd have her cupboards properly stocked. Then she went off abruptly into the next room.

"Well I at least am glad that Milord comes regularly to Shrewsbury," Benjamin said to Lucy. "The country can be mortal dull, especially in the winter. Milord comes for the races, always, which is fine sport; and sometimes we go to London, so that he can see the king, and go to all the plays and the balls.

"But now we have come in for the Assizes. Milord will be here next week, and all his friends – they have their junketings here, too, though not so many folk as there is in London. The judges and lawyers come up from the Royal Court, and put the country bumpkins all on trial." He leant forward, teasing. "You want to watch out – have you got a licence to sell your fancy waters?"

Lucy shivered, and pushed her plate away. He reached to pat her hand, but she flinched.

Mrs. Rundle, returning with a plate of cold plum pudding for Lucy, broke in. "Now then, young man, less of this slummocking about – get your elbows off the table, get that new coat off before you soil it, and fetch me a pail of water, there's a good lad."

So here was a new problem: Lucy realised that she had no idea about what these great ones did with the poor prisoners at their Assize, about the workings of the court. She opened her mouth to ask, but Benjamin had unfolded his length from the stool and was lazily shrugging his shoulders out of the canary coat. His long-sleeved waistcoat and breeches were of the same bright silk. "I only do this as a favour for an old friend," he explained to Lucy. "Being an upstairs man myself, and no kitchen slavey." He sauntered away and came back without his coat.

"I canna wait all day," said the cook sharply.

Ben smiled at her as he picked up the wooden pail and strolled out, leisurely.

Mrs. Rundle's stern face relaxed into a smile. "He's a good lad at heart," she said to Lucy. "Too much to say for himself, but so have all young folk these days. He and I arrived in Milord's house the same day. It must be fifteen years ago, and me newly made head cook."

Her face softened as she looked into the past. "I can see him now, poor wee scrap. Barely six years old – a sad, frightened little soul he was, and great eyes on him like lamps. New-landed from the colonies, and hardly a word of English a Christian could understand. So I fed him in the kitchen, and kept him by the fire day and night – this is at home, mind, where you can tend a bairn or a sick dog in the kitchen and never notice they are there. And pretty soon he was as tall as the gardener's boy, and twice as much trouble.

"You've done with these?" She picked up Lucy's empty cup and plate and gave them to little Bet, who vanished into the scullery.

"And now he is servant to Milord?" Lucy prompted.

"He is now. A good footman, and valued as such," Mrs. Rundle agreed. "But at the first, my old Lady – Milord's mama – took a fancy to him, and had him for a page. He was quick and pretty, and he would fetch and carry for her. Mind, she spoiled him terribly. He would sit on a little cushion at her feet, and be petted by all the ladies. If you ask me, 'twas no bad thing when she went to live in the Dower House, down by Hereford. Benjamin had outgrown a silk cushion by then, and Milord kept him here. He's a good boy." She smiled at Lucy. "But it's best not to tell him so."

It was a long time since Lucy had been so warm or so full of food. Once or twice she was surprised when Ben or Mrs. Rundle spoke to her, and realised she had been dozing. But she came broad awake when the cook said, "Was that the clock? I must lift that pudding out. Will you stay for a bite in the servant's hall, lassie? We dine at five."

Five? Lucy was catapulted back into the real world. How could it be so late? She had not taken her stock back to Mrs. Mountain. She had washed no bottles today. And worst of all, she realised with horror, she had completely forgotten about Bron.

Thirty

The pits of hell could not smell worse. Lucy gagged. Setting her teeth, she squinted, peering into the shadows. Something scuttled over her foot. Nearly out of range of the lantern's flickering flame there was a black, unmoving mound.

Bron lay face down on the straw in the corner of the dungeon. She did not move or speak. Lucy was sure that she was dead. Wilding's boy held up the lantern and Lucy ran, slipping on the slimy flags, throwing herself on her knees, reaching out to embrace the lifeless body. But Bron was not dead. Her fingers dug into the straw and she heaved and twisted to throw off the touch. As her back hit the wall, she opened her eyes and recognised Lucy.

She stared, then, without speaking, flung herself down again, burying her face in the filthy straw.

Lucy said, "Bron. Bron, what is it? What ails you?"

Bron's shoulders heaved, but she did not speak.

Lucy felt frightened and angry at the same time. "I thought you were dead! Tell me what ails you! Has something happened?"

Bron rolled on to her back and lifted her manacled hands to wipe her face. In a low voice she said, "I thought you'd given me up."

"Yesterday?"

"I thought you wasn't ever coming back."

"Oh, I'm sorry! I'm so sorry! I left it too late, they wouldn't let me in. And this morning I thought they wouldn't again, for they said you were ill and couldn't go to the day-room, and then he said I could come down here if I wanted, but he looked so strange, and he didn't want any money, and I was so afraid, I thought..." She faltered to a stop.

Bron struggled to sit up. In all her trials, Lucy had never seen her weep, but now her eyes were red and swollen. "No one could have blamed you," she said roughly. "You got no cause to come here."

"Don't speak so," said Lucy. "You are unkind. I am your friend, and I thought you were mine." Now she was crying, too. Blindly, she reached out a hand and, to her surprise, Bron clutched it.

They sat on the filthy floor, holding hands, looking helplessly at each other.

The boy coughed nervously. "You got to go now, miss. No visitors allowed down here, see, in the regular way." He gestured with his lantern towards the stairs.

Bron said, "You better go."

"But –"

"Come tomorrow." The ghost of the old smile flickered on her face. "I bain't going nowhere."

Lucy smiled back.

"You'll come tomorrow?"

"Of course I will," said Lucy.

And so she did. Bron was back in the day-room by the window, where she took the pie Lucy had brought her and smiled. But she looked like a ghost, nothing but long bones wrapped in rags, her skin a greenish colour with shadows like bruises round her eyes. Yesterday, in spite of everything, Lucy had gone away warmed by the thought that Bron needed her, but now she felt that Bron was slipping further away from her every day. Had the lady visitor been right about the fever? She was beside herself with worry, but powerless to help.

If Bron was ill, there must be medicine to aid her, but Lucy had no money for doctors or apothecaries, and no one to ask. Madam would be useless: the Elixir might help those who believed in it, but Lucy was not one of them, and she was sure Bron would not be either. And apart from Mrs. Mountain and Benjamin, she knew no one here.

Ben appeared most days while she was working, though she knew she would see less of him once his master came to town. "There'll be less drinking and gaming and running after wenches then," Mrs. Rundle had said sharply. But for now he seemed to lead an idle, pleasant life, running about the town carrying messages or fetching trifles for the cook or the steward, and never too busy to spend a few minutes with Lucy.

He always seemed to have pence in his pocket. After the next Thursday wool-market he took her for a drink in one of the coffee-houses on the square. Milord was expected that very evening, and was soon to give a great dinner for all his friends in the town.

"That will put a stop to your rambling, then," Lucy said.

"Bless me, no! I get about, whatever's afoot. Free as a bird, that's Benjamin!" He winked at her over his ale-mug.

Sometimes, as now, his smugness annoyed her. "You call it freedom," she asked sharply, "to belong to your master, like his dog or his monkey?"

He froze, the mug still at his lips. "And what do you call freedom, little sister? Freedom to starve in a gutter?"

But nothing could dent his good humour for long. Next day he stopped at the stall again. He had a dozen letters to deliver, invitations to the great feast.

To his surprise, Lucy gripped his arm urgently. "Tell me how letters are sent, Benjamin. Not the ones you deliver, but letters that go to other places, by the mail coach."

"Are you writing letters, now, like a lady of quality?" he teased.

But she was in deadly earnest. "I shall write one, yes, if you can help me," she said.

When he finally understood that she was serious – and that she knew reading and writing, which he regarded as a great prodigy in a girl like her – he helped her to some ink and paper. And that night, while Madam was asleep, Lucy wrote to Hope.

As she struggled to think how Bron might be saved, it had occurred to her that, although she had no friends at hand herself, there were those who cared about Bron and might help her. Hope, who had taught Lucy to write, might not want even to read a letter from her, after their bitter parting on the morning after Twelfth Night, but Bron was her old friend; and Bell, whom Lucy had never seen, was a wise woman, skilled in herbs and healing. So Lucy wrote to Hope, begging her to help. She spelled the words to herself over and over, to make sure Hope could read it, and addressed it to the Two Crosses, because it was on a road where coaches passed.

Next day she asked Ben again how it could be sent.

He frowned. "Where is it to go? The best way is to get a cover, from a gentleman – a great man, such as Milord, who can frank a letter for the post. Otherwise the people who receive the letter must pay when it arrives – it costs a deal of money, I believe."

"It goes to the Two Crosses," said Lucy, "an inn on the road to Ludlow. Is it a very great deal of money?"

He looked at her as if she had said something wonderful, and smacked the table so that the Elixir bottles jumped. "Ludlow, did you say? On the road to Hereford, is it not?"

"I don't know," said Lucy. "But the Two Crosses is this side of it, about six miles."

"Then I can take your letter," he said.

Lucy gaped.

"Yes, truly. I came to tell you that I am to go with the carriage to fetch my old Lady, Milord's mother. She lives near Hereford, and comes here for the assembly and to see some company. We go tomorrow. Trust Benjamin."

He grinned and held out his hand for the letter.

Thirty-one

Bell put Lucy's letter down and looked at Hope. Her eyes were full of questions, but all she said was, "Then we must go at once, not wait."

Things were going too fast for Hope – something she had learned to associate with Lucy, she thought wrily. "But – Alistair?" she asked. "There's been no word yet from him, and we have sore need of his advice. Besides," she turned to Mercy, "we do not know if Harriet –"

"Oh, she'm willing, I have no fear o' that. Only tell her your names – she've heard them often enough from me! – and she'll be that pleased to take you in…"

Hope was pacing the inn parlour now, thinking aloud. "But if we go at once – tomorrow – we must walk, for the carrier does not go that way until Tuesday next. How can we take all we need?"

"Leave my box here for him to fetch after us," said Bell promptly. "William will see to it. Will you not, William?"

"Most gladly," said the big man. He twisted a napkin in his hands. "Would there was more we could do to aid you."

Hope picked up the letter and scanned it again.

"To hope Bishoppe I do begge you as you are bronns good frend that you come to her Aide for she lies sick the Prizen is dark and fole" – Full? Foul, most likely, Hope thought. No doubt the prison would be foul – *"and what ails her I know not she has no Stumick for meat her*

Flesh wasts her face Pale and somwhat green she Pynes for her Dogges and to be again on the Hills but tis more that ails her and I fear she wil Dye Hope I do not ask this for frenships sake that do not desarve it but for bronn please help her there is none else can Lucy."

There was no date, and no address.

How long had Lucy been in Shrewsbury? Was that why she had run away, to find Bron? It made no sense. She turned to William. "It came this morning, you said?"

He nodded. "Towards noon. Mercy was all but laying the meat on the table, when we heard a great clatter of wheels in the yard. Gentry coach and pair, very fine. Joey ran out, to hold the horses, and beg them to step in –"

"But they would not!" Joey took up the story, eager to have the wonder of it over again. "Because there was no one inside it! The finest rig that ever I see, and not a soul in it." His eyes turned to the window, as if the coach still stood in the yard. "Arms in fine colours painted on the door," he said, "matched pair of greys – prime horseflesh as ever came here – and two men on the box. Their coats was yellow as egg yolk, and their wigs white as wool!"

"And one of 'em a blackamoor, and spoke to 'ee?" his mother encouraged him.

"Faith, he was the blackest I ever met! Not dark like a Welshman, more like our Lucy, but darker still. I called her to mind, soon as I seen him."

"Even before he fetched out the letter." Mercy beamed admiringly at her son. "William and me ran out, then, to see what were afoot. And the black man had got down off the box, and were talking to our William, very gentleman-like, with the letter in his hand, asking if this were the Two Crosses."

"And he bowed to Mam like she were gentry," Joey grinned, "and he said, Please to deliver this to the lady named – lady, mark 'ee! – and Mam did him her curtsy and he done another bow, and they was a-bobbing like morris dancers, and Mam were that hot and bothered, and then he got back on the box. The coachman whipped up the team, and they were away."

"All come and gone in a wink," said William, wonderingly. "Naught left but the tracks of their wheels. And that letter."

"'Twas a fine new coach, deep sprung," said Joey. "You should have seen them bounce on the box as they hit the deep ruts by the road."

"You did well, Joey." With a smile, Bell cut off the repetition of every last rivet and horse-line, which he had already told over once. "We owe you thanks all," she added, looking at Mercy and William. "And now we must make haste to ready ourselves for the journey."

They walked homeward in silence, until Bell said, "This Lucy grows more and more surprising. To go all that way to help someone she hardly knew! And hardly more than a child, you said. Perhaps she felt partly to blame for Bron's arrest?" She paused to negotiate the stile, then went on, "And you did not tell me she had book-learning."

Her tone was neutral enough. But she had a way, sometimes, of saying dangerous things in a deceptively light voice. Hope glanced sideways at her, but could not tell if this was one of those times. Bell was not looking her way; her eyes were on the stones at her feet.

Hope kept her own voice steady as she could. "Oh, did I not say? I taught her her letters, when she stayed at Brynsquilver." When Bell did not reply she added, "It gave us occupation in the dark evenings."

Bell's gaze shifted to the hills. "Well, 'tis fortunate that you did! Your work has borne more useful fruit than you could have guessed." They paced in silence for a few minutes. Then Bell added, "I had not realised she stayed with you so long. Or was she a quick study?"

Hope swallowed. "Very quick," she said.

*

The prison yard seethed like a cauldron. Bell was taken aback.
Nothing had prepared her for this concentration of misery. As she
and Hope had tramped the Shrewsbury road, her picture of Bron
had been one of gloomy solitude, dark and cold. But today the
prisoners were all outside – men, women and children penned in
like cattle in a barnyard – and the bright March sun shone merci-
lessly on rags and sores, prison pallor and hunted eyes. The noise
was dreadful: shouts and curses rebounded from the high walls,
punctuated by the insistent wail of a baby. A man pushed past,
cursing; Bell tightened her grip on the basket she carried and
moved closer to Hope. She could not see Bron anywhere.

Then Hope said, "There!" and began to shoulder through the
crowd, pulling Bell after her. A woman lay on the ground, half-
propped against the wall, another bending over her, talking
earnestly. With a shock, Bell realised that the woman on the
ground was Bron.

Hope called, "Lucy!"

The second woman straightened and turned. For a moment the
thin, dark face was blank, then recognition and relief flooded it.
"Hope! Oh, thank –" Her voice faltered as tears rose in her eyes.

As Hope hurried forward, Bell stood still, staring. This was
Lucy? The young woman did not at all fit the picture Hope had
given her, of a feckless, unpredictable child. She was young, certainly, but careworn, and serious beyond her years. Just then Lucy
turned towards her, and Bell saw her own surprise and apprehen-
sion mirrored in the young woman's eyes.

Hope had never said that Lucy was beautiful, but she was. The
large dark eyes that stared at Bell with such frank curiosity gave life
and beauty to Lucy's whole face. This was the "child" who had
shared a roof with Hope through a long winter? A shock of jealous
fear took Bell by surprise. She forced her attention back to Bron.

Hope was already on her knees beside her friend. "Bron, how

goes it with you? Are you ailing? Do they treat you badly? Oh, it is so good to see you!"

Bron looked from Hope to Bell, confused. "How did you – why have you come? I would not cause you trouble..."

"Fiddlesticks!" said Bell briskly, putting down her basket. "Are we not friends? Now show me those wrists."

Listlessly, Bron held out her arms. The manacles had rubbed the skin raw, and then stopped it from scabbing, so that there were running sores on both arms. Bell set to with ointment and clean rags, while Lucy jealously watched her every move and Hope struggled to keep up a cheerful conversation.

"I have greetings for you from two old friends," she said, smiling.

Bron looked up with a puzzled frown.

"Gwennie and Gelert, of course!" said Hope. "I believe they would be here with us if they had not had your flock to keep while we are away. The Wayland lads are helping them, but you know Gwennie – she'd not leave her sheep to hirelings!"

Bron sat forward, her lean face suddenly more animated. "You have seen them, then? They are safe?" she asked eagerly.

"Have no fear of that! I see them daily. They are at Brynsquilver, sheep, dogs and all."

Bron gave a great sigh, as if putting down a burden. "I have not deserved such friends," she said.

Bell looked up from her work. "I think you have a better friend yet," she said gently. "Has Lucy been here with you all this time?"

Noticing Lucy's look of surprise, she thought, the girl does not expect me to like her.

Bron nodded. "I'd be dead already without Lucy," she agreed gruffly.

"Let us have no talk of dying," said Bell. "Your ankles now."

She was skilled in not showing her feelings in the face of pain and sickness, but she drew a sharp breath at the sight of Bron's feet. The shock turned quickly to anger. How could this be necessary? Did they think the woman would break through all these stone walls and iron bars, that they weighted her down with iron? She schooled herself to gentleness as she unwound the stinking rags and began to clean the wounds.

"'Twas a good lambing," Hope was saying. "Only one still-born, and two that died after. But we had a pair of twins that both lived. By my reckoning your flock is increased by eight and twenty, more than half of them ewe-lambs. No bad count for a novice shepherd, you'd own?"

Bron nodded her agreement, but it was plain her heart was not in it. There was a moment's pause before she said, "'Tis well you have them, and the dogs too. I reckon I'll not see them again."

Bell woke slowly, surfacing from a familiar scene of dread. It was the same dream she had always had when she was worried. She was sitting in the great hall in her father's house, waiting for someone to come home, unable to move, while the rushlights burned down and down, threatening her with darkness. As she woke, she realised that this time it had been Hope she was waiting for, Hope who had gone away. She reached out across the lumpy bed to touch Hope's reassuring back. Without waking, Hope shaped herself welcomingly and pulled Bell's arm round to hold it against her breast. Bell snuggled into her warmth, pushing her dream away.

When she opened her eyes again, Bell saw that it was already broad daylight, and that she lay under the beams of an unfamilar roof. After a blank moment she remembered: she was in the attic of Mercy's cousin Harriet's house in Fish Street. In Shrewsbury, where the terrible gaol was.

They had been to see Bron every day since they arrived. Bell was sure now that she was not suffering from any serious bodily ailment. She was dirty and unnaturally pale, as were all the prisoners, and bore the mark of too little sleep, but freedom and wholesome food would soon put that right. The sores from the manacles were bad, but not festering, and Bron had not taken the gaol fever, as Bell had feared she might.

Yet Bell could not put out of her mind the fear that Bron was near to death. She moved her eyes only slowly to meet yours and when she spoke, it was as if from the far side of a running river, or across a great gulf of darkness and cold. Nothing that any of them had said to her these last three days seemed to have persuaded her that there was any hope.

Bell simply could not believe that the London judges would find anyone guilty on a charge of witchcraft. The idea was uncouth, antique, in savage contrast to the bustling, fashionable life of this town, where silken ladies strolled with well-dressed gentlemen to elegant shops and coffee-houses. Shrewsbury was sophisticated, worldly; how much more so, then, would the great men from London be. No rustic superstitions for them, surely? But a little nagging fear persisted, and even if the judges spared her, Bell feared that Bron had condemned herself. Defeated by her own strange self-doubt, she could die, quite simply, of despair.

And today, Harriet had said, the judges would come, entering the town with great pomp and ceremony, and all the world would be out to see them. Harriet was too busy with a houseful of paying guests to spare the time, but she had urged Hope and Bell to go out early and find a place where they could see the procession. Her guests in the house in Fish Street were only the humblest of those who had come in to Shrewsbury for the weeks around the judges' visit.

The town was overflowing with the best county families – gentry such as Bell's own family had once been – leaving their scattered country seats and opening up their town houses for a brief season of merriment. The grim business of the Assizes was an excuse, it seemed, for a great round of concerts, balls and parties. Harriet said there was scarcely a family in the county that had not come to town – especially those with marriageable daughters. And certainly Bell had seen more French lace and figured silk walking the streets these last three days than she had seen since her Jacobite days in Bath. The contrast with the squalid prison sickened her. It was enough to give her a new sympathy with the Friends and their sombre disapproval of the doings of the great.

There were other things troubling her, too. They had never had any reply from Alistair, for instance. And then there was the business of Lucy. Ever since she had set eyes on the girl, the vague fears and jealousies that she had suppressed before had taken new shape and force. She was haunted by the new knowledge that Hope's winter visitor had been not the pathetic and infuriating child that Hope's stories had suggested, but a spirited, striking young woman. Foolish fears, perhaps, but she could not share them with Hope, and her unspoken questions hung uneasily between them.

Before Bell could begin to brood, Hope stirred and reached out for her.

Bell wriggled away. "Hope! The household is stirring. Would you make a scandal?"

Hope pursued her, grinning. "I promise to be quiet. Let us see if you can be."

But this morning, Bell's thoughts were not so easily distracted. Evading Hope's outstretched arms, she slid out of bed and pushed her feet into her slippers.

As they were dressing, they heard banging at the street door. Bell, in stays and petticoat, put out her head to see what was happening. Above the house tops, bright clouds scudded across a blue sky; below her, the street was already full of early shoppers, and the now familiar smell of fish was strong on the air. But the upper storey of Harriet's house leaned out so far that Bell could not spy on the visitors. She closed the casement and reached for her gown.

Only minutes later they heard steps on the stair, and Harriet erupted into the chamber. Breathless and wide-eyed, she bore a closer resemblance to Mercy than Bell had noticed before.

"There's a gentleman and lady below asking for 'ee," she said. "Will you come down? 'Tis a Quaker gentleman. He says he's your brother."

Thirty-two

The ballad seller elbowed and bawled his way up Wyle Cop. "Last dying speech!" he bellowed. "Last words of the Scotch child-murderess! Last dying speech of the Edinburgh whore at the gallows foot!"

Lucy turned to Sal, who was struggling with the cart. "Come on, girl, put your back into it! If they'll part with good money for that rubbish, they should be ripe for picking. Come on, do."

Sal opened her mouth to speak, then looked at Lucy's face and changed her mind.

Just as well, Lucy thought: she was in no mood for nonsense this morning. She glared across the crowded street, then dodged out in the eddy behind an empty dray. Fetching up under the windows of the Eagle, she leant back and closed her eyes as she waited for Sal. Another day to be got through; she had begun to think that the Assize Court itself could be no worse than this endless waiting. She opened her eyes and surveyed the crowd. Is it just my fancy, she thought, or do they all look uglier today?

As if to answer her, a burly man with a leather apron trussed up under his armpits let out a stream of curses at Sal and kicked out at the cart. Only the steady downhill pressure of bodies carried him away. Lucy pushed out into the crowd again to rescue Sal and the stock. At least the old mother had stayed away today, in the back parlour of the Plough most likely, leaving them to work this edgy, dangerous mob. She looked around. They could always abandon the cart and the stock if things turned nasty. The way she felt today, she didn't care if she never saw the Elixir again, or any of its poxy customers.

But Sal was bursting to succeed. As Lucy's mind had become more and more filled with worrying about Bron, she had let Sal hang around, wiping bottles, helping to set up the stall. Even Mrs. Mountain had seen that Sal was not trying to snatch the takings and had given her a civil word or two. Today, she was allowed to push the truck, and now she ran it into the wall and surveyed the crowd.

"Don't look like customers to me," she said. "Faces long as sermons, most of 'em."

"Are you surprised?" said Lucy roughly. "Half of them are waiting to see their friends hanged when these judges arrive – or transported at the very least."

Sal grinned. "Look'ee here, then." She jumped up on the cart. "Step up, ladies and gents," she yelled, in a fair imitation of Lucy's voice. "Mountain's Elixir cures all ills! Sovereign for them as is going on a long voyage! Settles the tripes and guards against sunburn!"

Lucy grabbed at her skirts. "Come down, you sad drab, that's no jest!"

But down at pavement level Sal persisted. "Cures the sea-sickness and the scurvy! Buy the 'Lixir here!"

Heads turned, and one or two passers-by stood still. Then without warning a woman spat full in Sal's face. Sal stopped, stunned, in mid-flight. As Lucy lifted her apron to wipe the girl's cheek, the woman said something to the man beside her, and he turned towards them, scowling. Lucy looked round for a way out. Any minute now the whole of Wyle Cop would set about them. She started to mouth apologies, while edging Sal and the cart away.

Just then a trumpet brayed. All heads turned towards the noise.

A wedge of soldiers, dressed in black with seven-foot staves in hand, were forcing their way up the street. Steel helmets half-hid their faces. In the ripple of silence that went ahead of them, Sal's stifled gasps could be clearly heard.

The man at their head cried, "'Way! Make way for the Lord High Sheriff of Shropshire! Make way, in the king's name, for the lord justices!"

Sal buried her face in Lucy's shoulder as the pikemen pressed forward through the crowd towards them, like a boat cutting its way upstream. The tramp of their boots echoed off the high houses; its drumming hit Lucy under the breastbone like a wave of fear. All around her, people turned unsmiling faces towards the suddenly empty cobbles.

Twenty paces behind the pikes, more men marched, this time two by two. They wore a red livery with crossed belts of gold, and each carried a thick black stick upright in his hand. When the soldiers had passed, the crowd began to stir and mutter, so that these liveried servants had to spread out and shove people back to make room for those who came behind. First were a crew of ordinary enough footmen – the judge's men, Lucy thought – wearing heavy travelling boots and carrying white staves. In their midst was a covered mule-cart, splashed and filthy from the open road. The men kept their heads down, as if to ward off the hostile stares and low jeers of the crowd, steering the clumsy cart and prodding their beast to go faster over the cobbles.

"What is it?" asked Sal.

Lucy shook her head, but a carpenter in his white cap standing by them answered.

"Those be the judge's papers and parchments. Filthy lies, for the most part, if you ask me. Sworn papers setting neighbour against neighbour and master against servant."

"And stealing the bread from honest tradesmen," said a woman behind him. "Once your name be writ in them papers, it be there for evermore. They do carry them to and fro, to London and here again every mortal year, and they never cast 'em away."

The carpenter spat. "And there go the lawyers, damn their eyes. Following upon their papers like flies on a rotten carcass."

His neighbours seemed to agree; the jeers and jostling increased as the gentlemen of the law passed by. They wore rusty black and plain white bands like low preachers, and were as travel-stained as the footmen. They rode in a close huddle and seemed to have a great deal to say to each other, but they looked nervous, twitching the heads of their scrubby ponies and pressing up close to the cart.

Behind them, two more rows of red coats marched; Lucy's eye was drawn to a black face and she saw with a shock that it was Ben. He marched along, blank-eyed, as if his mind was far away, his yellow breeches sticking out under the borrowed red and gold livery. The red coats led the way for a train of gentlemen on fine, tall horses. Real gents, these were, with gold lace on their coats and waistcoats, their boots and spurs shining. The people left off cursing, and passed their names from mouth to mouth; one or two even doffed their caps.

"Look!" squeaked Sal as a short man rode by on a high horse covered with plates of gold. "There's the Lord Mayor. Look at his chain!"

Lucy looked, but said nothing. Were these proud, hard-faced men the lords Ben had spoken of, come to give a judgement? There were twenty or thirty of them, mostly with their running footmen at their stirrups, struggling to make a way through the press of people. One young man in green velvet rode a raw stallion that sidled and snorted, scattering people at its heels. Scowling, he jerked its head brutally back into line. Hatred rose up like bile in Lucy's throat.

The London judges came last of all, in a fine painted coach drawn by four horses and hung about with gold-laced footmen – two on the box, two standing up behind. The coach moved slowly, the horses tightly reined in, almost prancing up the hill. Lucy caught a glimpse of a stony face, nearly as pale as the full powdered wig that framed it. A white hand, laid on the window ledge, gleamed with rings on every finger. As the coach passed close to them, she could see that there were two men inside, and that both judges were dressed in red. Deep folds of scarlet wrapped them round, filling the inside of the coach as if they sat bathed to the eyes in blood.

"So how soon will the trials begin?" Bell asked anxiously. "The judge arrives today – listen to the noise outside." They were sitting in Harriet's best parlour. Her windows overhung the street, and the uncertain hubbub of a holiday – or a mob – had been wafting up to them for hours.

"Will Bron go to court tomorrow, think you?" she asked.

"Possibly," said Alistair. "No one can be arraigned before the court until the Grand Jury have done their work. Thy friend must wait, I fear, until Friday, or late tomorrow at the least."

A surge of helpless fury brought Hope to her feet. She went quickly to the window and looked out, mainly to hide her face. "But what can this Grand Jury do," she asked, as levelly as she could, "before they see the poor folk who are accused?"

"Why, they see those who accuse them," said Alistair.

Amazed, Hope turned to see whether he spoke in earnest. She sat down on the window-board.

"'Tis true, upon my word. I had the clearest account of it from Richard." He turned to Bell. "I had hoped Richard might be minded to come here himself, but no doubt his business in London is heavy. I wrote him when I first had thy letter, for I guessed thou would feel it too delicate a matter to approach him."

Bell was sitting in the morning light, just opposite, and Hope saw her colour and look down. Hope set her teeth on her jealous panic, and looked at Alistair. He's pleased, she thought;

Bell's discomfort at the man's name pleases him. She clenched her fists in the folds of her gown, and tried to listen for the meanings of what they said.

Alistair went on, "If the judges come here today, then the prosecutors and their witnesses will be called and sworn first thing tomorrow morning. Their charges will be heard and copied down by clerks, and then they are sent in to the jury."

"The written bills are sent?" Bell interrupted, "Or the prosecutors?"

"Both," said Alistair. "The Grand Jury must look at the charge and hear those who make it, before they decide if there is a case to answer."

Hope tried to bite her tongue, but her anger burst out. "You call that justice? To listen to the likes of Hamer and Noll Wethered, and never even to see the poor woman they accuse? How can that be right?"

Bell put out a restraining hand, and she sat down, flinching away.

Alistair sighed. "Friend Hope," he said, "I am of thy mind entirely. But that is how the king's justice is carried on. By tomorrow afternoon we shall know whether the accusation against thy friend has been put aside, or found to be a true bill, to be answered in open court."

Hope turned her head away. The distant hubbub had died down, and she heard a cart rumble beneath their window, and then silence.

Bell said quietly, "Did Richard say what chance Bron might have?"

Hope looked round at the mention of Richard, but Bell was waiting for her brother's reply.

"In truth," Alistair said, "We know too little of the case to judge rightly. But 'tis an antiquated charge, this of witchcraft, hardly heard of in these days. I pray that the gentlemen of the Grand Jury have more sense than to listen to such superstitious wickedness."

His wife – Susannah, the little Quakeress who had scarcely raised her head from her sewing since they had sat down together – spoke up. "And so do I pray," she said. "May providence guide them."

They fell silent. Hope thought bitterly of Bron in the prison, prayed over by well-meaning ladies and slowly fading from the light of day.

Bell spoke first. "We should go to the gaol tomorrow morning, then, and be with her when the news comes, whether good or bad."

Susannah put down her sewing. "If she is arraigned, it would be well for her to be clean-dressed, and have on a fresh cap and apron," she said.

Hope wondered if she had heard aright. How could anyone be concerned at this moment about the state of a gown or petticoat? And were not the Quakers meant to be above such fripperies?

But Susannah went on seriously, "The world sets store by such things, more than thou would think. Friends in their sufferings under the law have always found that a neat appearance and respectable demeanour did much to allay the fury of a judge. If thou will tell me thy friend's height and girth I will go tomorrow and find a plain gown for her here among the Friends in Shrewsbury." She looked at Bell. "It is little enough, I know, but I would do something."

Bell took her hand. "And so you do," she said, "for I know you hold her in your prayers. And now there is nothing more that any of us can do but wait. Let us try to think of other things a while."

This seemed to act as a signal to Susannah. She looked speakingly at her husband, and Hope saw him nod. He turned to Bell. "Well, sister, we do have other news to share with thee."

Bell smiled at Susannah. "I think I have guessed it. You look thrivingly, which half-tells your secret, even if you were not sewing such a very small cap!"

Susannah blushed as Bell got up to hug her. "It is true," she said, disengaging herself. "I am with child indeed – how clever of thee! I have so lately known it myself, I did not think it could show." She turned to her husband. "But that is not the news Alistair meant."

Hope saw him hesitate, as if ordering his thoughts. She was filled with sudden foreboding – what did they want from Bell now?

"Thou remembers, sister, the American John Goodman, who travelled with cousin Richard?"

Bell nodded. "But I hardly saw him – he stayed but one night, as I recall?"

"He has been staying with us again these past weeks, and we have both had much conversation with him. He is greatly favoured in his witness, so that through him the word of God truly enters all hearts. Susannah and I have heard him, at Meeting and at home, and we find ourselves growing to the same determination." He paused, and the girl put down her half-made baby cap deliberately and looked at him. Hope was struck by the certainty and the authority with which her straight, childlike gaze fixed on the older man.

He went on. "In short, Bell, we are both determined to seek approval from the Meeting to accompany Friend Goodman when he returns to Pennsylvania."

Bell gasped. "You go to America?" She turned to Susannah. "But is that wise, in your condition? It is your first – how long will you be on the sea?"

Susannah smiled serenely. "My mother has been a touring preacher. She was on horseback most of the time she carried me, and testified in Chester market the day before she was brought to bed. A sea voyage can be no more hardship, I trust. And we shall be in America long before the child is born."

Hope looked at Bell, who was frowning. Hope could see her

hurt at the idea of her brother thus snatched away again, just as she had found him; in her own heart, relief at such a prospect was tempered by a suspicion that he had not said all his say.

With a sad little smile, Bell gave him up gracefully. "If it is right for you both, then of course you will go. But I am sorry to lose you again so soon, Ali."

"We may not be away for ever," he replied. "Two or three years in the first place, by my reckoning. But we are in the hand of providence."

And you are in the hand of yon smiling girl, Hope thought; but she waited with a sense of uneasiness as he weighed his next words. At last he began again.

"I have great hope that Richard will go with us to America. When this business of the Act of Parliament is completed, and he has finally reported himself back to his father, then I think there is nothing to keep him here in England." He paused.

Hope followed his eyes as they met Bell's across the little room.

Susannah broke in. "Oh, Bell," she cried, "we should be so glad if thou too could go with us! Wilt thou think on it? Wilt thou go with us and Richard to the New World?"

Thirty-three

Lucy could see the court-house from the stall. In truth, she saw little else that morning. The market hummed around her, the Welshmen came and went, and even more customers than usual came to seek Mrs. Mountain's reassurances about the future, but Lucy was oblivious to everything but the comings and goings of the court. The word in the gaol yesterday had been that the first of the felons would be brought before the judge today, and she watched like a hawk for any sign of the trial beginning.

She knew the judge wasn't there yet. She had seen him arrive in the market place, with a whole mob of other gentlemen, very early in the morning, while she and Sal were setting up. But they had gone into another building over by the High Street, and although lawyers' clerks had come in and out, nothing else had happened. As the morning wore on, the knot of fear tightened in Lucy's stomach until she felt she might be sick.

Once she saw Bell across the market, talking seriously with a woman who sold vegetables. Lucy prayed Bell would not see her. Against her wishes she had taken a strong liking to Hope's friend, who knew so much of herbs and healing. On her second day in Shrewsbury, Bell had discovered a druggist's shop where she could buy a hundred things that Lucy had never heard of before, like orris-root and coriander seed. Bell had been as excited as a child to discover this treasure-house, and had shown them the handbill the druggist had given her with all his stock and prices. Flower of brimstone, juniper water, cinnamon bark... It had made Lucy even more ashamed of peddling the awful Elixir. She knew Bell would be shocked and disapproving of Mrs. Mountain's quackery; the last thing she wanted was for Bell to see her here. But she need not have worried: a few moments later she saw Bell heading off towards the Buttercross with a plain-dressed young woman carrying a bundle.

"No greeting for a friend this morning, miss?" The voice in her ear made her jump. It was Ben, his usual quizzical smile replaced for once by a look of real care. "You look sickly, little sister. What ails you?"

"I just wish I knew what was happening," she said. "What are they doing in there? When will it all begin?"

He followed her gaze. "Why, the Grand Jury are hard at work now," he said. "Milord called for his breakfast before I was well awake this morning. He has been at the Green Room yonder since before eight o'clock. Faith, they do brisk business this year! I wager they will call the first of the prisoners directly after they have dined."

Lucy stared at him. So long? It was unbearable. She untied the purse from her waist and thrust it at Sal. "Take care of the goods, squib. Tell Madam I'm sick."

As she drew near to the gaol, the crowd was suddenly thicker. There was a noise up ahead, shouting and cheering. A fight? Lucy edged towards the wall and kept going. Then someone shouted, "Make way for his lordship the Chief Justice!" and her heart thumped painfully. She strained to see what was going on, but a sea of backs obscured her view. Furiously she started to push forward, worming her way between the jostling people.

A woman's voice shouted, "A pox take the old tyrant!" There was laughter, and more cheering, Ducking under a man's arm,

Lucy suddenly found herself at the front of the crowd.

They were following a high cart, on which a great fat man in red was seated with his back to Lucy. At his feet a young woman, in a low bodice, with painted tears on her cheeks, wept and grovelled, begging for justice. The monstrous judge, his hat over his eyes, seemed to sleep as she suffered. The other players pranced ahead of the cart, or pushed it along. They carried slapsticks instead of the staves Lucy had seen in the hands of the judge's servants yesterday. One man strode ahead, a huge chain of office made of pots and pans clanking down to his knees. Standing on the edge of the cart another, dressed in black with pens stuck in his wig, gloated in dumbshow over a huge bag of money.

"Rot in hell, and all lawyers with you!" screamed a woman in the crowd.

The player grinned and waved his money bag.

Lucy stared.

It was Mr. Stukely. She knew him again as if they had met only yesterday, just as she knew the cart, and the red cloth that served as the judge's cloak, and the face of the woman who knelt at the justice's feet. And at once, in spite of herself, she was searching the faces of the other players for Mr. Brown.

At that moment the judge awoke with a roar and staggered drunkenly to his feet. The crowd howled with laughter as he belched and scratched himself.

"Mercy! Mercy!" screeched the woman at his feet.

"Give her what she deserves!" yelled a prentice boy near to Lucy. His mates sniggered and whistled.

The judge silenced them with a waft of his hand, and looked at the kneeling woman. "Pox take the strumpet," he drawled, "I want my dinner. Send the slut to the colonies."

And of course Lucy knew his voice, too. She watched as Mr. Brown, holding up his huge cushion of a belly, turned slowly round, acknowledging the cheers and jeers of the crowd. A couple of lads, egged on by their fellows, tried to jump up on the cart to join in the play, clasping their hands and crying for pardon. One pawed at the judge's gown, and as Mr. Brown turned sharply to brush him off, his eyes met Lucy's.

He recognised her, she could tell at once. She stood, stunned, as he raised his hat in salute. Then, settling it again, he put his hand lightly to his lips and blew her a kiss.

The crowd screamed with delight; someone called out that the old whoremonger was a good judge of a drab if nothing else. One or two people tried to grab hold of Lucy to lift her on to the cart. But the other players stepped in. A tall red-haired woman Lucy did not remember scolded them off, giving Lucy a hard look as she did so. The ragged procession moved on, leaving her staring after them.

Her mind reeling, Lucy dragged herself down the hill to the gaol. She had dreamed so often of seeing Mr. Brown again, but now it had happened it only added to her feeling of living in a bad dream.

Well, there was no waking up from this one. Squaring her shoulders, she braced herself for one last effort at cheerfulness.

The prison was oddly quiet. There were far fewer people than usual in the day-room, and they sat silently for the most part, avoiding each other's eyes. Bron was not there. Lucy found her at last in the yard, sitting on one of the benches against the wall. She had to look twice to make sure it was Bron, because she was dressed in different clothes: a grey gown and a plain white cap that half hid her face. Lucy plumped herself down on the bench beside her.

"What a day!" she said as brightly as she could. "I've a tale to tell of what I saw in the street just now. But first you must tell me where everyone has gone. And how you came by this new-fangled gown – you look as if you was going to a Quaker Meeting!"

Bron did not look up. She said, "The first paper of names came from the Jury. Some of the prisoners were released straight away." She paused briefly. "They found a true bill against me."

She was staring at her hands, not looking at Lucy.

"I'm to go to the court today, so they say. Our Dame was here, and that little Quakeress that married her brother. They put this upon me, to do me good with the judge." Her mouth twitched in the shadow of a smile. "They meant well."

Lucy's fear was like a pain in her gut. She fought to keep her voice steady as she said, "The judge will see the truth. That's what he's for." She did not believe it, and she knew Bron didn't either.

The door across the yard opened and Wilding appeared. "Come up now, mistress, you are to go with the first gang to the court-house. All in here, now!" He passed along, to find others in the room.

Bron did not move.

Lucy asked, "Will he let me come with you?"

Bron shook her head. "They will chain and guard us. But first I must ask a favour of you. And then there is a thing I must tell you before we go. I have been thinking of it, all night."

"Anything," said Lucy.

"Will you be there? When I am tried?"

Lucy almost laughed. "Of course! Of course I will. Where else would I be?"

Bron nodded to herself. "Thank you."

"And the thing you wanted to tell me?" Lucy prompted. "That man will be here again to fetch you if we are not quick."

Bron frowned, ordering her thoughts. Then she said slowly, "I was never wanted."

Lucy frowned, not understanding.

"When I was a child. And after. No one ever wanted me. I have thought about it, while I have been here. Mam died bearing me, and my Da, he cared for no one, least of all me. Davy was... like Da." She paused, searching for the words. "So I never knew what it was to have anyone care about me. And I thought, that's no bad thing, if I am to die. No one will suffer by my going, see?"

"Don't speak so!" cried Lucy. "Stop it, Bron! I cannot bear it!"

Bron went on staring at the ground in front of her. "I don't say it to hurt you," she said carefully, "And it is not true any more. Because of you. You have cared for me. You have come here every day. And you fetched Hope and the Dame to me, I know that. This is what I wanted to tell you. To thank you." She still stared at the ground. "I don't know why you care for me, but I thank you."

Lucy tried to speak, but tears choked her.

Bron plunged on, "When you are not there, I think about when you will come again. And when you come in, it is like the sun coming over Hergan Hill. So now I am cared for, and I find that I care for someone. And that is... hard."

"Hard? What do you mean? Of course I care for you, and if – if you care for me, I am glad."

Bron raised her head and looked at Lucy. "It is hard," she said, "because now I do not want to die."

The crowd outside the court-house was dense and ugly. It was quite clear there would not be room inside for half of the desperate folk who thronged around the door, but every one of them was determined to get in. Lucy did her utmost, pushing and kicking with the best of them. As they neared the door, the press was even thicker. Squeezed between struggling bodies, she elbowed her way painfully towards the front.

Two burly pikemen were doing their best to control the entrance, but seemed in danger of being swept away themselves at any minute. As Lucy came within earshot, one shouted to the other that the room was full, and they began to try to close the doors.

"Let me pass, let me pass!" she shouted, clawing at backs and arms. "I promised! I promised!" With a last desperate effort, she flung herself forward. A massive wooden pike barred her way.

"No more room, sweetheart," grunted the man who held it. "Take my advice and forget the rogue. If he's before this judge he's past praying for."

The door was nearly closed. With a roar of fury the man directly behind Lucy surged forward, knocking her off balance. Then she was scrabbling helplessly among legs and feet that threatened to trample her. Biting and kicking, she fought to free herself. With a final lurch, she stood up and tumbled out on to the cobbles.

Defeated, she dragged herself to the safety of the wall. She had failed. Bron would be before the judge and she, Lucy, would not be there. Bron had never asked her for anything, only this. And she had failed. Burying her face in her torn apron, she cried and cried.

"Madam, are you ill? May I be of any assistance?"

The voice was kind, and not unfamiliar. Lucy looked up. The gentleman bending over her wore an elegant brown suit and a shirt with many ruffles.

"Damn me!" exclaimed Mr. Brown softly. "If 'tis not the nut-brown maid! What ails you, child?"

Lucy clutched the gloved hand. "They will not let me in," she sobbed. "My – my friend is to be tried, and they will not let me in."

Mr. Brown's golden eyes hardened. "No fellow is worth this grief, sweetheart. Forget him as soon as you may, and keep your heart for a better."

Lucy looked up. "Oh, no," she said. 'Tis no fellow, but my dear friend. She who saved my life, and now I cannot even be at her trial." She began to cry again. "I promised her I would be there. And I could not bear it if –"

Mr. Brown gave her a searching look, and the expression on his face softened. "In that case," he said, "be of good cheer, for I can assist you."

Taking Lucy's hands he pulled her to her feet. "Wipe your pretty face," he said briskly, "and come with me."

Leading her round the corner of the court-house into a narrow alley, he stopped before a small door. "The powder-room is above here – an upper chamber where we high-born gentlemen," he raised one eyebrow very slightly, "repair to prettify ourselves. Though today it will be a waiting-room for their servants, I warrant."

As Lucy gazed uncomprehendingly, he went on, "Last time our company were in Shrewsbury, the court-house was our theatre, and this chamber our green room. We gave the *Beggars' Opera*, I remember." He grinned. "Though I say it myself, I was astonishing as Macheath. Stole all the ladies' hearts."

It was the same smile, Lucy thought, but he looked somehow older and more tired than she remembered. The brown suit, she saw now, was shiny with wear.

Seeing her hesitate, Mr. Brown pulled open the door. "Only skip up these stairs, sweetheart, and you'll be in the best box in the house, my word upon it."

She began to stammer her thanks, but he waved them aside. "A favour for a fair one," he said airily. Then, just for a moment, his face became serious. "Thou art a beagle true bred," he said softly. "Your friend is fortunate in you."

Taking Lucy's hand, he bowed low and lifted it to his lips.

"Mr. Brown!" said a sharp voice. "You are waited for, sir."

It was the red-haired actress Lucy had seen outside the gaol. She did not look pleased.

Mr. Brown dropped Lucy's hand and pushed her a little hurriedly towards the door.

As she pulled it closed behind her, she heard his voice again.

"Your servant, Mrs. Brown, my dear. I was coming directly."

Thirty-four

The small, close room was already crowded with serving-men and a few women. As she hesitated at the door, Lucy saw Ben talking to a man in a green livery. He spotted her almost at the same moment and came to her side, gathering her up and steering her to a bench next to a little latticed window in the far wall.

"Bird's eye view of the whole proceeding, little sister," he explained.

Peering through the wooden screen, Lucy found herself looking straight down into the court-room.

Perhaps it was because of what Mr. Brown had said, but to Lucy it looked like nothing so much as the makeshift theatre on the Wrexham road where she had first seen the players. The high, dusty roof-beams, streaked yellow with birdlime and festooned with crumbling nests, were just like the old barn. It was noisy and surprisingly dark; the windows were narrow and the day cloudy, and this time no one had thought to hang up a cart-wheel stuck with candles. Peering out from her spyhole as if from behind the stage, she looked down past the judge's high seat at a crowd of faces.

Just as on that hot night long ago, there were seats for the gentry set out at the front, many of them occupied just now by the peacock liveries of servants saving places for their masters. A few ladies and gentlemen had already claimed their seats. Lucy scanned their faces: they seemed unconcerned, even enjoying themselves. One girl, in a jaunty hat and a lace cap with long kissing-strings, laughed piercingly at everything the man next to her chose to say.

Then, with a jump, Lucy saw Hope and Bell. They sat silently side by side in the third or fourth row. There was a man with them, a Quaker by his dress, who Lucy thought must be Bell's brother. As she watched, Bell turned and spoke to him. Her lovely, serious face looked troubled. The man said something in reply and patted her hand. Lucy looked away, past them to the packed benches behind the gentry seats, full of the good citizens of Shrewsbury, out to see what there was to see. Lucy recognised one or two of Mrs. Mountain's customers.

And beyond them, standing at the back and packed around the walls, were the people who had fought their way in, those who, like Lucy herself, were there because it mattered. They stood dumbly gazing about, or argued among themselves, still trying to convince themselves they had done all they could for the friends or relatives whose fate would be decided that afternoon.

The room was so crowded that the only two empty spaces in it drew the eye. On one side of the judge's chair, a couple of benches were fenced off by a low wooden wall, like a rich man's pew in church.

"Jury box," said Ben, following her eyes. "Those are the petty jury, there, look, waiting to be called. All in their best coats, feeling important. But they're only tradesmen or farmers. The judge tells 'em what to say, you'll see. The real gentry are on the Grand Jury, like Milord." He settled himself more comfortably and unwrapped a bundle. "Have a bite?" he offered, holding out a knuckle of ham.

Lucy swallowed the queasiness that rose in her stomach and shook her head. Turning back to the lattice, she forced herself to look at the other empty space. She knew what it was for. A black cage, barred and empty, waiting for the accused prisoners. Set along its top was a row of vicious iron spikes. Dragging her eyes away, she noticed what she had not seen before, that there were more spiked railings along in front of the judge's chair. To keep him apart. Or to keep him safe, Lucy wondered, from the anger and hatred of the people in the back rows?

There was a stir at the far end of the room. The double doors had been thrown open and a stream of ladies and gentlemen began to push their way down the crowded centre aisle. The servants keeping their places jumped up and bowed themselves away.

"Dinner's over," said Ben. He turned back in to the room. "Shift yourselves, fellows, they're on their way up!"

"And here's the judge's carriage," shrieked a girl at the far side of the narrow room. Perched on her lover's knees, she had a view through a narrow side window to the street.

Lucy heard a trumpet sound outside, then a rumbling and stamping as everyone in the court-room rose to their feet. She turned back to her vantage point, just in time to see the great doors open again.

Silence fell on the crowd. Trailing his blood-red robe, the judge walked down the room. He looked at no one, treading the path his servants made for him as if he were all alone in an open field. The people pushed back, jostling each other like frightened sheep to make way for him. He climbed slowly on to the platform, raising his skirts to show thin black silken ankles. He was hardly more than an arm's length from Lucy; she could see his pale, lined face, and the wig-powder on his scarlet shoulders. His eyes were dark, expressionless. He turned and stood for a moment, gazing at the crowded room before sinking into his chair. Someone began to read out a list of names, then the door behind the dock opened, and the first prisoners came in.

They were treated like stupid cattle in a market. They were herded into the cage by Wilding the gaoler, all dressed up for the day in a deep-cuffed coat and red stockings. A man in black, who handed papers about and was the judge's mouth, barked relentlessly at them like a dog snapping at their heels. They were still chained together, but at the black dog's command three were separated from the herd and pushed forward in front of the judge. Black dog barked to make them answer to their names, to listen to the charge against them, to say if they were guilty or no, and how they would be tried.

Lucy recognised one of the prisoners: he was one of the card-playing gentlemen. He answered up in a startlingly loud voice that he was not guilty of stabbing someone – could it have been his mother? Lucy was only half listening, craning her neck to find Bron.

Bron stood at the back of the dock, chained between a big, shambling man in the washed out rags of a ploughman's smock and a bold-faced young woman who stared vacantly about her. She looked awkward and unlike herself in the borrowed clothes. Her face was set and grim, but her eyes roamed restlessly about the court, as if she were looking for something. With a pang, Lucy realised that Bron was looking for her. She wanted to cry out, to tell her to look up at the little window and see that she had kept her promise. But Bron, not seeing her, dropped her head and her face was hidden by her cap.

At the clerk's orders, Wilding had struck off the chains of the first three accused men, as if to dare them to make a run for it now, in front of all these people come to see their shame. They did not. They stood huddled together, shivering like calves in the auction ring. One of them was very young, no more than a boy. The crowd were quiet now, the only noise the bark and drone of the indictments and accusations, the rustling of papers and the clink of iron as the waiting prisoners shuffled and shifted. The judge was like a whip or a wasp: his questions lashed the prisoners with fear and shame.

The jurymen were named and sworn in, as roughly as the prisoners, Lucy thought. The whole business went so fast that she lost the thread, until the judge suddenly instructed the jury to find all three guilty as charged, and their leader duly gave the verdicts he had asked for.

After the verdicts, the judge gave out the punishments in the same dry, stinging voice. The card-playing gent was to be hanged, and so was the young fellow, who was found guilty of stealing a bolt of cloth. The boy was still screaming as he was led away, and Bron and her two chain-mates were brought forward.

The black dog growled and worried his papers, and Wilding gave Bron a push. She stepped forward to the bar and looked up at the judge. Lucy felt sure Bron must see her through the lattice of the window. She held herself quite still, so as not to startle her.

"Bronwen Richards, hold up thy hand."

Bron did so, dropping her arm again immediately and holding on to the spikes in front of her. Lucy saw that they were shiny from the grip of many hands.

This time Lucy fastened on every word the clerk said.

"Thou art here indicted by the name of Bronwen Richards of Cloudborry in the parish of Clun, spinster, for that thou didst invoke evil and wicked spirits, sometime in the form of a black lamb, and by enchantment, charm or sorcery did injure John Hamer, yeoman, of Cloudborry Heath, from afar, so that he fell down in his own yard and his arm was broken, it being the third week of December in the year of Our Lord seventeen thirty-five. And that other harms and injuries were done by you through witchcraft, especially that you did overlook the child of Lucy Weaver, spinster, lately residing at Coldheath in Cheshire, being newborn, so that it died."

At the sound of her own name, Lucy cried out. She felt Ben's arm round her shoulders and saw Bron look up as if seeking her. Then Bron shook her head, but whether at Lucy or at the wicked words the black dog spoke, Lucy could not tell.

Bron looked at the judge. "Not guilty," she said in a low voice.

"Culprit, how wilt thou be tried?"

"By God and by the country."

They all said that. They must have taught them in the prison, Lucy thought.

"God send thee good deliverance," said the clerk, in a sing-song that robbed his words of any vestige of meaning.

Wilding stepped forward, turned the key and peeled the filthy fetters from Bron's wrists. Slowly, Bron turned her hands over, looking at them. Then she let herself be led aside.

The ploughman was charged with poaching, and the young woman with stealing a pair of gloves from her mistress. Lucy could hardly bear the delay as their indictments were read and the judge counted out another jury and committed all three prisoners to their charge, the black dog droning out their names and crimes once more. Then, at last, Bron held up her hand again and all eyes turned to her as she stepped up to the bar.

Lucy had not seen John Hamer in the court, but he appeared at once when his name was called. With a sudden chill, Lucy looked for Noll. There he was, in the shadow of the jury-box, his eyes gleaming as they flickered from Hamer to Bron. At the sight of him the old terror gripped Lucy. For a moment she forgot that she was hidden from his stare, and cringed back from the window, heart racing with fear.

When Hamer had gabbled through his story, the judge called Noll as witness, and asked him about the broken arm.

At the sound of Noll's voice, Lucy began to shake. She reached out and held on to Ben's arm for support.

"This woman," he was saying, "is a notable witch, my lord. I saw her myself with her black familiar spirit, and another known witch in her company. She flies in the face of nature, living alone with no man, and is known by all to have strange power over men and beasts. I swear this good man's injury is as clear a case of malicious sorcery as ever I came upon."

"He wasn't even there!" hissed Lucy. "He never came near the place until past New Year. It's all wicked lies! Why doesn't someone tell him she didn't do it? She didn't hurt him, and she didn't kill my baby." She was shivering uncontrollably.

"Hush, now," said Ben. "If there's any man will speak up for her, he'll be given the chance."

Indeed, the judge did wave Bron forward, and ask her if she had any answer to bring against the charge.

Bron looked at him for a long moment before she spoke.

"I am no witch," she said, the calmness of desperation in her voice. "I did not harm John Hamer. He fell down drunk in his own yard." She shifted her feet, squared her shoulders and went on. "I did not harm the child, neither. He died in the way of nature, being weakly from birth." She fell silent.

Lucy choked with pride. She knew how much such a public speech had cost her friend. And now the judge must see the truth plainly.

But the judge gave a roar of fury, and banged his hand on the arm of his chair.

"'Sdeath! What manner of testimony is this? Have we no sworn witnesses? No bailiff or constable? 'Tis no matter – we have heard half the village already! And no doubt she would bring all the beldames of the region, to swear she cures warts and eases the headache. We shall be here all night. Enough. We have heard enough to pass verdict."

If Ben had not held her, Lucy would have been down the stairs and into the court in spite of Noll. But suddenly there was a stir in the court, and a man's voice came from the back of the room.

"By your leave, friend. I bring news of some import."

Heads turned to watch the young man who strode the length of the room, a paper held aloft in one hand. He was tall and his unpowdered hair was red as a fox's tail. Like Bell's brother, he wore the unmistakable dress of the Quakers. Lucy saw Bell clutch Hope's arm, and Alistair say something urgently to his sister.

Stopping before the seat of judgement, the man smiled, first at Bron, and then at the judge. He bowed neither head nor body, but stood, calmly and quietly, looking at his lordship.

"What means this interruption, sir?" snapped the clerk. "Who are you and what is your business?"

"My name is Richard Farley. I come here post haste from London, where, among other business, I have been attending Parliament. As you may know, friend, the statute on which this charge of witchcraft rests has been the subject of debate this very month."

He paused, as if to be sure that his words were heeded. The court-room was so quiet that the wheels of a cart on the cobbles outside were loud in the silence.

"The news I bring to our friend the justice," said Richard Farley, "is that the statute against witchcraft is rescinded. The bill was to be signed by the king yesterday."

The room broke into clamour, buzzing like an overturned hive.

"What does it mean?" asked Lucy urgently, gripping Ben's arm. "What does rescinded mean?"

"Silence!" barked the clerk. "Silence for his lordship!"

Slowly, the hubbub subsided.

Lucy could not see the judge's face, but she heard the ice in his voice. "If you wish to give evidence, sir, you may be sworn. Clerk to the court, administer the oath."

"Nay, friend," said Richard calmly.

Lucy gazed, open-mouthed. The young Quaker stood and spoke as easy as if he and the judge were taking tea together. If he had not looked so solemn, she would have sworn he was enjoying himself.

"Thou can see by my dress I am one will take no oath, in this or any court. I am of the Society of Friends, and as such I will give you my word."

"'Sdeath, sir," roared the judge, "if you will not swear before God to tell the truth, I will hear none of your news, be it from Parliament or anywhere else. Clerk, have him removed!"

For a moment no one stirred. Then the two troopers guarding the dock clattered forward.

But Richard did not take his eyes from the judge's face. "John Maud Montague," he said quietly, "would thou wrong this simple woman, for the sake of inflicting indignity on a well-meaning man who has vexed thee? For shame, friend! I tell thee the truth. The statute against witchcraft is repealed. And there is more." He looked hard at Noll Wethered. "The new bill forbids us to believe in any such wicked superstitions, or to attempt to persuade others of them." He held out the paper. "Here is the proof, hot from London. Read for thyself what I say, if thou will not take my word."

The judge held his gaze for a long moment, then reached out and took the paper.

The pikemen shuffled back into their places. No one spoke.

Lucy looked at Bron, who stood like a statue; at Bell, one hand to her mouth; at Hope, her jaw set grimly and her eyes on Richard Farley. In all the room behind Lucy and all the court before her, no one moved.

At last the judge spoke. "You have told the truth, Mr. Farley. But not, I fear, as you must have done under oath, the whole truth." He looked down at the paper in his hand. "According to this bill, no prosecution may be made against any person for witchcraft, sorcery, enchantment or conjuration. And the bill was indeed to be made law yesterday. What you seem not to know, my good sir, is that the law does not take immediate effect. Three months must pass before the new law comes in. Prosecution for witchcraft is legitimate until the twenty-fourth of June next. And, tedious though this case has proved, I wager it will not take that long!"

There was uproar. Richard began to speak, but no one heard; half the gentry sprang to their feet, and the packed room boomed with angry voices. The clerk banged on his desk for order; the soldiers' staves thundered on the hollow floor. Only when the judge rose to his feet did a hush settle on the room.

His voice was cold as ice. "We have wasted time enough," he said. "Continue with the trial. If there is no one to speak in this woman's defence, proceed to judgement."

As he sat down, Lucy saw Bell stand up and move towards the front of the room. The hand that held her petticoats from brushing the floor trembled slightly, but her head was up and her expression was determined. She really is a lady, thought Lucy. It is true. But what can she do?

Taking her place beside Richard, Bell met his eyes for a moment, with an expression Lucy could not read. Then she faced the judge and sank into a formal curtsy that drew a murmur of surprise from Ben.

"Quite the thing," he said, as one who knew gentry when he saw it, even when it wore an old wool gown and no jewels.

Bell turned to the clerk and held up her hand. She repeated the oath in a clear, ringing voice. The folk around Lucy nodded and smiled appreciatively; this was how a lady behaved.

Bell looked up at the judge. "My lord, I stand to witness that this woman is innocent." She spoke calmly, as if she talked with men of his rank daily, and there was only the slightest tremor in her voice.

She turned to face the jury. "My name is Isabella Wiston," she said clearly. "My father was Sir Walter Wiston, of Wiston Bassett in Somersetshire; my mother was descended from the Pembertons of Coldbatch, in this County."

Lucy fretted. What had Bell's family to do with Bron? But she saw that the jurymen liked to hear it. At the mention of

Coldbatch, they nodded and whispered to each other.

"Bronwen Richards has no father or brothers to speak for her," Bell continued, her voice gaining strength and conviction, "no blood-kin at all that I am aware, and few friends. Does that make her a witch? Because she lives remote, and quietly, so that few people know her well, is she a witch? Because she is an orphaned daughter and sister, whose father left her but a few poor fields to live on, and no dowry to buy her a husband, is she to be called unnatural?"

Bron never wanted a husband, Lucy thought suddenly; she is master in her own house. But of course Bell was too clever to say that. Gripping the wooden lattice of the little window, Lucy fixed her eyes on Bell's face, willing her on, hanging desperately on each word.

"Mr. Wethered," said Bell, her voice tinged with scorn, "speaks of Mistress Richards' strange, malignant power over animals. He miscalls her gift, my lord, for gift it is. I know her to be without equal for curing the cough in sheep, or the flux in a calf. It is known up and down our valley. But who here would not value a neighbour whose skill can aid a crippled ewe or a cow gone dry? Only malice, my lord, could call it the work of evil spirits."

There was a murmur of assent, then the court-room was quiet again. Lucy could not see the judge's face, but he was very still. The jury were listening intently. Bell ventured a small smile at the judge before she continued.

"And if I speak of neighbourly charity, what of Lucy Weaver and her baby? A poor, friendless girl, driven from her home by who knows what cruel chance, brought to bed in a strange house. Her travail was long and hard –"

How does she know about me? thought Lucy. Hope must have told her. Did she tell her everything? she wondered uncomfortably.

Bell had paused. "These are women's matters, my lord, and I

need not speak of them here. Suffice to say that Mistress Richards was friend to the girl when she was most in need. Who would not extend such help to the unfortunate? If there is evil in this matter it is not in her, my lord, but in the heart of him who brings this wicked accusation."

Lucy's hands were numb from gripping the lattice; but Bell seemed almost relaxed. "To speak of smaller matters – how many of us have warmed a newborn lamb at the fireside?" she asked the jurymen. "How often has a little creature, hand-reared by your wife or daughter, slept as quiet on your hearth as the old dog does?" More than one man nodded solemnly. Bell looked at the judge. "Is this what Mr. Wethered means when he talks of familiars? I fear he is no countryman!"

She turned from the judge to the dock, and smiled at Bron. Then her gaze swept across to the accusers.

"Of Mr. John Hamer," she said, and an edge came into her voice, "I can say but little. Little is known in our valley about his family." She paused a moment. Lucy thought she sounded just as if she were the lady of the manor, disapproving of a ragged wanderer squatting in her village.

"He was not born in the county. He is an incomer from the south. He rents a cattle walk from Sir John Waldron and it lies alongside the Richards' ancestral holding."

The people shifted and whispered.

"I am sorry to have to say that Mr. Hamer is thought by many to be an unthrifty farmer," Bell went on. Once again she looked aside, this time at the jury.

Then she turned a grave face to the judge. "I must confess to you, my Lord, that it is said of this same John Hamer that he is not above moving the ancient boundary stones, to improve his own land."

Murmurs of shock and disapproval filled the court-room, but the people fell silent again as Bell turned towards the jury.

"I see here in the court many of our neighbours – men of the Clun Forest and of Bryn. They might be called to witness what I have said. But I am sure his lordship understands without our poor aid the importance of the ancient marks of property."

This time there was a rumble of approving voices – someone at the back began to clap, quickly hushed by his friends. Everyone, it seemed, understood the importance of landed property.

"Of Mr. Wethered," Bell went on quietly, "I can say nothing. He has been in the district but a few weeks, I believe. Anything he has to say about Lucy Weaver's baby can be hearsay and gossip only. Such gossip, indeed, as will soon be outside the law. But Mistress Richards, my lord, I have known these twenty years. She is a good neighbour and my true friend. I cannot think her a witch." She paused.

"But then" – and she looked straight at the judge with a lovely, guileless smile – "I oppose all such wicked superstitions, and disapprove any attempt to persuade others of them, as his majesty the king has so wisely advised."

She stopped, and curtsied again.

The judge cleared his throat. "Thank you, ma'am. A valuable testimony." Avoiding Richard's eye, he turned to the jury.

"You may give us your verdicts on the three cases before you," he said brusquely. "The poaching and the theft you should regard as proved. The case against Bronwen Richards you should dismiss."

Thirty-five
April

It was a spring morning, rich and warm as new milk. At Brynsquilver, when they woke, the flock lay under thick mist, on fresh wet grass that rippled like green waves.

"Hot day coming," said Hope, as she and Bron ate their porridge on the bench before the door.

Bron, gazing out, nodded.

She looked much more like herself. Her cheeks were still hollow, but the last three weeks had laid a flush of wind-burn over her prison pallor. Sitting here, watching her ewes graze the lush meadow, she had slowly come back to herself. Bell had salved and dressed her sores, and the devoted company of Gwennie and Gelert and the quiet beauty of the hills had made her well.

Hope followed her gaze as the familiar outline of trees rose above the soft mist into sharp sunlight. She saw that Bron's thoughts were away over the horizon. Today they would go home – Bron, her dogs and her sheep – with Hope to help on the way. It was time.

Bell came from the door and Bron turned to smile up at her. Bron smiled more than she used to, Hope thought.

"Here's something to eat when you get home, and for a day or two while you settle," Bell said, dropping a stuffed satchel at their feet. "And I've put in the last of the strengthening draught. It would be good if you could take it a few days more. Will you be sure to do that, Bron?"

Hope got up and bent for the bag. "Time to go now, then," she said, "before the sun is any higher."

The dogs sat up, alert, but did not move for her. When Bron stretched and stood, they were up and away at once.

Bell watched them climb the bank, then bent for the pitcher that stood by the door and set off to fill it at the spring. Everything was settling into its old place. She and Hope were home again, this time for good, and now Bron was going back to her solitary life in the hills. So why did Bell still feel an undercurrent of anxiety?

Perhaps it was simply the unfamiliarity of having someone else in the house. Bron had been a welcome enough visitor, but Bell and Hope had hardly been alone together since they set out for Shrewsbury. Even in Harriet's attic chamber, they had been aware of the other people in the house, footsteps and voices on the stairs, and had spoken almost in whispers. They had even argued in whispers, on the last evening before the trial, when they fell out over the idea of Bell's going to America.

She frowned now, thinking of it. A foolish, unnecessary dispute, for there had never been the slightest possibility of her accepting Alistair and Susannah's offer. But she had been completely unprepared for Hope's jealous fury, for Hope's thinking – after all these years – that Bell might choose family loyalty before her love. Far from home, in a strange house, with the threat of the trial hanging over them, they had been suddenly like strangers. And since the trial itself, they had had few moments to themselves to talk.

It had been late, that night, by the time they tumbled out of the waggon in the yard at the Two Crosses. They had all been exhausted, Bron seeming more dead than alive, and Mercy's clean beds were all they could think about. Next morning it had been quite clear that, even after a night's rest, Bron was in no state to return home alone, and Bell had taken charge, insisting that the invalid should come to Brynsquilver to be nursed.

Picturing again that moment in the inn parlour, Bell remembered the silence that had fallen when she issued the invitation. Bron had looked not at her but at Lucy, who was clearing the table, and Lucy had put down the plates she was holding, and stood quite still, as if waiting, staring at Bron with an intensity that hushed them all. Then Bron looked abruptly away, uttering her thanks to Bell and Hope, and the moment had passed.

What had that been about? Did Lucy think *she* should have been the one to care for Bron? After all, she had looked after her all those weeks in the gaol. Bell shrugged, knowing she had done the right thing by Bron, who had indeed needed skilled nursing.

And Mercy had certainly taken it for granted that Lucy was back at the Crosses for good. By the time they had set out to bring Bron to Brynsquilver, Lucy was back in her tapster's apron, serving breakfast to the other guests.

It must be hard work at the inn, yet Bell had been surprised at how often Lucy made time to visit them at Brynsquilver – especially since those visits seemed so awkward and unrewarding. In spite of their shared adventures in Shrewsbury, Lucy and Bron seemed almost uneasy in each other's company. Bron had never been the person to look to for conversation, Bell thought affectionately, but she had seemed particularly tongue-tied of late. It had not escaped Bell's notice, either, that Hope usually found some task to take her out of the house when Lucy was there; but in spite of everything, Bell herself had begun to like the girl.

She was surprised at this, for she had not completely suppressed her jealous curiosity about Lucy's winter stay at the cottage. But Lucy was quick and lively company – restless and sharp, as some would no doubt say – and she was hungry for knowledge. She wanted to know about the work of healing, and Bell found she was pleased to teach her.

When Bell told Lucy that Bron was going home, Lucy had said nothing, looking again at Bron with those great dark eyes. Bell shook her head, impatient with herself. She might be reading the girl quite wrongly. In any case, she could not live other people's lives for them. They must sort things out for themselves.

Hope padded behind as Gwennie and Bron turned the flock expertly into the steep green lane. Gelert, slavering eagerly, wove to and fro behind her, shepherding her to keep up with the ewes. Soon the whole cavalcade was moving steadily forward and Bron dropped back to Hope's side.

They plodded along in companionable silence, Hope thinking about the events of the last few weeks. Her pleasure at Bron's going home was partly selfish, she admitted guiltily to herself. Perhaps when Bron had gone, they would see less of Lucy, too. Her presence still made Hope uneasy, and her growing friendship with Bell made it worse. She wondered if Lucy would stay at the Crosses now, or travel on again.

Bron spoke suddenly. "We'll all be back in our places, then."

It was unlike Bron to start a conversation.

"You two back at Brynsquilver," Bron went on. "Me and the dogs at the farm."

She looked away up the lane. "And Lucy's settled at the Crosses. So I hear."

Hope looked at her curiously, but Bron's eyes were on a bunch of black-legged lambs butting madly at a weak spot in the hedge. Gwennie gave them a sharp nudge, and they sprang back down the bank into the flock, bouncing off all four feet at once.

"Settled isn't how I think of Lucy," said Hope, "but, yes, Mercy says she's very quiet since she came back. Not at all her old sharp self. She reckons Lucy's had enough of gadding and answering back. Says it's time Lucy settled down with some fellow."

"Gwennie! Steady!" cried Bron sharply.

The old bitch, padding quietly along, looked up, puzzled.

They were at the top of the lane before Bron spoke again. "What's to settle down for, at the Two Crosses?" she said scornfully. "A scullion's life. Pawed at by every man and his dog, and indoors more than out. Wouldn't suit me. Nor Lucy neither, I'll warrant."

Hope grinned. "Well, Mercy might agree with you there. She has some fancy in her head about Lucy and the black man in the lordly carriage." She chuckled. "But then, Mercy always did love a ballad story, especially the ones where maidens are carried off by elf-knights on fine horses!"

To her surprise, Bron did not reply. Scowling suddenly, she forged to the head of the flock and stomped off uphill. The sheep spilled out of the lane into an upland meadow, the first of the Waylands' fields, and there was no more time for talk as Bron and both the dogs circled left and right to keep them from spreading across the hillside.

At the far hedge, Bron led them into a steep stony track to pass by the farmstead. A round-headed apple tree leaned over the hedge by the farm gate. On one side the blossom was out already, so that the tree blushed pink on the sunny side like a great single apple. Looking up, Hope saw Mary Wayland looking over the hedge, her arms full of wet linen.

"Good morrow, Hope." She nodded at the bobbing rumps of the ewes. "They'm looking well."

Gelert barked excitedly at the sound of her voice, and Bron looked back and waved. Hope stopped, hushing the dog. "How are you, Mary? How do you fare, all?"

"Well, indeed, my dear, very well. Young Georgie thrives – he'll have his teeth before long, I'll warrant." She disappeared briefly behind a sheet, spreading it out along the hedge for the sun to dry and whiten.

"And tell Mistress Bron," she said, reappearing, "the best news is that Cefn Bank is empty. He'm gone, John Hamer. Back to Leominster, to his da. Hitched up his cart and drove his cattle, nigh a se'nnight back. And a good riddance, say I."

She heaved another sheet on to the hedge. "He told my Ned he'd come into money, but I'll warrant 'twas because no one in these parts would have aught to do with him" – she nodded after Bron, disappearing up the track – "after that business. What's sure is, Sir John will be after a new tenant come Michaelmas."

Up at Cloudborry, Hope left Bron at her gate. She smiled and thanked Hope, but seemed to want her own company now. Hope was happy enough to start for home. Her garden called to her. It would be dry enough to get another row of peas in, and she might even sow some cabbage this afternoon. Unencumbered by the sheep, she set off directly across the open fields.

The pasture was still wet. Kilting up her skirts, she strode through carpets of spring flowers. In the depths of the untrodden grass, dew-soaked pockets of spider web caught the sun and shimmered with rainbows. Celandine, primrose and violets studded the banks under the hedges. Over on the edge of the hill, the farm deserted by John Hamer stood quiet, its windows blank. As Hope glanced that way, she was surprised to see a thin skein of smoke coming from the chimney. It had not taken long for some passing traveller to make a temporary home there, she thought.

The sun was strong now. Hope's heart lifted as she plunged into the head of their own lane, half a mile from home, and saw the chimney of Brynsquilver through the trees. There was a fine patch of primroses under the big oak and she paused, thinking to bring a posy home for Bell. Stooping to gather the soft stems, she thought how glad she would be when Bell's brother had finally sailed for Pennsylvania. Bell had said she did not want to go with him, but Hope still felt edgy and worried. Whenever Bell was quiet, Hope wondered if she was missing Alistair, wishing herself back with him. And then there was Richard. She remembered with a jolt how he had smiled down at Bell, so easy and familiar, as she took her place alongside him in the court-room. When they were all embarked and away on the ocean, then she would feel safe again.

Clutching the flowers, she strode briskly down the rocky lane. A hundred yards from home, she saw the horse tethered at the garden stile.

She stopped dead. At the same moment the door opened and a man in a brown coat hurried out.

Not Alistair. There was no mistaking the tall, red-haired figure. It was Richard Farley. Without looking back, he mounted his horse and rode quickly away.

"Marry him?" Hope yelled. "He asked you to marry him? And will you tell me what encouraged him to think you might accept? Or am I to think that the fancy just came into his head? That he rode for two days across country on the mere chance that you might be at home, and might say yes? I think not!"

Bell, still sitting at the table, did not speak.

"You must have encouraged him," Hope insisted furiously. "What was between you two? There was something. I knew it."

Bell was deathly pale and her eyes were red from crying, but Hope's rage was unstoppable.

"And, what, pray," she continued with angry sarcasm, "what did you say, when he asked for the honour of your hand? Or is that none of my business either?"

Bell twisted her fingers in her lap. "How can you ask me that?" she said in a low voice. "I refused him, of course. I had refused him when he asked me the first time, and then – after Shrewsbury – he came to see if he could change my mind."

Hope was stunned. "He asked you before? When? In Coalbrookdale. Of course. And you never told me! Why?" She could hear her voice rising uncontrollably again. "Why did you not tell me, Bell?"

Bell drew a long breath. "Because," she said wearily, "I knew how you would be. And I was right. And because there was nothing to tell. It was not you I hurt."

She looked past Hope, through the window. "He is a good, clever, generous man, and I have hurt him. I thought we could be friends, simply. I was wrong. And now he is to go to the New World with Ali, and I shall never see either of them again." She hid her face in her hands.

Hope knew that she should stop, but there was a kind of luxury in this release of pent-up jealousy and rage. "You are sorry you refused him, then? You do feel something for him. I knew it when I saw you together in the court. Small wonder you would not tell me, but kept your feelings secret!"

The chair scraped the stone floor as Bell stood up, gripping the edge of the table. She was shaking. "Don't talk to me of lies and secrets!" she cried. "What of the stories you kept from me?"

Hope froze.

They stood for a moment looking at each other, while the room filled up with danger. The game was up, thought Hope. She was about to fall into a pit of her own digging.

Then, quietly, Bell asked, "What exactly happened here last winter, between you and Lucy?"

It was a terrible afternoon. When everything had been said, and most of it wished unsaid the moment after, Bell put on her hat and went out into the mocking spring sunshine.

Hope took her spade and tried to exhaust herself in the garden. Every time she raised her head she could see Bell, sitting quite still by the Dames' graves at the edge of the wood.

At night, Bell put food on the table without speaking. Neither of them ate it. When it was finally too dark even to pretend to read or sew, they climbed the ladder, undressed and went to bed. Hope lay on her back in the darkness, aware of Bell beside her, not touching, not speaking.

We are not practised at this, she thought miserably. There are people who seem to live and thrive by fighting, who throw pots and pans and then clip and kiss the next minute. We have never been willing to join battle, and now we are in, we do not know how to get out.

A memory came, unbidden. She turned to Bell. "Do you remember my great grandmother?"

"Anticipation Liddell," said Bell softly. "She meant much to you when you were young."

"And ever afterwards," said Hope. "I hear her voice still at times. She used to speak out of the Scriptures, as if it was her own thought."

"I remember," Bell said. "She used say, 'Perfect love casteth out fear.'" Her voice had an edge of bitterness.

"It was anger, though, more than fear, that plagued me as a child. I was so often angry, especially with my mother. And Anticipation always said, 'Let not the sun set upon thy wrath, lest death call thee before the dawn.'"

Bell did not answer, but Hope thought the bed shook slightly. She reached out a hand: Bell's face was wet.

Hope said shakily, "Nothing is more important to me than you are. Please, Bell? Please forgive? I think I was a little mad without you. I love you more than my life."

There was a long moment of silence, and then Bell reached out for her and clung on.

Much later, when they lay exhausted, still clutched together, Hope said, "I never stopped loving you. You do know that? I was never in love with Lucy."

Then Bell did a surprising thing. She giggled. "Just as well," she said, "for I fear you'd have been jilted. I was thinking about it this morning, and 'tis clear to me as the nose on your face, beloved, that Lucy is in love with Bron."

Thirty-six

She's at home. She wakes quickly, like she always has. Home. Her father's house. The hard black arms of oak above her, the skitter of rats in the roof, the poking straw-stalks in her back.

Then Gelert thumps, below, and Gwennie whines at the foot of the ladder. They must have heard her cry out. She has been back in the depths of hell all night, in the dark earth under the city, the dungeon; buried, cold, alone. Awake, she is home, and Gwennie is calling to her. Her heart goes out, as always, to the lovingness of dogs, welcome, undeserved. Rolling from the mattress, she sticks her feet into boots and tumbles down the ladder.

"What, Gwennie? Good girl. All's well. Good girl." The bitch rears up, and she holds her, the rough warm coat sliding between her fingers, the warm wet lick on her face. She is home, and she is happy.

She stands, surprised by her own thought, cracking her knuckles.

Happy?

At home?

She opens the door, like always, and goes to blow up the embers of the fire. The dogs rush out. The sun falls in across the threshold, warm, again warm. She goes to stand on the threshold of her father's house, stretching long limbs, looking up at the sky of china blue.

In the prison she looked at the sky. Rain or shine, from the moment the first light crept down the hard black roof across the yard, to the last glints in the pool of filth at the foot of the grey wall, she would look up to the sky. She had told herself it was the same sky as this, the sky over Hergan Hill, and while she believed it she stayed alive. After that, when she stopped believing, the only thing that saved her was the girl. Lucy.

Behind her the fire spits into life under the old black pot. When the water is hot she will throw in her handful of meal. Like always. As she goes about her work now, she thinks about Lucy, the same thoughts she has had for days, ever since she came home. Is this why she can be happy here now? It is not as if the girl will come here again, but she did come once. And then followed after her, to the prison.

She understands now, having thought about it for so many days, that she owes this happiness to the prison, where she learned that she could be loved, and not only by dogs. Straddled in the yard, pumping hard for the deep spring water, she numbers the friends that the prison gave her. Hope, who understood about the dogs, and kept her ewes. Bell, who tended her wounds and spoke up for her before all the world. And Lucy.

Bent sideways by two gallons of water, she carries the pail to the hearth, and remembers Lucy, here in this room. By this window, sitting, watching her. Asleep, in that bed. It is her father's bed. She looks at it now and sees him, lying there like a great stinking black spider in its web, catching her every day of her life as she came and went, calling her to within reach of his hands. Her flesh flinches from the thought. But there is Lucy, in that same bed, sweetly asleep under the worn patchwork that was all that remained of Mother. That, and the black Bible that none of the rest of them could read. She has left it on its shelf, just as she has left the old man's coat on the peg behind the door. And his boots still stand in the corner of the great hearth. Like always. She looks at them for a long time.

Then she stoops and reaches out. The boots are hard and greasy, and heavy; but the coat, when she takes it from behind the door, is strangely light. Rotten, it rips as she tugs it away from its stiff folds on the peg. A whiff of the old man's smell. Her lip curls. She walks out of the house and deliberately, strongly, she hurls the boots one by one into the deepest part of the midden. They keel over, slowly, and are swallowed in the stinking slime. The coat sinks more easily into the sludge; she pokes the last fold under the surface with a stick. She stands up, looks at the sky, the hills; and goes into her house.

Only then does she see a mark on the door which she has not seen before. She reaches out. Sticky. Two thick smears in a rough cross, with a feather sticking between two boards. And to one side, on a nail, a horse-shoe, upside down. She frowns: she does not remember that. And the mark is fresh. But after a moment, she shrugs. She will wash it away, get rid of it, when she chooses. Now she is at home.

"Certainly not!" said Bell sharply. "I should have thought you would have known better, Will, than to believe such nonsense. No, I cannot make you a charm to make the fish swim into your net, and neither can anyone else. Who put such things into your head?"

The little boy shuffled, avoiding her eye. "Aren't you a witch, then?"

Bell frowned, troubled. Then, more gently, she asked, "Who told you I was?"

"Josh did. He says a man told him you were a black witch as could put the evil eye on folk."

"Well that's nonsense," said Bell firmly. "You tell him so, and this man too. Who was the man?"

"Dunno. A stranger." The child looked shamefaced now.

She smiled at him. It was not his fault, he was only repeating what others had said. "Now don't forget to remind your mother about tomorrow," she said cheerfully. "You men must let her have an hour or two's holiday to come and visit me, for it is the day before May Day, you know."

May Day would see all the usual revels on village greens and in the yards of inns, but it had become a habit over the years for Hope and Bell and some of their neighbours to meet on the morning of May Eve, and go together to tidy and decorate the graves at the wood's edge. After they had done their work they would sit on the grass under the trees and eat the bits of food they had brought with them, and talk.

It was a gentle remembrance of the first Dames, long ago inhabitants of the cottage, a ritual with no name and no importance to any but those involved. Although they made light of it to their husbands and sons, and spoke as if they might not find time to climb the hill, Bell knew that the women would come. She watched Will Wayland until he disappeared into the lane, then went indoors to make gingerbread for the morrow.

As she moved about the room, she let the happenings of the last weeks come and go in her mind. She thought of her brother, on shipboard now, tossing on an ocean she could only imagine; of Susannah, waiting for her baby; and of Richard. She held them all in her mind, willing the ship safe to harbour, and each of them to contentment in their new life. So far away. One day she might have news of them, but until then they must inhabit the landscape of her imagination.

She stared through the open doorway at the real, solid landscape of her home. The pieces of her life, so shaken and stirred about, had finally settled again. Not quite into the old pattern, perhaps, but all the more precious for that. My ship is this valley, she thought suddenly, and all of us in it have been on a voyage. Here we are at last, storm-tossed, a little weary, but safe come to port.

She thought of Lucy, the restless, passionate spirit who had so nearly shipwrecked them all. What would become of her? Would she stay now, or wander away? Well, time would tell.

She began to shape the little cakes. She, at least, was safe home now. She would not go away again.

Lucy watched the scrubbing brush disappear into the scummy water for the hundredth time, and cursed furiously. She was seriously considering running away. Now. Today. Walking away from this washtub, from the inn, taking to the road again, leaving it all behind. Washing! She hated it. Why was she here, up to her armpits in dirty water? Again. Still. The work was unending. So was Mercy's chatter, and Nance's handless idling about. And as for Joey, with his daft questions and his moonstruck stare...

Lucy had the belly-ache and the headache, and no one cared, she thought moodily. She clung to her memories of Shrewsbury, where she had been important. She had saved Bron's life. The Dame had said so. She had told her, you saved our friend's life. Some might have thought it was Bell herself who had done that, or the red-haired Quaker man, but Bell had understood what Lucy had done. No one here understood anything, she thought bitterly. Looking back, it was hard not to feel that those weeks in Shrewsbury were the only time she had ever been really happy. She had been wanted, needed – she had had something really important to do, a sense of who she could be.

Now it was all over, no one needed her any more. Bron had just gone off with Hope and Bell, she thought bitterly, as if nothing had happened. And now Bron had gone home on her own, with her dogs and her sheep, up the hill where it was so beautiful. A sharp vision pierced Lucy of the spare, clean room, Bron's home; a quiet and purposeful life that she had glimpsed – shared – before they were dragged off to the gaol. It had been the same at Brynsquilver: a glimpse of how Hope lived, a moment of feeling needed, and then she was out on her ear, the Dame back in charge, the two of them snug and smug in their cottage with their cat. And me back here, she thought savagely, groping yet again for the brush, bent over a tub like me mam, washing other people's bedsheets in a poxy inn-yard for the rest of my life.

She was back where she started, at the bottom of the heap. Mercy and Nance had gone out a couple of hours ago, up to Brynsquilver. Some women's business, William said vaguely, something to do with the old Dames' graves. For May Eve. And had they asked her? They had not. She was only fit to do the washing. She looked down at her hands, gone all bloated in the grey water. She would run away.

A movement caught her eye across the yard. Joey again, hanging round her. She had had enough of him, too. Yesterday he had surprised her while she was gathering eggs in the half-light of the hay-loft, and scared her half to death. She flinched again from the fear – the fear of Wethered. She closed her eyes, and then opened them quick as his mad, glaring face appeared inside her eyelids. She took a deep breath, and told herself again he would not come back. But it wasn't true, was it? He could come. And he still haunted her, lurking in her mind, if nowhere else, ready to jump out whenever she was off guard.

A pox take Joey, why couldn't he fix his calf's eyes on some local girl and leave her alone? It wasn't as if he had any conversation. He either gazed in goggle-mouthed silence, or asked daft questions. This morning he had asked her if it was true you could take away a witch's powers if you drew blood on her. She wondered what company he was keeping, to put such nonsense into his head.

And where was he when she needed a hand? She dragged the fifth sheet out of the water and straightened up.

"Joey!" she shouted irritably. "Joey! Come here."

Sure enough he came, lolloping out of the stable like a great eager dog.

"Get hold, here. Don't drop it! Now, twist. No, back off, can't you, stretch it out first. Now twist."

The heavy rope of linen, dripping all along its length, slid suddenly from the boy's grip and came down, splat, on the yard.

"Oh, Lucy, I'm sorry!" He was scrabbling it up, mud and all, into his arms. She shut her eyes.

"Codshead. Stupid, handless, poxy mooncalf! Put it back in the tub." She opened her eyes. "And now you can wash it yourself." She stripped off her sodden apron and flung it at him. "You wash the stinking sheets. I'm going out."

Where?

Just out.

Anywhere. Up the bank. Away.

An idea struck her. If it was the season for grave-tending, then she had a grave to see to of her own. She ducked into the coachhouse, and found a hedging glove and a broomhook to hack away the brambles. Its heavy, curved blade was clean and sharp – Joey had put an edge on it when he finished pleaching the lower hedge. That was something he was good for, anygates. She headed for the road. She would go and say goodbye to the baby, and then she would run away.

It was cool in the high woods. The air was alive up here, moving, full of birdsong and insects flying by. The pale new growth under the beech trees rustled with life as she passed. She slowed her stride, and began to breathe more easily.

She was not quite sure of the way. She had purposely avoided the usual path, so as not to meet the women coming from the other graves. In a gap in the trees she paused, trying to get her bearings from across the valley. She could see a roof and chimney on this side – she did not think it was Brynsquilver, but she knew she had not come far enough for it to be the Waylands' place. She stood still, considering.

And heard a rustling behind her, quite loud.

"Joey?"

What was the bumpkin doing now? He'd be the death of her, reeping up on her like this all the time.

"Joey Jones! Come out, now!"

Silence.

She turned to look.

"Joey?"

Thirty-seven

She looks up.

Noon.

The bunched shadow of the three ashes falls just clear of the barn. Her barn. She smiles, stows the old broom and goes to sit in the shade at her door.

All is tidied, completed for the day. Soon she will take a drink. Her hands hang over her knees.

Gwennie flops, panting, at her side. And Gelert? Off down the lane an hour ago: there is a bitch in heat at the Mardu.

"Much good may it do him, Gwennie." She fondles the old one's ears and Gwennie pushes against her hand.

And now, what?

The gate-post in the lower field has been working loose for months. There is a new cheese in the dairy she must remember to turn. Tonight will do for that. Nothing calls urgently.

In the house?

She hesitates. What should she do in the house?

Something to mark the change.

For there is a change, and she is restless. There is something she needs to do.

Or something she needs?

Considering this question, she gets up slowly, goes to the mossy half-cellar and draws a mug of her own cider.

She needs something...

Someone.

Lucy.

She pictures Lucy. Coming into the prison, smiling always, but with her eyes full of fear. Thrashing in agony on the floor at Brynsquilver, that first night. Sleeping, here by the fire. She remembers the feel of her as she carried her home from the hill, light and cold, her hair wet. And the night at the Two Crosses, in the barn. Twelfth Night. She has not let herself think of this before. She thinks of it now.

Agitated, she pushes shut the cellar door and walks out into the yard. She pictures Lucy now, down at the Two Crosses, working indoors on such a day as this. Lucy, quick and warm, a white apron tied twice round her, bringing food and drink. Smiling for strangers.

She should have spoken when they all came home.

She puts her mug down on the bench.

"Stay, Gwennie," she says, and walks out from her door.

Above Brynsquilver she stops. She can hear voices along the bank. Women, laughing a little, chattering together like swallows on the wing.

She frowns. May Eve. There will be a dozen there. She will go round about. She strikes off the path into the wood, stepping quickly on the mossy cushions between the trees.

She is thinking only of Lucy, so that for a moment she is not surprised to hear her voice. She stops. She is dreaming. But no, it is Lucy's voice, calling. She turns, finding an opening in the trees, and moves quickly towards the sound.

When the screaming starts, she runs.

Then in the distance she sees them. Lucy has her back to a tree. She is screaming and struggling, almost hidden by the black-coated figure of Noll Wethered. Their hands, spread wide, are locked together; there is the glint of steel. There is blood on the knife.

"Stop!" She is shouting, bounding down the slope.

Wethered seems not to hear her, but Lucy's head comes up. She calls, "Bron! Bron!" and starts to buck and struggle more fiercely, kicking, twisting, her arms still braced wide.

It is too far, she will be too late. But as she leaps over a stream, Lucy breaks free, kicking him so he staggers back, bent double, screaming curses. Now Bron can see his crazed, contorted face, and the blood running from a cut on Lucy's bared throat.

A stream of filth is coming from Wethered's mouth. He falls and gets up again, clutching himself, and he calls them the devil's whores, cuntspawn, breath-suckers, child-eaters. His eyes are red, spittle froths at the corners of his mouth. He is still holding the bloody knife. As he lunges at her again, Lucy stoops, and then straightens up.

Bron, still ten yards away, sees them quite clearly as he raises his knife – and Lucy swings the heavy broomhook over her head, and fells him with a blow.

With a high, bubbling scream, he falls. His body jerks, the knife falls from his hand and a terrible cry comes from him as he rolls over and over on the ground, thrashing like an ill-stuck pig. And suddenly there is blood everywhere. On the grass, on Wethered, on Bron's boots. And on the hook, lying in the grass, its gleaming edge dulled with gore. Lucy stands very still. Her own blood is trickling down into her dress. Bron steps over the shuddering body of Noll Wethered and takes Lucy in her arms.

And it becomes simple.

Women stream into the clearing, as Bron holds Lucy against her heart. Mary Wayland is first: she puts her hands to her mouth. Wethered has come to a stop, sprawled on his back, the blood still welling from the wound in his neck.

Hope, shocked, drops to her knees beside him. Mercy is there, and Nance, and the others. The women part to let Bell come to him. She kneels too, and looks at him. She says, "We must stop this bleeding."

But when she touches him he screams, "Witch!" and throws her off. He is weak, but he finds strength to curse her. He will not be touched by witches, hell-hags.

There is little Bell can do to help him. His tortured life is running away into last year's bracken. As they watch, his body stills. Bell reaches out at last and feels for a pulse, then, after a moment, she closes his eyes.

Bron is still holding Lucy. She is never going to let her go again.

Bell says in a low voice to Hope, "She has killed him."

The women look at Bron and Lucy. An uneasy silence falls.

Hope picks up the bloody hook. "Never fear, Lucy," she says, in a strange voice. "We will do something about this carrion. Never fear." But her face is troubled.

In Bron's arms, Lucy straightens up. Her voice is strong. "I shall never fear him again," she says.

She has not understood.

"Lucy," says Nance, beginning to cry.

Then, from the group of women, Mercy speaks. "Well, m'dear, good riddance, that's what we all say." She takes the hook from Hope's hand and puts it carefully in the basket on her arm, with her other gardening tools. "No call for you to trouble yourself either, Hope."

She looks around the circle of women. "We'll fetch Bailiff Gilroy. Any on us can tell him," she says carefully, "how this loon came to kill hisself with his own nasty old knife." She looks down at Wethered's knife. There is still blood on it. With her foot she pushes it nearer to his open hand.

There is a silence, and then Mary Wayland says, "Daft old bugger. Fell on his knife, didn't he? Serves him right, say I."

Nance grins and shakes her head. "Melancholy mad, I'd say, and cut his throat – look, you can see. Tell that to the baily."

The women begin to murmur, to weave the story they will tell to the bailiff. "Terrible thing... By his own hand... Ted Gilroy won't be sorry to see the end of him, either..."

Mercy sniffs. "'Tis only a pity he should do for himself so near the graves of our old Dames," she says piously.

Hope smiles.

Bron takes Lucy by the hand and looks into her eyes. "Come home now," she says.

More new writing from DIVA Books

Breaking Point
Jenny Roberts

Cameron's back!

When Cameron McGill stumbles across a vicious knife attack, the victim begs her to pass on an email address, then slips into a coma. Cam starts to investigate, and meets animal rights militants, local thugs, a mysterious dyke called Beano, the troubled Angel who only wants to get her into bed... and the very unhelpful chief executive of an animal research establishment. Determined to get to the truth, Cam finds to her horror that she has now become the prey.

In this eagerly awaited follow-up to Needle Point, Cameron has fallen out with Hellen, and landed up in Hull. More than one person wants to kill her. If only she'd never left Amsterdam.

Praise for the first Cameron McGill mystery, Needle Point:

"A very pacy mystery... we look forward to more"
Lesbians on the Loose

Spring 2001 RRP £8.95 ISBN 1-873741-58-8

Needle Point
Jenny Roberts

The first Cameron McGill mystery

"Completely enthralling" Amy Lamé, BBC London Live

"The bruising and the torn skin were worse than I had ever seen before – even the most hardened users protect their veins."

Cameron McGill is on a mission: to find out why her sister, who never touched drugs, was fished from a canal with needle marks all down her arm. Tearing through Amsterdam on her Harley-Davidson, Cam encounters radical squatters, evasive drug agencies and a particularly alluring policewoman. But it's hard to know who to trust in a quest that could claim her life as gruesomely as it took her sister's.

**"Deserves to be read by more than a niche market...
An excellently paced, well-plotted thriller"**
Guardian

"A fast-moving tale of revenge and retribution"
Time Out

"Rivetting and well observed. Recommended!"
Gscene

RRP £8.95 ISBN 1-873741-42-1

Mush
Kathleen Kiirik Bryson

**Mush charts the progress of an Alaskan threesome
in a Gothic fairy tale for the 21st century**

When Nicky and Carol meet Ellen in Seattle, the girls are drawn into
an intense bond. But their triad is destined to disintegrate as linked
memories of the Alaskan wilderness turn simultaneously erotic and
horrific...

A haunting debut, *Mush* examines childhood ties and the dynamics of
a *ménage à trois*, weaving dreams and myths into a very modern setting. If Courtney Love had got it together with Angela Carter, *Mush*
would be their love-child.

"Bryson is Alaskan born and bred and thus, unlike someone
from Essex, has immediate access to a unique, intense landscape
that is unsurpassed as a setting for eerie fiction. She perfectly
captures the never-ending, powerless quality of childhood"
Time Out

"A well crafted tale... It has a dreamlike surreal quality, with a
very real terror coming to the surface. I read this in one go.
Excellent book for those long dark winter nights" *Gscene*

"She's no mean poet and storyteller"
queercompany.com

RRP £8.95 ISBN 1-873741-46-4

Emerald Budgies
Lee Maxwell

From the New Zealand reviews:

"This is the other side of *Fear and Loathing* – the morning after"
North & South

"A darkly comic book about Ruth, a difficult, funny anti-heroine who falls for manipulative, beautiful Tracey and a bastard ad director called Martin. Ruth tries to sort herself out but is running too fast from too many things... With its stream of consciousness riffs and easy violence, Emerald Budgies could be influenced by Beat writers such as Burroughs and Kerouac" **Emily Perkins,** *Pavement*

"If Bridget Jones was into dildos, heroin and cruelty to animals, her diary might read something like this... But [Maxwell's] laughs don't come from the quirky, knowing humour of a Helen Fielding or a Nick Hornby; her vision is much darker, more frightening and more real... A raw, thoughtful and very funny novel that just happens to feature a disproportionate amount of hard drugs, rubber underwear and poor housekeeping" *Listener* (New Zealand)

"She's witty and she gives good dialogue" *Grace*

"A dark and suspenseful tale of psychological disturbance and a shadowy malevolence" *Metro* (NZ)

"Sex, drugs and lots of laughs" *Waikato Times*

RRP £8.95 ISBN 1-873741-44-8

The Comedienne
VG Lee

"A very funny book"
Lesbians on the Loose

"I couldn't believe it at first – that Susan could switch from padded Valentines, eighteen inches high with 'Be mine forever', to not even stopping her car for me to cross on a zebra. If she hadn't recognised me with the added weight, she must have known it was my shopping trolley."

It's time for Joan to try her luck on the London comedy circuit. After all, everybody always said she was a funny woman...

"The Comedienne has an intrinsic truth that pulls you in before you know it" *Time Out*

"A sympathetic protagonist in the tradition of Lucky Jim – Grade A" *Girlfriends*

"A touching evocation of loneliness and the complex relationship between an ageing mother and daughter" Andrea Levy

"An easy, feelgood, summery read, and a joy to behold" *What's On* (Birmingham)

"Straddling the knife edge between funny and sad, it leaves you giggling, days later" *Gscene*

RRP £8.95 ISBN 1-873741-43-X

The Diva Book of Short Stories
edited by Helen Sandler

"Look out for the Diva Book of Short Stories"
Observer Magazine

"This wonderful collection presents fresh work from familiar names –
including Emma Donoghue, Stella Duffy and Jackie Kay – alongside
the best from a new generation of British talent. In tales of pride and
jealousy, cruelty and community, the characters find themselves eating passports, healing horses and running for cover when the gossip
gets out of control. The selection and originality of the work makes a
refreshing change, with situations that the majority of lesbians can
relate to – there are plenty of characters here that you'll think are
based on people you know or at least recognise from the scene.
Recommended!" Gay's The Word website

"Many [of the stories] are good and some have universal appeal"
Guardian

"Audience participation opportunities, as well as 28 stories,
make it good value... you will be able to take it home to help
you through the most closeted family Christmas"
Time Out

"A brilliant collection of stories" rainbownetwork.com

RRP £8.95 ISBN 1-873741-47-2

It's a Family Affair:
The complete lesbian parenting book
Lisa Saffron

Indispensable help with the littlest big decision of your life

Are you planning a baby by yourself or with your lesbian partner? Or perhaps you have a more conventional family but now it's time to come out to your husband and children about your 'other life'?

What will life be like after your big decision? How does self-insemination work? How do children cope with being part of a non-conventional family? What will your mother say? Will things change between you and your lover?

All these issues and much more are explored in this thorough and readable book by a leading authority in the field. Lisa Saffron has run parenting workshops for many years and writes a regular column in DIVA magazine about lesbian families.

In this unique illustrated handbook, she uses interviews with lesbian parents, gay donors and their kids to bring alive the issues.

Spring 2001 RRP £15 ISBN 1-873741-62-6

Girl2Girl:
The lives and loves of young lesbian and bisexual women
Edited by Norrina Rashid and Jane Hoy

The only book written by and for young women
questioning their sexuality

In this lively illustrated book, girls from across the UK write from the
heart about being gay or bi, coming out or falling in love:
• "The first time I kissed a girl I could have collapsed... it felt like
I had always imagined a kiss should feel."
• "I don't remember when it was that I actually thought, Oh my
god, I fancy the bridesmaid!"
• "People say bi-try is a big student thing – well it is, and I'm loving it!"
• "I asked my dad if he had ever considered sleeping with a man. He
said no. I said, Well neither have I."

"Anything that helps minimise the stigma people are subjected
to for being different gets my vote"
TV's Trisha

"This anthology with its excellent resource section
is a must for any young woman" *Time Out*

"Fun reading and a lifeline to the young and isolated,
[a] very important book" *Gscene*

"Life-saving and inspiring"
Skin, Skunk Anansie

RRP £8.95 ISBN 1-873741-45-6